The Devil's Music

The Devil's Music

JANE RUSBRIDGE

BLOOMSBURY
LONDON · BERLIN · NEW YORK

FT

First published in Great Britain 2009

Copyright © 2009 by Jane Rusbridge

Illustrations by Penelope Beech

The entries in the glossary are from *The Ashley Book of Knots* © 1944
Clifford W Ashley, used by kind permission of Doubleday, a division of
Random House Inc, except the entry for the Royal Crown, which is from
Knots, Ties and Splices by Tom Burgess and Commander John Irving, used by
kind permission of Taylor & Francis Group, and the entry for the French
Shroud Knot, which is from *Knots, Splices and Rope Work* by A Hyatt
Verrill, used by kind permission of Dover Publications

The moral right of the author has been asserted

Bloomsbury Publishing, London, Berlin and New York

36 Soho Square, London W1D 3QY

A CIP catalogue record for this book is available from the British Library

ISBN 978 0 7475 9869 5
10 9 8 7 6 5 4 3 2 1

Typeset by Hewer Text UK Ltd, Edinburgh
Printed by Clays Ltd, St Ives plc

The paper this book is printed on is certified by the © 1996 Forest Stewardship
Council A.C. (FSC). It is ancient-forest friendly. The printer holds
FSC chain of custody SGS-COC-2061

FSC
Mixed Sources
Product group from well-managed
forests and other controlled sources
www.fsc.org
Cert no. SGS - COC - 2061
www.fsc.org
© 1996 Forest Stewardship Council

www.bloomsbury.com/janerusbridge

For David, with love

Glossary

 Carrick Bend: When under stress pulls up into easy loops, which may be readily opened with a few light taps from a belaying pin, fid, or other implement. It may be water-soaked indefinitely, and even then it will not jam.

 Celtic Shield Knot: Ancient knot designs thought to have had spiritually significant meanings. Continual looping of designs suggests themes of eternity and interconnectedness, and various knots have been made at one time to foil evil spirits.

 Cross Fastenings: Used when one spar is vertical, the other horizontal.

Fiador Knot: Sometimes used as a hackamore or emergency bridle, although very few cowboys can tie it. Those who can might earn considerable revenue by charging for each knot made.

Five Strand Star Knot: A Star Knot is perhaps the most distinguished of sailors' Button Knots, and certainly the most individual. The purpose of Multi-Strand Button Knots is to prevent unreeving. {to unreeve: to withdraw (a rope) from an opening (as a ship's block or thimble).} Multi-Strand Knots are never untied.

French Shroud Knot: A shroud knot is a method of joining two ropes together permanently.

Granny Knot: Questionable knot that is often tied as a bend. Its use is inexcusable . . .

Harness Knot

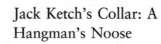

Jack Ketch's Collar: A Hangman's Noose

Manrope Knot: Tied in manropes, which are ropes leading to either side of the gangway. A man who can make a Manrope Knot is an object of respect.

Matthew Walker Knot: Sometimes called the Single Matthew Walker by the uninitiated, it is the most important knot used on board ship. Amongst knots proper, the Matthew Walker is almost the only one which it is absolutely necessary for the seaman to know.

Midshipman's Hitch: A semi-permanent loop, one of the strongest.

Monkey's Fist: Used on the end of a heaving line; commonly tied over a small, heavy ball of stone, iron, marble or glass. The heavy core is required to carry the weight of the heaving line.

Overhand Knot: The simplest of all knot forms and the point of departure for many of the more elaborate knots.

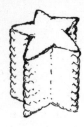

Pentalpha (see Sinnet)

Reef Knot: A true Binder Knot, for which purpose it is admirable, but under no circumstances should it be used as a bend.

Royal Crown: An ornamental method of finishing a rope's end.

Sinnet: A three-strand flat Sinnet is commonly known as a simple braid or plait. A Solid Sinnet is larger and more complex, resembling crochet or French knitting. A Solid Sinnet, in cross-section, may be triangular, elliptical, hexagonal, and so forth. In cross-section, a Solid Sinnet that is a Pentalpha will be a five-pointed star.

Two-Strand Lanyard Knots: Sailors use these lanyards on knife, marling-spike, whistle and pipe lanyards.

Part One

I'M ALONE UNDER A high sky. Clouds race across the blue, skim in reflected shoals over puddles and hollows in the wet sand. I'm holding Susie's rubber bucket. Far away, made small by distance, a man digs for lugworms.

You're in charge, Andy, my mother said. She picked Susie up and put her on one hip. They went to get ice creams.

My shorts are wet and clinging. I have tipped out Susie's morning collection of slipper shells, bits of razor shell, the joined pairs of purplish shells she calls butterflies, and now the bucket is filled to the brim with water. Tiny cracks appear in the stretched rubber handle. The water's surface glints, tilting like a flipped coin; the slanting O almost reaches the lip. It will spill.

I put the bucket down. At my back the sea heaves and drags.

The rubber bucket is old. Once, it was mine.

I look up towards Jelly's carrycot, a long way away on the pebbles. Then down to the edge of the wet sand where Jelly lies on my towel by the pool I've dug for her. She was lumpy as a bag of coal in my arms and nearly as heavy; my chin knocked on her head and my bare feet burned on the pebbles. But she was too hot and squashed in her carrycot. She couldn't stop crying. Further up the shingle bank my mother's empty deckchair billows red and white stripes.

Honey is circling, nose down. Round and round Jelly and our pool. I see Jelly has rolled on to her stomach. Honey sits down. She barks once; twice. The man digging for lugworms pauses and looks up, a foot on his spade. Goose bumps rise on my arms.

And now my mother is racing, skidding down the steep shingle slope, a clutch of ice-cream cornets held high. Pebbles bounce and slide. Far behind, by the row of beach huts with their shuttered doors, Susie holds her arms high, hands like starfish, stiff in the air.

My mother reaches the pool. She stands rigid. The ice creams topple and fall. She bends to scoop Jelly from the sand and wraps her arms around her. My mother lifts her face to the pale sky, her mouth wrenched open.

And that's when I hear the high-pitched sound, a keening that goes on and on and doesn't stop. It doesn't stop when the lugworm man throws his spade to the ground and begins to run, doesn't stop when the bucket drops at my feet, doesn't stop when I'm crouched low, hands covering my ears.

I HOIST MY RUCKSACK on to my back and step across the gap between the train and the platform's edge. Fag butts and a paper cup marked with lipstick lie on the grey chippings below.

Susie's not expecting me. I sit on a metal bench on the platform and wait for a plan to materialise. Cold seeps through my cut-offs. Becomes an ache spreading across the surface of my skin then deeper, into my thigh muscles. My toes grow numb. In the rucksack there are only odds and ends of clothes. Leaving Triopetra was a sudden thing. I packed Ashley's *Book of Knots* and Grandfather's sailor's palm; the new length of rope. Not much else.

Last time I came back – two, maybe three, winters ago – it wasn't great. Susie and I yelled and screamed at each other. I manhandled her, shoulders like bundles of twigs under my hands, out of Richard's study, locked the door and held the key up above her stretching reach. Richard walked in the front door. A whining child in pyjamas was crying 'Mummy, Mummy, Mummy,' from the top of the stairs; Susie pushed and slapped at my torso. We were both breathless. Richard slung me out. Not physically, of course. No. He gave me a lecture, delivered in his vicar's voice. Wax melting on a church candle. Susie must have told him things. He won't want me back at The Vicarage.

On the opposite platform, a sign over a door says 'Lost Property'. I imagine the stifle and weight of shelved belongings: suitcases, umbrellas, overcoats, scarves. Parts of people's lives they wanted to leave behind.

A train pulls in. A slam of doors; a voice on the tannoy. The shriek and clank of wheels on the track, leaving. No one else left on either platform.

The daylight is fading. I'm fidgety, missing the Cretan mountain smell of wild thyme and baked earth, the cicadas' pulse. I could catch the next train back out of here.

Running a palm over my face tells me the beard is thick. I finger through pocket fluff for some string to pull my hair back into a ponytail and walk up the slope to the exit. The road is slick with drizzle. After some trouble with coinage, I phone Susie from an old red phone box at the station entrance.

'*Andy?*' Her voice is hollow. 'Where are you?' Breathing and gurgling saliva down the line; she must be holding one of the kids.

I tell her.

She says, 'Stay there. I'll come and pick you up.' Her words are clipped, as if she doesn't quite have the time to pronounce the sounds. Or perhaps it's the way I'm hearing them.

'I'll need a few mins to get organised. But . . . Andrew?'
'Yes?'
'*Please* don't disappear. Stay put.'
I wait with my back to the red brick of the station wall. The rain stops. A blackbird clucks and tuts. Trees stir in the dusk. Bare branches of a silver birch are joined and black and the limbs of other trees grope upwards, rooks' nests anchored in high clumps: a cluttered sky. No horizon. No

stars. I wrap the cracked rawhide of Grandfather's sailor's palm around my hand, fit my thumb through the thumb-socket, press my index finger into the metal needle rest.

That last time, I'd caught Susie bent over the computer in Richard's study. She was chewing on a fingernail, a frown line scoured between her eyebrows. She leapt up; a glass of water tipped. Her hand shot out to grab it and water sloshed over the papers on Richard's desk. She flapped both hands at me, eyes popping, and rushed from the room. I went round the desk to see what I could save from disaster. There was a Google search: FIND MISSING MOTHER.

Zeros, too many of them. *Results 1–10 of 10,900,000 for Find Missing Mother.*

I bent and pulled the plug. A fizzled ping and the screen shrank away.

'Why don't you want to find her? Why won't you help me?' she'd sobbed, pummelling my chest.

I catch sight of her hurrying across the station forecourt, a slight figure in a cardigan that's too long in the sleeves. She's dragging a protesting blond kid and drops her keys twice. When she sees me, she starts to cry, mouth twisting. Her head turns from side to side. I ease the rucksack from my back, wondering if I should put my arms around her. She leans into me, so I do. She's skeletal, back ribbed and bony beneath the cardigan. But her belly is firm, pressing into me, the only substantial part of her. She must be pregnant yet again. She wilts, head bowed against my chest. Beads of drizzle hang heavy in her hair.

The blond kid drapes himself around Susie's leg and scowls up at me, tugging insistently at the bottom of her cardigan. Eventually she rubs her cheeks on her cuff and straightens, holding me at arm's length.

'I always forget how big you are, the way you sort of *loom*,' she says. 'And you look like a tramp, as usual.' But she's smiling, her heart-shaped face looking up at me. She curls her fingers around my wrist. 'I've left the twins in the car. Come on.'

A cassette tape playing a song about ducks – QUACK QUACK QUACK QUACK – is audible yards from Susie's old Volvo estate. A caravan covered with green algae is hooked up on the back. Presumably Susie has hatched a scheme to park it up somewhere as my temporary accommodation. In the back of the Volvo, two half-dressed blond kids in matching jumpers bang on plastic buckets with spades and an assortment of toy cars. The seat is littered with discarded socks and apple cores and the boot is crammed with stuff. Susie straps the bigger kid in the back, speaking to me in breathless half phrases. I'd forgotten how she talks.

'Aren't you going to get in?'

I hesitate. A decision seems required. Right now it's neither here nor there where I am but it must be warmer in the car, so I fold myself into the front seat. Inside, the car is steamy and smells of hot plastic. Susie fiddles with the ignition.

'Andy, I'm really, really glad you're here.' Her hand touches my knee, patting. 'I was worried about space in the car. I half thought you'd be with someone.'

There's usually someone, but never for long. The girl who has started cleaning at the taverna often looks my way, curling a strand of hair behind her ear and smiling, but she's related somehow to Vasilis, or perhaps she's just the daughter of a friend. Either way, it's not a good idea. I stick to tourists.

I can't concentrate on what Susie's saying because the tape is on full volume and the three boys in the back aim guns that fire nothing but a noise like a siren. The twins are in nappies. Babies with guns. And still she talks, raising her voice: Richard this, Dad that; the boys; church jumble sales. She talks at me as if there isn't much time to say it all when really she's saying nothing. I wonder if she talks like this to everyone or if she simply talks to fill the gap there is between the two of us.

In Crete when I think of Susie, she's wearing white school socks yanked up to her dry little knees and folded over. I picture the way she used to stand on the pouffe singing along to Dana, watching herself in the mirror above the fireplace. She didn't talk much then. Hardly at all, to me. She'd just give that little tilt of her head and flounce out of the room whenever I lifted the needle from her record to put Hendrix on instead.

We stop at a red light.

'He's dead.'

Her words startle me. I wipe my mouth with the back of my hand.

'Three days, he lasted.'

Father wipes the soles of his polished shoes, shakes out an umbrella, stoops to place his bag by the radiator in the hallway. I can't see his face, only the rain in spatters on the shoulders of his gabardine Mac.

So he hung around. When Susie phoned a couple of weeks ago, the splat and whiz of a cartoon in the background, the official prediction was twenty-four hours max.

He's gone.

I shift down the seat. My rucksack takes up most of the room in the foot-well. Coiled in there, waiting for me, is the new length of yarn-tarred hemp, its smell of salty, windswept miles. The dip and curve of the strands is thick as muscle. This is what gives rope its strength, the laying together of strands which have been twisted in opposite directions. Rope is bound together by the friction of its parts.

'Andy, where on earth have you *been*?'

I wish she'd concentrate on driving, instead of turning around in her seat all the time to look at me.

'Thought I said.'

'What?'

'On the phone. That I wasn't coming back.'

She rolls her eyes. 'Yes, but. Now. Here. You. Are.' Each word has exaggerated emphasis. 'Besides, when I phoned the taverna again, what's-his-name said you'd left Crete more than a week ago.'

'Vasilis, his name's Vasilis.' But the windscreen wipers scrape and thud and Susie's still talking.

'– yet *another* of your well-timed disappearing acts. The next thing you're going to tell me is that you walked all the way, dressed like that!' She gestures in the general direction of my sandals and cut-offs. 'I suppose you've forgotten what England's like in October?' Shaking her head, she lifts both hands from the wheel and drops them.

I take a breath, to make some sort of reply, but can't think of one. Nobody asks the questions I want to answer. The last October I spent in England must have been the autumn after 'O' levels. The autumn I bought an afghan coat and hitched across Europe. Susie was all teeth and braces. She had a crush on Bobby Moore and practised kissing her own reflection.

When Susie phoned Triopetra to tell me about Father's stroke, there was the hiss and crackle of long distance. It got me thinking about the distancing effect of time. I lay in my hammock strung across the balcony, watched the moon set, the sky throng with layer upon layer of stars. I thought about ways to use rope to connect my ideas about time and distance with the stars, moon and sky. Before I left, I'd sketched out some knotwork, bought the yarn-tarred hemp. Shroud laid: four strands, right-handed, around a central core of plain laid rope. My fingers itch to hold it.

Susie clicks her fingers in my line of vision. 'Andy?'

'Yes?'

'You know this is tricky. The Vicarage . . . Richard . . . Guess there's no way you'll stay at Dad's? Even now?'

'No.' My fingers tremble.

'*So* . . .' her voice holds a bubble of anticipation, 'I thought we'd drive down to The Siding!'

I concentrate on the swish of the wipers across the dark windscreen but see mudflats at low tide, a rushing sky. My teeth chatter. I can't manage my limbs. I fold my arms across my body and clamp my hands under my armpits.

Thirty years. I thought I would never go back.

'Richard thinks it's a good idea to give the whole place a lick of paint before it's sold.'

She still does as she's told then. Daddy's Good Girl. But The Siding cannot be Richard's to sell. There's something she's not saying. A hot nausea washes over me. I push up the sleeves of my sweater and reach for the toggle on my rucksack.

Susie eyes the marline spike warily as I pull it out. 'Do you have to wave that thing about in here?'

I ignore the question, twisting the rope firmly to the right to angle the point of the marline spike between the arch and swoop of the strands. The rope's too new for me to use my fingers to force an opening. I'll work a multi-stranded Button Knot, the knot sailors used to prevent un-reeving; a knot that will never be undone. This one will be a Star Knot, one of the most distinguished and individual of the Button Knots. To make a five-strand Star Knot, I'll need to splice another strand to the core of the rope. It has to be a five-strand Star Knot. The reason will come to me, sooner or later.

Rain splatters on to the windscreen from the tunnel of trees above. It's dark. I separate the strands. The kids whine and demand biscuits at regular intervals. The tape is still on full volume. Yet again, Susie's left hand reaches up to adjust the rear-view mirror, drops down – fingers stretching over the plastic stems of indicators, wipers, lights – falls lower, groping to check the hand brake is released, up again to fiddle with the fan and heat setting on the dashboard.

'That all right for you, Andy?'

'Fine.'

I want to lash out at something. My knees are wedged up against the plastic dashboard, which makes cracking egg-shell noises every time I shift position.

Susie glances over her shoulder at the kids before lowering her voice. 'He'd been eating black cherry yoghurt, Andy, all alone in that big empty house. He must've sat there all night by the time Mrs Hubbard found him. Spilt across his lap, it was, his trousers; the pot on the floor. Dad was always so . . . He'd have hated it, people seeing that. I tried to clean him up. With my hanky.'

I focus on working the knot snug. Sudden death: the easiest way to draw a crowd.

Susie glances my way. 'Say again?'

I must have spoken out loud.

'Houdini. Houdini said that sudden death is the easiest way to draw a crowd.'

'Well,' Susie shoves hair behind one ear and glares ahead at the road, 'in this case there were the usual absentees.'

YOU ARE EMPTY, BRITTLE as a shell, the blood in your ears the sea's ghost. The clock ticks; your lungs rise and fall.

Her cry comes from a long way off, like a breath catching. It's a struggle to get up off the bed and go to her. In the box room, she lies on her back in the cot, her body rocking a little from side to side, not thrashing about or screwing up her face as the others used to. Jean says she's just a placid baby; undemanding, but you know there's something. Not something wrong; less than that. Something not quite right; an absence. Michael won't speak about it.

The house is cold; it's late. You lower Elaine back into her cot and pat the blankets down around her. The pallor of her face with its high forehead reminds you of the head of a china doll.

In the bedroom, you lie again on the candlewick bedspread, limbs limp, hands motionless, only the edges of your mind alive. There's greyness; a desire to sleep that creeps up on you even as you finish dressing in the morning. Beneath you, the freshly laundered sheets are tucked down tight as the grave.

After a while you summon the energy to hitch up your skirt, unclip your stockings and haul yourself upright to roll them down, pushing the flimsy fawn-coloured rolls until they slip past your knees, your toes, one after the other, like so much shed skin. You fall back on to the bed, eyes closed. Sleep is easy. Dreams are colour and energy; in them you are present again.

It's exhaustion, Jean says. Not enough rest. Getting up to both Susie and the new baby in the night, finding yourself with your hand on a door handle, not knowing where you're going. She says it in front of Michael, flicking open her compact and powdering her nose, her eyes darting towards him. She loves to get him riled.

'Wretched uptight Presbyterian,' she mutters behind his back. 'Don't know how you put up with it.' She twiddles the dial on the wireless to find the Light Programme and sings along with Max Bygraves at the top of her tinny voice.

You must get up soon and tidy away the children's game. Perhaps Jean is right, it's just exhaustion. Two babies in less than a year – you'd felt so foolish discovering you were pregnant again. You'd conceived the very first time after Susie's birth. Michael came in from seeing a patient, woke you, and everything was over before you even thought of fixing yourself up. Afterwards you lay awake thinking about his hands on other women's bodies. His hands gentle against a woman's distended belly as a contraction comes, or firm on the inside of her thigh as the crown appears. You wondered if it had been a breech that night, or an umbilical cord around the neck; perhaps a stillbirth or the fluid chaos of haemorrhage. You imagined the mask, the gown, the lunge of his forearm. *Imperative to ensure that the mother survives.*

And after that night, as if your body was resolutely sealing itself, your milk had started to dry up. For Susie's bobbing head at your breast, the urgent searching lips squaring to scream, you'd felt a dream-like detachment. So different from when Andy was born.

Into your mind comes a picture of Michael. He's outlined against light streaming in through the bay window of your bedroom, head bent towards Andrew, only a few hours old, cradled in his arms. Michael looks back towards you on the bed. His face is wet.

'Look at him,' he says. 'Just look at him: our beautiful son.'

The front door: a slam. You must've dropped off. You hear the rubber seals of the Frigidaire, the scrape of a pan on the stove. Michael. He'll be making hot milk – a difficult delivery then. Chair legs against the lino. The metallic twist as he opens the whisky bottle. He's drinking downstairs. Elaine's quiet. A car going up the road throws its headlight beam across the wall; the curtains not even drawn yet.

Then, splintering wood; a thud on the landing.

'BLOODY HELL.'

It's Michael, grunting as if he's been punched.

You stumble to the door in time to see him rise to his feet and disentangle himself from the mess of sheets and wash-ing line that was the children's game. They have spent the afternoon sailing across the landing in the two halves of a cardboard laundry box. Andy snatched up the blue tissue paper wrapping the clean sheets and tore it into strips which he wrinkled and spread all over the landing linoleum to make the sea. Susie joined in, shrieking as she scooped shreds of tissue in her chubby arms and flung them into the air. Michael must have slipped on a wave.

Andy pushed Susie to and fro across the landing in her half of the laundry box, his socks slipping on the lino. You'd helped him hang the dirty sheets, huge as mainsails, between one bedroom door and another, meaning to take them down before Michael got home. Skipping ropes are still strung out across the landing and the two halves of the laundry box are moored to the banister with Midshipmen's Hitches and Crossed Fastenings. Now washing line hangs from the newel post, the banister broken.

'Michael! It was my fault. I fell asleep. I forgot to clear this . . .'

'Go back to bed. I'll deal with it.'

'But it's not . . .'

'GET BACK TO BED.' He kicks the laundry box and shoves open Andy's bedroom door. Wood cracks and shudders against plaster.

'Michael!'

He rips the covers from Andy's bed. You hope the mute curve of Andy's sleeping back will stop him and he does pause, his hand slowing as he reaches down. But then he drags Andy out of bed, across the floor on to the landing.

Andy, half-asleep, clutches on to his pyjama bottoms with his free hand.

'Look at this! Look at what you've done now!' Michael's face almost touches Andy's.

You try to move towards them, but your thighs have no bones.

Michael shoves Andy towards the banister, jaw hard against his ear. He mutters through gritted teeth, tendons in his neck taut and swollen.

'Clear it up. Just DO it.' The words spit out and he lurches down the stairs. Andy kneels down.

Your bare feet make no sound. Andy freezes when you kneel to pull him towards you. His body heaves with silent sobs and his face is sodden with tears. You cradle his head and stroke his hair but he struggles away, his fingers reaching for the hitches and fastenings around the banisters. Neither of you says a word. You start on the knots too, fingers gradually becoming surer. You both pause when you hear the clink of bottle on glass, and you half rise, but there's no other sound and you're almost finished.

Andy is shivering, so you squeeze into bed beside him and curl your body around his, feeling the occasional shudder of his rib cage. You breathe in his sleepy skin smell of salt and pencil sharpenings, the faint perfume of washing powder from his pyjama top. His breathing steadies. Warmth spreads through your body. A door closes downstairs; Michael will be sleeping on the sofa tonight.

You must be careful not to fall asleep here. You slip out from between the covers and creep across the landing to peer in at Susie's sleeping form. Back in your bedroom, perched on the edge of your bed, your mind is jerking and snapping.

When, eventually, you sleep, you dream Andy is lost and while a policeman stands with his clipboard in your sitting room, you run to the rope walk, your mind seeing him there, but when you get there the walk is covered with a long shed where chickens scratch and squawk. Andy stands at the far end, silhouetted against light that comes in through a door. He turns when you call his name, but he can't see you.

You must keep calling.

WE'RE ON A LONG car journey. Susie's leg is next to mine on the seat. We're squashed in the back with Elaine in her carrycot. It's hot. All the way we sing *We Love To Go A-Wandering* and *Casey Jones, Steaming An' A-rolling*, me and Mummy and Auntie Jean. We're all going to The Siding.

Honey is in the back of the Traveller. Her nose is up to the gap at the top of the window. Her ears have blown inside out and she smells of wet pebbles.

My legs are stuck to the seat. I lift them up, one at a time, like pulling off plasters. Susie copies me and we lift our legs up and put them down again, watching our skin stretch. Auntie Jean passes us sherbet lemons to suck and Susie cries when her mouth gets sore.

When we get there, Honey pushes out of the Traveller, her tongue curly and panting, her whole body wagging as she gallops round and round, knocking into chair legs and door frames and skidding on the lino, her claws clicking and the tip of her tail bleeding because it hits things when it wags so hard because she loves it here. Me and Susie want one of the special plasters from the tin to put on Honey's tail but Mummy says she will be better off without it.

Susie doesn't like the pebbles yet. I help her but she is too slow so I run over the pebbles and kick my new stripy canvas shoes off at the edge and run and run over the wet sand towards the sea.

The sky is huge and high, up from the sand and up from the sea. Wind and sky rush in my ears. I can breathe in whole sky. I run, stop, fill myself with sky right up to the very top until I am fat and full like a balloon. Then I shout it out. Susie copies. We can shout at the tops of our voices and still the sand and the sky go on being big and flat and happy.

Father has not come down to The Siding with us. Patients don't have holidays from being ill and babies come when they feel like it. They don't wait to be born. Usually they don't even wait for the night to be finished. Father might come down on Saturday or Sunday.

Father says when their bedroom door is shut we must not go in there. *Do as I say, Andrew.*

Back up the beach I can see Auntie Jean stand and stretch her bathing cap over her head, pushing her hair up inside, the rubber straps dangling over Mummy, who sits in one of the stripy deckchairs with her pot of Nivea, putting a blob of white on her arm and rubbing it in. The hospital blanket with Mummy's old name sewn into the corner is spread, lumpy on the pebbles. Mummy's old name is the same as Grampy's and Auntie Jean's. There is a tartan vacuum flask with tea for Mummy and Auntie Jean and sponge fingers in the plastic picnic bag, lemon puffs and crisps with blue paper twists of salt. We don't have to wash our hands first.

If Father does come down to The Siding, he does not wear canvas shoes or have bare feet on the beach like the rest of us. He wears his shiny lace-up shoes and socks.

I can run with bare feet on the pebbles. I have bare feet all day but Susie does not like the sand between her toes. She stands with her legs straight and cries.

And sometimes we eat fish and chips with our fingers, or tea will be poached eggs and mash. Me and Susie make nests with the mashed potato and mix in the gold top creamy milk with our forks and Mummy and Auntie Jean smoke Senior Service and say let's not tell Daddy. Auntie Jean has made an ashtray out of a chipped cereal bowl with blue and white stripes. It sits on the glass top of the green wicker table.

Father threw a packet of Mummy's cigarettes on the bonfire. His neck was lumpy with shouting. *How many times do I have to tell you?*

I like the sand between my toes when I slip them down in the cool between the sheet and the edge of the mattress and listen to the wood pigeons, fat and gentle. My bedroom has a curvy ceiling and rope shelves for luggage because it was once a carriage in a Pullman train. I put my box of cars and *The Mountain of Adventure* and my book on Houdini on the rope shelves above my head. On the window it says 'SMOKING' in back-to-front capitals and I can smell the smoke from Mummy and Auntie Jean's cigarettes and they laugh. This is what I can hear: the creak of the wicker chairs and Mummy and Auntie Jean laughing and Honey's tail thump thump thump on the floor.

THE CLICK OF THE indicator wakes me. We turn left into Sea
Lane, entering the village. A sign over a café, 'Fish 'n' Chips',
flashes on and off. Two ride-on toys, a pink elephant and a
yellow giraffe, are chained together, and a Mr Whippy van is
parked up on the forecourt by some stacked picnic tables.

'This is what people mean when they say a place is
"dead" in winter.' Susie speaks under her breath. The boys
are still asleep.

'I suppose.'

'But,' her voice is flat, 'it makes it easier, that it's so
different.'

I say nothing. I don't know if it will make it any easier.

We reach the T-junction with West Beach Road. 'Strictly
Members Only' announces a sign for the sailing club.
Behind us, the caravan jolts and sways along the pitted
mud track as Susie negotiates puddles hiding craters in the
road. The twins loll in their car seats, mouths drooping and
soft with dribble; a sock dangles. The older boy has undone
his seatbelt and is curled among the empty crisp packets
and plastic dinosaurs. He's clutching a red beaker with a lid
and a spout. It has leaked on to his trousers.

I crane forward to peer out at the low buildings huddled
behind tamarisk and hydrangea bushes. The headlights

pick out a line of white-painted breeze blocks evenly spaced along the verge, a metal beer barrel with 'NO ARKING' in black and gold stick-on lettering and, further on, lumps of concrete. The drizzle gives way to a sudden downpour.

'Goodness!' says Susie between gritted teeth, whacking the windscreen wipers on to full speed. 'I suppose there used not to be so many cars.'

'What?'

'All these "No Parking" signs.'

A couple of lobster baskets on the verge are lit up, garish with fluorescent tape, in the beam of the headlights.

'They certainly don't want anyone stopping, do they?' Susie tosses her head. She's pissed off.

I used not to feel a trespasser here. I belonged. But every place has several histories, both personal and collective. During the war, Grandfather told me, this was a 'No Go' area. The permanent residents were shipped out of their railway-carriage homes and the specialist army and navy engineers moved in, to carry out top secret work on the concrete Mulberry harbours. Here, trespassers must be particularly unwelcome.

Many railway carriages have gone, or are unrecognisable. We pass a sprawling bungalow. The caravan's bulk sets off the intruder spotlight. Displayed in the brightness is a Spanish-style 'villa', fenced and gated with black metal rods topped with golden spearheads. There's a huge water feature, Cupid dribbling water from his chubby penis, El Vienza in looped writing across a white wall.

Susie snorts. 'At least it's not Dun Roamin.'

'It's grim.'

'The estate agent says the few remaining Pullmans are worth a bomb. There's one up for over 350,000. Amazing, when you think they tried to demolish the lot in the sixties.'

Not so amazing though that Richard wants it done up in order to sell. If I'd met the bloody man before Susie married him I'd have warned her off. Stood up at the wedding and shouted my protestations.

Ahead an official-looking sign says 'Car Park Closed. Turn Back Now.'

Susie changes down into first gear. 'I don't think I can turn this thing around here.'

'No, no, keep going a bit further—'

I stare out into the dark. The Siding is just before the track turns into a footpath; the last house but one. 'There!' A low roof above the tamarisks. 'There it is!'

Susie steers the Volvo on to the grassy verge, watching in the rear-view mirror as the caravan tilts and follows. Just before she switches off the headlights, I notice gates across the end of the road, chained and padlocked.

We sit and gaze out at the shadows of the tamarisks flailing in the wind. The car ticks.

'Well, the rain's stopped, at least,' says Susie, as she turns to check the boys. 'But listen to that sea.'

Pebbles shift and rumble, like distant buildings collapsing. Susie hugs her arms and rubs her hands up and down them, although the car is very warm. The windscreen is misting over.

'Come on then.' She flings the door open.

Wind hurtles through the car. Crisp packets and chocolate wrappers fly up from the foot-well and out into the night. We totter towards the sea, the sound of it drowning everything. At the top of the shingle bank, we stop. Foam surges phosphorescent in the black. It's a struggle to breathe, like being smothered with too much air. Susie tugs on my sleeve, hair across her face, as she mouths words that are snatched away. I nod, and we allow ourselves to be buffeted back towards the car.

The twins sleep on, legs akimbo, but the older boy is stirring. I stand by the car while Susie rummages through the paraphernalia in her shoulder bag. Through the car window, I watch her pile things on her lap: a blue dummy with a fraying ribbon, a baby wipe smeared with chocolate, a half-sucked rusk. The skin on her knuckles is chapped and sore, and she's wearing her wedding ring on her right hand because of the eczema on her left. She jams her thin hair behind her ears.

When I can't wait any longer, I open the car door and duck my head in. 'The key?'

'It's here, I know it is, somewhere.'

'There'll be one in the coal bunker, almost bound to be.'

Fumbling in the glove compartment I find a torch, and switch it on. It goes out. I bang it on the car seat and light flickers back.

The sliding door at the base of the bunker is stuck. The rough edge of the concrete grazes my fingertips, but then the door shoots up and jams halfway. The torch beam dims. I switch it off and, groping in the dark, find a loop of string in the coal dust just inside the opening: the key.

Susie has unhooked the caravan and is winding down the legs. I should help.

'Susie!' I shout, waving the key.

She nods and sticks a thumb in the air. 'Great. I'm going to get the boys into their beds. You go and have a look.'

The paint has cracked and peeled from the front door and, where the pebbled glass should be, there's a square of hardboard. Susie is moving about in the caravan, dealing with the boys.

The key turns, but the door won't open. I kick once or twice, then throw myself against it at shoulder height. I'm in the hallway. A peppery smell. And something sweet, like rotting apples. I reach for the light and find the familiar dome of Bakelite casting, the switch with its rounded end. I wipe my fingers on my jeans, swaying in the sudden brightness. The hallway stretches away like a tunnel. There's a ting from the light bulb and darkness again. I grip the radiator with one hand.

'OK?' Susie is at my arm.

'Yes. It's nothing. My sandals are wet; slippery.' I smile to reassure her but in the wavering torchlight, patches of brown linoleum in the hallway are disintegrating. In places it lifts away from the floorboards, shifting and treacherous beneath my wet soles.

Susie flicks a switch in a doorway. Nothing happens. Again, she flicks the switch up and down. Click click click.

'Why don't we do all this tomorrow, in the light?'

The batteries are almost out. Each time I hit the torch with the flat of my hand, the beam lasts only seconds before fading. The last time, nothing.

'It's no good getting belligerent with it. I'm going back to the boys. You sleeping in the car?'

'Probably.' I put a hand to the wall. It reverberates with the pounding of the waves.

'Don't forget the kids'll have us up at crack of dawn. Night.' She kisses her hand and waves it at me, then trots across the wind-flattened grass, head down.

In the kitchen, the noise of the wind is louder, gusting against the window. The glass panes rattle. Moonlight comes and goes through tamarisks. I edge through the moving light and shadow to the sink and try the cold tap. It's stiff and then loose. No water. I try the hot tap. It wobbles on its pipe: nothing.

I stand, perfectly still in the middle of the room. The walls creak. Wooden boards shift under my feet. The sea's turmoil surrounds me. Raindrops streak down the glass and collect along the bottom of the window pane. With them, images from family cine films, black and white, jumpy, cluster in my mind. My mother, dark hair waved and parted to the side, holds out a birthday cake: four candles.

Then, wearing lipstick and pearls, she bends to kiss my head goodbye. And Grandfather rides me down the garden in a wheelbarrow. The wheel rolls and bumps; my shoes bang on the metal. Grandfather holds up a piece of rope and tells me 'cnotta' is an old English word that means to join together.

FATHER SCREWS UP OUR blue tissue waves. He pushes them into the metal thing with legs in the garden. He stamps with his wellingtons on Susie's boat until it is the cardboard lid of the laundry box again and he squashes the lid into the metal thing too, on top of our blue tissue-paper waves. Then he strikes a match and sticks it through the metal cage. Another match and another until all our waves are on fire. There is smoke. Susie cries and rubs her eyes. I hold her hand and wish very, very hard for our tissue-paper waves to get huge as a house, and crash down, to grow into huge roaring waves that can knock down even a grown-up and fill their mouth and ears and nose with the rush and burn of salty water. I wish for a storm. A storm with waves like the ones in the painting halfway up the stairs, big and black, making everything else in the whole wide world silly and small.

But our tissue-paper waves are soft, like at low tide when the sea is shallow and warm and I lie on the sand while the sea washes over me, quiet as if it's dreaming.

Father is burning our dreaming waves.

'They were only little waves,' I say, nearly to myself.

'I beg your pardon?' He holds the top part of my arm. His mouth is wet and red. I say it again, moving my lips to make the words come out.

'They were only little waves.'

Father walks me fast to the kitchen. Mummy looks up at his face and starts to get out of her chair, but she has baby Elaine in her arms and before she can be properly up, Susie runs to put her head in Mummy's apron and pushes her back down on the chair.

In the hall, Father opens the door of the cupboard under the stairs with the toe of his Wellington boot and bends me through the gap. He kicks the door shut. I am in the dark. The key turns with a clunk.

The cupboard under the stairs smells of shoe polish.

I am in the dark until I can see sense.

I hold my breath and close my eyes. Grampy tells me about the Lapland witches who tied wind knots to sell to sailors so they didn't have to whistle for a wind to sail by. Whistling is the Devil's music. It can make a storm come.

I don't have any enchanted knots in the cupboard under the stairs. It's dark. I don't have any string to tie even a Reef Knot. Left over right, right over left and under, his fingers on my fingers, Grampy tells me the Reef Knot is one of the simplest and best of the uniting knots.

In the cupboard under the stairs I suck hard on my thumb, my teeth on the bone.

After this is the first time I run away to Grampy's.

I WAKE TO THE sound of the sea, the ripped lino of the
kitchen floor slippery beneath my hip. I roll on to my back.
The white painted wood of the railway carriage ceiling
curves above me. Last night's gust and surge of wind and
waves has ceased. Today, there's a distant sighing *shuuush*
followed by a pause like an intake of breath, a gathering of
the next long curl of water.

No sounds of movement yet from Susie and the boys in
the caravan; it's early. No voices. No rain. A grubby
sheepskin jacket and the old binoculars hang from a nail
in the wall. I get up.

But once on the pebbles I can see the tide is far out, the
sea yawning back over damp stretches of sand. Wet sand:
gleaming and ridged for miles and miles. The smear and
squelch of it, thick as wet paint. Adrenalin flares. My
body wants to be far away. Fast. I press the heels of my
palms to my eyes. I'll have to turn back. But then, at my
feet, are the pebbles: black, white, grey, tan, brick-orange,
dark red. Ahead, the shingle banks appear more uniform
in colour, predominately orange-brown. The stones are
glistening wet and slide beneath my weight. Smaller
stones, like gravel, roll and bounce down the slope. I
focus on the crunching sideways slip of each step. Unable

to look across the sand towards the horizon, I can walk parallel to it.

The sea has sculpted the shingle banks into curves and scoops. I will collect the smooth black pebbles. They warm in my hands and lend a weight to my pockets as I clamber over the rough wooden breakwaters. The breeze invigorates. Perhaps, after all, this will be all right.

I tramp for a while then, testing my courage, lift the binoculars and look up. Careful to keep the blue arc of sky in my circle of vision, I move the binoculars steadily downwards until I find the smudged line of purple. The horizon: that distant place which both does and does not exist. Sunlight catches on the slow roll of a distant wave and throws into sharp relief the shadowy underside of its curl. Two flocks of *Calidris canutus*, Canute's favourite bird, perform their characteristic aerobatics. One flock shows the dark plumage of their upper parts, the other forms a loose diamond of white as they turn and reveal their silvery undercarriage. Towards the mudflats another dense flock is feeding, long bills plugging in and out. Their continuous low twitter sounds close, intimate. A woman in a bulky waxed jacket and wellingtons is striding across the mudflats. She's tall. Long, slender legs. I glance at my watch; time to head back.

Muffled thumps and shrieks come from the caravan. The boys must be up.

The twins are wearing nappies and vests. They bare their teeth and roar at me from under the table, scratching at each other with clawed fingers. They chase around the caravan, waving bits of toast and jam. The caravan rocks. I stand in the doorway, reluctant to step inside.

'Why are *you* here again?' the biggest kid asks, peering sideways at me up through his blond fringe.

'Andy, sit down. I know you don't like to be inside for more than five minutes, but you haven't stopped fidgeting.'

Susie's hair is shoved back behind her ears. She's surrounded by towers of folded bedding, miniature pairs of jeans and T-shirts, piles of what looks like shiny wads of folded plastic. Disposable nappies, I guess. Her voice strains, bright and brittle, above the kids' noise. Her tea has skinned over. Her egg sits untouched in its egg cup. Now she's crying again, leaning her forehead on one hand, face hidden in a scrunched-up tea towel. Her other hand, nails bitten, cuticles ragged, lies on the narrow table amongst a collection of multicoloured socks neatly sorted and rolled into pairs. How can she stand all this?

When she was about six, Susie used to press straight lines into the sleeves of her bottle-green school jumper. Every Sunday. The way our mother had done. And she pinned back her fringe with a round plastic slide. It irritated the hell out of me, the way that slide dragged down because it was too chunky for her thin hair. She was always fiddling to get it just right.

Susie's still in the tea towel. Buses and Beefeaters. I slide in beside her at the rickety table and contemplate putting a hand over hers. Instead, I dig a teaspoon into the sugar and load it.

'Susie.' Crystals tumble over each other. I tip the spoon. Sugar sprinkles from the edge of the spoon back into the bowl. 'I shouldn't have come.'

'What?' She lifts her face from the tea towel. It's a mess, bloated and wet. 'Aren't you going to help me?'

I can't imagine why she might need my help. I get up to cut myself a slice of bread and open the caravan door wide. The biggest boy tumbles out on to the wet grass. Susie seems not to notice. Getting to his feet, he stands with a hand shoved down the front of his pyjama bottoms, clutching his willy.

Susie has stopped talking. She's gazing out at the tamarisks, a hand on her belly. It reminds me.

'How long . . .?'

'The baby? Oh ages. I just look enormous because, well, I'm not exactly voluptuous, am I? That's why it shows so much.' Susie strokes the swell of her belly. The self-absorbed caress makes me think of masturbation. That focused concentration.

'And have they, you know, said anything?'

She laughs at me, hand covering her mouth. 'I can't believe you still do that.'

'What?'

'Pull your ear lobe about! Look at you.'

I slide my hand into my pocket.

'I'm sorry. It's just so . . . weird.' She bites her lip. 'Where were we?' She reaches for a balled pair of socks and separates one from the other. 'I expect you're thinking about Elaine,' she says, not looking at me.

My hand fists in my pocket. I concentrate on opening it, stretching my fingers one by one to touch the edge of the pocket seams. A curlew mews, plaintive and invisible, somewhere in the pale sky outside. The boys are lugging buckets filled with pebbles. Even though it's freezing cold, one of the twins has taken off his vest and dropped it on the grass. One of the adhesive tabs on his nappy has come unstuck.

Susie picks an imaginary piece of fluff from a sock. 'No. It was nothing hereditary. It was the labour – way too long. Something like thirty-six hours, Dad said. It all went wrong then. Maybe lack of oxygen, I don't think they knew. No,' she tosses her head, 'I may be small but I can push them out easy as peas from a pod.'

She's not all here, is what they said about Elaine. I'd lick the soles of her fat and placid feet to bring her back, giggling. Or so I thought then – that I could bring her back.

And I used to lick colours too, to feel them. Beige linoleum and the thick spread of red polish on the front step. The float and slide of pale blue Formica and the kitchen table's silvery edge that swooped like a slope. Bakelite door handles, dark as chocolate. Also, smells: the powdered down of my aunt's cheek, my mother's hair, sunburned after a day in the sun. *Stop that this minute.* I licked surfaces: the rollers on the Acme wringer; the sheen on the coal in the bunker; the humming fur of ice inside the refrigerator. *What is the matter with you?* It became another thing I did in my room with the door shut. I think there's a name for it now.

Susie wipes her face.

'Sorry, I can't seem to stop doing this.' She swallows and sniffs and rubs her nose. 'It's . . . Poor Dad. He went on loving her.'

Listen to her: Dad, Dad, Dad. She never got away from him. I pinch soft bread from the middle of the chunk of bread and roll it in my palm until it's a doughy ball I can drop on to my tongue.

'I looked, after he . . . I don't know what I was looking for, really, but I found a half-empty perfume bottle, "Tweed", in the dressing-table drawer with his shaving stuff. The top had corroded and it had leaked into the drawer. That must have been hers.'

She gives another little shake of her head.

'I was only five. There's so much I don't remember. Dad started to talk a bit at the end. He said they put you on liquid sedatives when it all happened. Would they *do* that to a nine-year-old child?'

I start on the crusty edges of the bread, tearing with my teeth. I stuff large bitefuls into my mouth until it's rammed. I can't speak.

Susie sighs. 'Well, let's not trawl through all that nightmare stuff now. There's enough to cope with in the present.'

She finally takes a sip of tea and wipes her mouth. 'Because there's his will. He's left her everything, Andy, including The Siding. Never divorced her – can you believe it? After what she did? So, unless she's dead, she's next of kin. We have to decide what to do.'

Bread is wedged to the roof of my mouth. I give it a poke with my tongue.

'I've never thought,' I use my forefinger to dislodge the bread, and swallow. A solid lump sticks in my throat, 'that she might be dead.'

A sudden riot and squabble of sparrows. What I've just said is a lie. I have thought my mother through many different scenarios, including death.

'Well,' Susie speaks under her breath, 'I just want to know, that's all. If she is still alive, she can bloody well go to hell.'

YOU SHOULDN'T LET YOUR father stand there so long in this heat. He's forgotten his walking stick again, left it at the post office or in his greenhouse, or somewhere he can't lay his hands on it. His head's bowed, the fingers of one hand loosely holding his panama hat as if he has just this moment lifted it in greeting. As he closes his eyes and his lips move, a lump of longing swells in your throat.

His face has the same distracted look as – more than five years ago it is now – the day your mother died. You'd been up very early, trailing along the streets with Andy in the pram because he was fractious with a tooth coming and Michael hadn't got to bed until half past four that morning. When Andy finally dropped off to sleep, you called in at your parents' for a cup of tea before heading home back along the river path. They were always up early.

But the milk bottles were still on the step, the newspaper sticking out through the letter box. The thought of their breakfast table with its seersucker tablecloth, the kitchen filled with sunshine and the smell of toast, made you realise how hungry you were as you rapped again at the door. At last, just visible through the yellow glass, Dad swayed along the hallway. He kept the door chain on, peering out through the gap.

'Dad, it's only me. Sorry it's a bit early.'

'I was unable,' he passed a hand over his face, 'to wake her this morning. Her heart's stopped beating.'

Your own heart flipped. You went to climb the stairs.

He put out a hand to stop you.

You sat on the edge of the sofa and Honey nudged at your hand with a wet muzzle as you stared out at the beads of dew on the lawn. The only sounds were Honey's whimpers and the heavy tock of the pendulum clock in the hall. Eventually, uneasy in the still of the house and desperate to see her, you went upstairs. Your father lay on the bed, cradling her head and stroking her hair, his lips moving close to her ear.

'It's all right,' he rested his forehead on hers. 'We're nearly there now; a few more minutes.'

Afterwards, you had wanted him to talk about it. But once she was buried, the tenderness was replaced by a tight-lipped anger. The only time you'd ever seen him really angry. He barely spoke at the funeral. You nodded when relatives commented: *He's taking it very hard, isn't he?* – didn't mention him swiping a hand along the mantelpiece, smashing the carriage clock to the floor.

He stayed with you for a few weeks until Michael complained about hearing him at night, pacing up and down. Then he wouldn't have Honey back. Jean had to keep her. There seemed to be no logic in it. And at first he hardly seemed to go out, beyond his garden.

You didn't know what to do to help him. You tried to think what your mother would have done, and realised there were many things you should've asked her. What was it like, to be loved so much?

She was tiny, much smaller than you. She'd dart around the kitchen making supper while your father, a hand on the door jamb, took off his boots and stood to watch her;

waiting. He'd put out a hand, place a palm, huge, at the small of her back, and she would pause, poised beside him. On the settee in the evenings, he'd lift her legs on to his lap and massage the insteps of her stockinged feet or circle an ankle with his callused fingers. Images of them touching, from your childhood, come back to you often now.

'Gynaecology and obstetrics,' you'd answered your mother proudly, when Michael first started courting you. 'And GP work at the Albert Road surgery.'

Your mother lowered her teacup. 'Well then, you'll need to get him off his pedestal right away.' She snorted. 'No playing doctors and nurses in a marriage.'

You laughed together in her steamy kitchen, wiping tears from your eyes. A suet pudding simmered in a pan on the stove, lid rattling. She'd paused in the doorway, slipped her arms around your waist, rested her head on your shoulder. 'You make sure he's right for you.'

How do you ever know?

Michael had swept you off your feet. You were still new to the hospital, nervous to prove yourself capable of a promotion to theatre sister which you hadn't thought you'd get. Your first Monday, and Michael sailed down a hospital corridor towards you, white coat billowing. He swivelled round as you passed each other.

'Nurse!' He whisked a black-and-gold fountain pen out of his breast pocket and rolled it between his fingers. 'Write it down for me,' he handed you the pen, 'your name. Have you a telephone number?' He put out a hand; his handshake was firm and warm. 'Michael.'

He tore a corner from a notice on the board for you to write on. His nib scratched; you were anxious about spoiling it.

'I'll take you for a drive,' he nodded in agreement with himself. 'In fact, I'll give you a driving lesson. What do you say to that?' His voice was just like James Mason's. And there was the wave in his hair, combed to one side. He pocketed the scrap of paper and leaned with an elbow on the window ledge as you walked away down the corridor. You hoped the seams of your stockings were straight. He watched, you knew he did, even though by the time you reached the corner and glanced back, he was gone. You splashed out on a visit to the hairdresser's for a Veronica Lake cut and set, shiny waves lifting to one side from your forehead and nestling at your neck, and spent an age worrying about which shoes you should wear for driving.

He called you a 'handsome' woman. You were flattered until you wondered why he hadn't said pretty, or beautiful. Jean said it was because you are tall and well endowed. 'It's always breasts with men,' Jean said, eyes narrowed as she lowered her head to light her cigarette, 'the bigger the better. He wouldn't tell you that.'

Michael strode the hospital wards and corridors, back straight, head up. He bent close to patients, looking them full in the eyes. Women smiled up in surprise when he cupped a heel in his palm, ran his fingers lightly either side of the length of a foot as he chatted about dates and antenatal care. They weren't to know the intimacy of his touch was an illusion; he was simply assessing pelvic width. Even the elderly female patients responded to him, fingering the ribbons at the neck of their bed jackets, fluffing up their bed-flattened hair if they glimpsed him sweeping down the ward.

He took you to the pictures to see Hitchcock's *Strangers on a Train*, boating on the river at Henley. He bought sheet music: Mario Lanza's 'The Loveliest Night of the Year'; 'Unforgettable' by Nat 'King' Cole. That won your mother over straight away, those gatherings around her piano while you played and Michael and your parents sang.

He drove you to the little church at Cookham where, walking in the graveyard, he pointed out the gravestones with his family name, lichen-covered and leaning, one or two of them going back as far as the 1700s. He bought expensive flowers and chocolates every week for the first two months. The other nurses exclaimed over the roses in crisp Cellophane brought to the staff kitchen by the porter almost every Monday. Often you took them to the wards.

The sex had happened too quickly. In your mind, Michael was still gowned up, in charge; the surgeon. Eyes closed, you wondered how to kiss him, where to touch him. The harsh graze of his stubble made your face sore. And the brown circle of rubber, powdery in its box – you never thought to put it in until it was too late, a halt in things, running to the bathroom and messing around while Michael lay on the bed talking and pulling himself about. It'll get better, you told yourself. You'd mentioned something to Jean. She said, 'Well, we're not supposed to enjoy it that much anyway, are we? Women, I mean.'

Your mother had. You're sure of it. Hoggie had once talked about being the single child, a mistake; about being excluded because her parents only really wanted each other. As she spoke, you remembered one summer holiday in St Leonards-on-sea, a fortnight in a furnished flat on the sea front, you and Jean running along the promenade to the ice-cream van, every day, coins clutched in your hands.

'Why not sit out on the wall and eat them so as you don't drip ice cream all the way up the stairs?' your mother suggested one day.

After that, you and Jean always did, you sat on the brick wall that scratched the backs of your legs and you looked across the promenade at the silvery railings and the stall with the multicoloured plastic windmills that rattled round in the wind. Once, you'd not had enough money, or Jean had dropped hers down a drain, you can't remember what made you turn back and run up the dark stairs. You burst in. Their flustered movements – your mother smoothing down her dress, your father coughing, his back to you as he walked into the bathroom – it came to you in later years that they had not been sitting drinking the tea that had grown cold in their teacups.

Your father picks up the freesias again, lifts them to his nose before laying them in the vase at the base of the headstone. Does Michael know now, freesias are your favourite flower, as they were your mother's?

'Time to go, Dad?'

When he nods, you have the sudden urge to prolong this weekly hour in the graveyard, this hour away from the children.

Beside you, your father limps between the gravestones towards the car. You lean over to open the door for him. He lowers himself slowly into the passenger seat, lifting up his leg to ease it into the foot-well.

'Going rusty.' He tut-tuts at himself, in the way your mother used to cluck her tongue at him. 'Have we time for The Copper Kettle, duck?' He pats your leg and nods. 'Talking to your mother has made me yearn for some tea and that chocolate cake they do.'

SUSIE LEAVES WITH THE boys to buy bottles of water and other 'essentials'. Silence settles like dust. I sit at the kitchen table. A leaf litter smell from the rotting lino; curled husks of dead woodlice everywhere. Bakelite door handles and chipped Formica surfaces; a blue metal cooking stove on legs. And a shadow in the room, like a warp in time. Nobody has been here for years, by the looks of things. Susie said Father paid out for someone to cut the grass and mend the roof if necessary; basic repairs. Not much else has been done.

She has written a list, 'TO DO' at the top, underlined twice. I'll look at it later. In the living room, I lower myself on to the faded cushion of a lopsided wicker chair and place my palm on the cool glass top of a wicker table. Then, through the salted glass of the window, I glimpse the roof of the shed.

'Flipping heck, Andrew! What a mess.'

Susie's voice makes me jump. As I turn towards her, the bottom of the cardboard box in my arm gives way. A jug and half a dozen striped beakers clatter on to the grass.

'What on earth are you *doing* in there?' She starts to pick her way towards the shed, stepping between rusted shears, cans of creosote, broken deckchair frames and an assort-ment of sagging boxes. The boys are thudding about inside The Siding, running up and down the long wooden corridor that's built down the side of one of the railway carriages.

'Ah – you're back already?' I pick up a beaker, remembering the feel of them, brittle plastic against my teeth.

The biggest kid appears at the back door and starts to follow her across the grass. 'Henry! Be careful.'

I point to the shelf at the back of the shed. 'There's a hammock.'

Susie peers in. The bulging canvas sack lies there like a cocoon. Henry strains to burrow his head in-between our legs across the doorway, tugging with a fist at the bottom of Susie's jumper. I try to ignore him.

'And look,' I tap Susie's arm. Hanks of tarred rope hang from the ceiling.

'A hammock? Is it a high priority?' Her voice is shrill.

I try to interrupt. 'I was looking for secateurs, to clip back . . .'

But she's talking. '—and I'll have to take the boys back tonight as I can't get hold of a plumber or an electrician today. You'd think this was the back of beyond. We'll have to get a skip for all this bloody rubbish.'

She grabs the kid by the back of his sweatshirt and hauls him out from the piles of cardboard boxes. Her mouth is a straight line. 'This is impossible.'

'I can sort the electrics.' Rubber gloves, a hammer and nail – that's all I need to bypass the meter. 'I'll put the kettle on.' I'm heading for the house as I speak. 'Got any water?'

Susie follows me and starts slamming cupboard doors in the kitchen. 'Anyone would think you grew up in a barn.' She raises her eyes heavenwards. 'I'm going to have to buy a few bits in Maidenhead, I guess. Nothing is in stock down here. We'll have a clear-out, make a start on the cleaning, then think about how much we need to do to jazz the place up before we put it on the market.'

She shoves her hair behind her ears and avoids my eyes as she pulls on rubber gloves. 'I'm going to have a go at the windows,' she announces and reaches for the bleach. 'May as well achieve something useful. Can you take down all the curtains and chuck them outside? And keep an eye on the boys with that junk from the shed.'

There's so much material. Although the vivid blue of the cornflowers has faded, the fabric feels heavy and substantial. The pattern is so familiar, the extravagance of the cornflowers splashed over the pale blue background, it's as if I saw it only yesterday. The linings are ripped and stained with damp.

I carry the pile of curtains outside. Something about the soft weight in my arms and the swathes of fabric make me think of lifting a woman, cradling her in my arms. I stand in the long grass. My mother must have made these curtains.

I negotiate the stuff that litters the grass. It looks as though the remnants, the discarded and broken household utensils and tools, the disintegrating pieces of lino, have been vomited on to the grass.

Folding the curtains loosely, I push them into a back corner of the shed. Clouds scud over a pale blue sky. I find I'm glad not to be getting back into the Volvo for the return journey. I stack boxes and cans and carry them back to the shed. There seems to be too much to fit back into the space. Tangled coils of rope swing against the back of my neck. Later, I'll investigate the shed contents more thoroughly.

When I stick my head around the kitchen door, Susie is scrubbing mould from the deep grooves in the carriage window frames with a toothbrush.

'Half an hour and I'll be finished,' she says, blowing her fringe out of her eyes. 'Then we'd better make a move.'

She's trembling with exertion. 'I'll feed the kids in that café on the corner.'

At the last minute, over fish and chips at the café, Susie has a change of heart and tries to persuade me to leave with her. 'At least until the water's sorted out,' she says, fiddling her wedding ring round and round. 'And the phone. Otherwise how will I get hold of you?'

'I'll use the phone box. Or the pub'll have one.'

'Well,' she stands to wipe the twins' mouths, one after the other, a hand on their heads to stop them squirming away. 'And you're OK for money now?'

I nod. She's already handed out cash to tide me over. She wants to sort an account for me to use while I'm down here, to buy paint and odds and ends; and food. Some warmer clothes. I wish she'd stop fussing.

The kids slide down from the table. Outside, a guy has turned a hose on the window to spray off the salt. The three kids line up inside and stare as water pounds and sluices the glass.

Susie sniffs and takes a breath. She's going to start all over again.

'There's so much . . . Richard kept saying she was bound to come to the funeral. But she didn't.'

'No.'

'In the church I looked for her, kept turning round, thinking, I know she won't look the same and I might not recognise her, but I didn't know how to imagine her, except from *ancient* photographs. I don't even know how old she is. Andy, I don't even know her date of birth.'

'No. 1920s?'

'So, she's seventy-odd?'

'Sixty, I'd say.'

Susie frowns. 'Well, she was younger than Dad, but she'd have to be *late* sixties at least, surely.'

My mother is young and wears a headscarf, a navy Guernsey sweater over slacks, and she sits in a deckchair on the beach, squinting into a compact to apply her lipstick.

'Jean gave me Hoggie's address, years ago, when I was going through a crisis at university. She was living quite near me then, in Leeds. Remember Hoggie?'

Red hair escaping from hairgrips, the nurse's belt and starched white apron; a watch pinned upside down on the apron's bib. I nod.

The guy outside starts messing around for the kids' benefit, holding the hose away for a second or two, then turning it back on to the glass, thumb over the end so water smacks the glass. Two of the kids leap about, pointing and yelling, but the bigger one puts his hands to his ears. He takes a step backwards, picking his nose. He watches as the other two clap and laugh, pull faces and shove at each other. They turn in unison, mirror images of each other, to the window again.

Susie reads my mind. 'Henry gets excluded. Those two are in their own little world. People hyphenate them. Y'know, "Paul-and-Matthew, do you want a biscuit? Paul-and-Matthew, do want to play?" Even I often call them The Twins.'

The kid, Henry, takes another step back, away from the window and the noise of the water. The other two lean and roll together, a jumble of chubby arms and legs. Lost in each other. They shriek and point, eyes wide, when the hosepipe guy shoves open the door and strides in. Henry's lip wobbles. He staggers back to the table. The hosepipe guy rattles his bucket and cloth and pulls a face back at the twins. Henry clambers past my knees to bury his head in Susie's lap.

'Tired, sweety?'

Henry turns his head from side to side, slurping on his thumb. He lies with his foot thumping rhythmically up and down against my shin. I move my legs an inch or so but he wriggles, repositioning himself so that he can go on kicking me. Finally, I put a hand loosely around his ankle, half expecting loud complaint. Or a harder kick. But his foot stills. It feels such a delicate, breakable thing, his ankle. Like bone china. Susie gazes into the middle distance, a hand on his head. The leg I'm holding gradually relaxes, foot falling outwards.

'I went to have tea with Hoggie quite regularly before Richard and I got married.' Susie strokes the blond head on her lap. 'Where were you then? Don't think we knew.' Her hand on Henry's hair lifts and falls, lifts and falls.

He must be asleep now. His ankle's warm and still in my hand.

'Hoggie's in America now. We haven't been in touch for years. She showed me their old nursing snaps. Holidays abroad: Monaco, and so forth. Biarritz. It helped.'

I've got several photograph albums of my mother's – thick pages, black-and-white photos with white scalloped edges – her comments (that strange habit nurses had of calling each other by surname only, like public schoolboys) and scattered exclamation marks under each one. They're in a box in my room, in Triopetra. Letters too, from various nursing friends. I can't remember how I got hold of them. Susie will probably be pissed off.

'Now Jean's gone, there's no one left. Well, one or two of Dad's patients were at his funeral, of course. Can't believe there are still any around. That awful woman who gave me Big Doll one Christmas, remember? She hung around for years. And Mrs Hubbard still cleaned. But I felt like a child, really, an orphan. Bereft, you know?'

Big Doll. That awful walking, talking doll with orange hair. Something happened . . .

Susie gropes up her sleeve for a tissue and blows her nose. 'Know what I did? I came home from the church hall tea-and-bloody-cakes afterwards, marched down to the bottom of the garden, kicked the fence and shouted at her. Bloody selfish woman.'

Susie fusses with the twins in the back of the Volvo – innumerable belts and buckles and beakers with spouty lids. Henry is already strapped in. He's dropped his biscuit, is straining and stretching sideways to reach for it, biting on his lower lip. I open the door his side and retrieve the biscuit for him. From my pocket I take the small Monkey's Fist I made earlier and place it on his lap. He stares down, then up at me. Says nothing. He looks at his mother, who is busy offering a selection of toys to the other two. He balances the biscuit carefully on his knee and picks up the Monkey's Fist instead. Turns it in his fingers; lifts it to his nose. He closes both hands around it. I'm pleased to see I judged the size about right. It's a good fit, small enough. He lifts his cupped hands to his nose once more and his eyes flick to me and away. I close the door.

Susie pauses half in, half out, of the driver's door. 'You *sure* you don't mind being on your own here for a bit? I might be able to make it down next weekend but . . .'

'I'll be fine.'

'Well – rather you than me.' She reaches up to kiss my cheek. 'This place has always given me the willies. The *wind*!' She shudders, stretching her fleece over the distended belly.

'I loved it.'

'Yeah,' she pats my shoulder, 'I know.'

Once they've gone, things drift. I wander down the narrow corridors of the carriages and slide open the heavy doors to the train compartments we used as bedrooms. There's an old trunk in one, made of what looks like thick cardboard and covered with peeling luggage labels. Back in the living area I notice a grey rug spread across the sofa back. My mother's hospital blanket, her name stitched, red, into a corner.

NO ONE ELSE IS listening to Honey making wolf noises outside the back door because they are all rushing round the kitchen getting ready for Elaine's christening.

Auntie Jean is singing at the sink and washing up. Father is brushing down his jacket. Hoggie is helping Susie eat her egg with the special boiled-egg spoon that's made of bone, and making patterns on a plate with triangle sandwiches at the same time. Everything's all squeezed together and no one talks much.

Mummy is upstairs.

Honey makes two loud barks, and her nose sniffs at the bottom of the door. Father opens the back door to put the rubbish out and Honey pushes in between his legs. He gets her collar and drags her out again. Her claws make a skidding, scratching sound on the lino. Her tail is between her legs.

Auntie Jean pulls the plug out and dries her hands on the roller towel. She throws a tea towel at Father and says, 'Not today of all days, Michael,' in a cross voice. She puts a cloth on a breakfast tray and toast in the toast rack for Mummy's breakfast in bed. I follow her up the stairs. The bedroom door is shut. Auntie Jean stops outside.

'You've had your breakfast, Andy,' she says. 'Go and

play, I'm going to help Mummy get Elaine ready. We'll be busy.'

I go and look for Hoggie. Hoggie is her nurse name. Her real name is Harriet Amelia Hogg.

Harriet Amelia Hogg.

Harriet Amelia Hogg.

She is still in the kitchen with Susie. Susie has yellow egg on her face and hands.

'I've got some new knots to show you.'

She says, 'Sorry, Andy, can't play now, I've got to get this sister of yours into her pretty frock.'

The christening day was meant to be jolly like Christmas with jokes and laughing and treats. I go outside. Honey is tied to the railings by the French doors. Her collar and lead smell of hot car seats. She has her head on her paws and every time she hears Auntie Jean's voice her eyes go to the kitchen window. She lifts up her head and wags her tail when Auntie Jean calls me to come and put on my new shorts.

And then we go in Auntie Jean's car to fetch Grampy. There is a little metal lid to open and close the ashtray. Open. Close. Open. The silver has black on it that rubs off on to my hands.

'Leave that alone, please, Andy,' Auntie Jean says. 'Here we are now. Look.'

We're at Grampy's house and the tall glad flowers are out. Some have fallen over and lie on the fence. My fingers smell of cigarettes. I rub them on my new shorts and I say, 'Why?' when she comes round to open the car door for me. 'Why did we leave Honey behind? Why can't she come to the christening too?'

Auntie Jean slams the car door. She walks very fast down the drive to Grampy's black front door. I say, 'Wait for me,' and run and scratch one of my shiny brown lace-ups on the crazy paving. There are ants running round my shoe. They come out of a crack.

At the door I remember Honey tied up at home and say, 'Why can't Honey come too?'

'Because,' says Auntie Jean as she drops the keys into her handbag and snaps it shut, 'your Father doesn't like dogs.'

Grampy's house smells different to ours and today yellow light falls on the wall where the snake skin is hanging.

'Why is Grampy's hall a funny colour today?'

The yellow light is the colour of the snake's eyes in my animal picture book.

'Dad?' says Auntie Jean, looking down the hall for Grampy to come out of the kitchen. I look at my shoe to see if the crazy paving mark is still there. Auntie Jean is not saying anything back about the yellow light.

Auntie Jean calls again, 'Dad?' and goes up the stairs. She says, 'Stay there a minute, Andy, and don't go and get yourself all mucky, I'll just see where he's got to.'

I do not like the yellow light in the hall today, or the wooden bear with teeth or the snake skin from India and The War so I crawl on my tummy into the front room and there is Grampy sitting in his wing chair staring out of the window at people walking by. His hair is brushed over to one side like mine. He puts his hand over his eyes. He doesn't want to see any more. Auntie Jean's feet come down the stairs.

Auntie Jean says, 'Well, there you are, all ready for the off?' from the doorway in the loud sing-song voice she uses for Grampy. She says, 'I'll just check the back door's locked,' and she goes into the kitchen. I climb on to Grampy's lap. He doesn't have his bluey green jumper on today, the one that Granny Clementine knitted him. Today he has a tie on like me and he smells of the soap in his bathroom. The one with the black-and-gold label I keep in my box. The label says something LEATHER.

I say, 'Elaine is going to be wrapped up in the special white shawl that Granny made for my christening and I have a tie with secret elastic like Houdini, look, Grampy, look.'

Auntie Jean says, 'Come on, you scallywags, stop dilly dallying,' and she stops in front of the mirror and goes close to it. She makes a funny face with her teeth showing. She rubs one of them with a finger and makes the face again. Grampy walks slowly down the hallway. Today he has his stick to lean on. Auntie Jean opens the front door. All the outside brightness and air and birds singing come in. She rattles her keys and she says, 'Come on, your carriage awaits.'

Auntie Jean drives us straight to the church. Father is at the door talking to the vicar. Inside the church is dark, like a train tunnel. Our feet make echoes. I walk very straight. We walk past all the pews. People are coughing. Bits float in the light that comes in through the windows. Hoggie's red hair shows up because there is lots of it coming out from under her hat. She is at the front with Susie sitting on her lap. Susie's dress has puffy sleeves and coloured stitches that pull the material all together. Mummy is sitting next to Hoggie, and she's holding Elaine in the white shawl. She has a little hat made of feathers. It is the same shape as an upside-down bird's nest. I pull my new tie on its pingy elastic. She smiles at me. She is wearing her red lipstick and her hair is dark and shiny. She's all better now.

The vicar talks for a long time at the front and his words go round and round the church bouncing off the walls and the pews and the coloured windows and he says about at a christening the baby is given a name.

Our new baby is Elaine. She is a bit floppy as if she needs winding up or a new battery, and her mouth can't smile and her eyes stare and I think of the grey mullet we caught in the harbour. Perhaps after the christening, the nurse that comes will say her proper name, not is Baby feeding well? How is Baby today? Baby. Baby.

Don't be such a baby.

The vicar's voice is old and stony, like the walls. The ceiling is a very long way up. It's like being in a whale's belly. Like Jonah. Belly is a wobbly word. Whales are black and shiny.

And Granny's piano.

And beetles.

Into my head comes something about the black and shiny phone in their bedroom. *Andrew, you are not to go in there.* I'm hungry and outside their bedroom door. There is only me. The door is closed. Mummy might be in there. Or she might be away at the hospital for a long time to get another baby. The wind goes ooooo through the gap underneath the door. I want to see if Mummy is in there. I turn the handle and push the door. Inside their room the net curtains are flapping high. The windows are wide open. It is cold. Mummy is lying on her side on the counterpane. I can only see her back. She has all her clothes on except her shoes. She does not move. The black shiny phone by the bed begins to ring. It rings and rings. I look at Mummy's back. The round bottoms of her toes are squashed in the stockings. She turns over but does not answer the phone. It goes on ringing. I run out of the room and down the stairs.

The vicar stops talking. We sing 'All Things Bright and Beautiful'. Grampy's voice makes shakes in my tummy. After the church, everyone comes back to our house. There is a tea party in the garden and a white cloth over the garden table. Auntie Jean and two of Mummy's nurse friends go in and out of the back door with teapots and plates of triangle sandwiches and cheese and pineapple on sticks. There are butterfly cakes in the kitchen under a white thing to keep the flies off.

Mummy sits under the apple tree on a kitchen chair. Susie is high up in the pram with her harness on. The long white shawl is spread over Mummy's lap. Only Elaine's cheek is showing.

Auntie Jean has a new camera called the Ilford and she takes pictures of everyone standing around Mummy and Elaine. Then Hoggie takes a picture of Auntie Jean with Mummy and Elaine. Auntie Jean says, 'Thank God for that! Now I can get my feet out of these ruddy shoes.' And she kicks them off. Father turns his head away. The men take off their jackets and put their ties in their pockets. Mummy sits on the kitchen chair in her smart christening clothes. They are not red, not blue, not green. They are no colour and make her sit up straight. Usually on hot days like this she wears a sundress with lots of different colours that leap about. If she was wearing it today she could sit on the grass with her nurse friends and smile and lift her bare arms up in the air.

I keep my new tie round my neck for ages and ages and stand with my hands in the pockets of my new shorts, same as the men. Then I run to look for Auntie Jean and she is in the kitchen.

'Auntie Jean, Auntie Jean! Please can I have some pennies to jingle?'

'Just a minute, Andy, stop jumping up and down, it's rude to interrupt.'

I stand on one leg and she talks to the vicar about the spaceship called Sputnik. She says, 'That poor dog the Russians sent up, a female, wasn't it? Uprooted from its life.'

In space Honey would have no one to give her chocolate drops from the box in Auntie Jean's pantry. And no one to shake her lead and call Walkies and take her along the towpath to bark at the ducks or sniff the litter bins.

'She wouldn't like it,' I tell them. 'Honey wouldn't like it one little bit. She'll make wolf noises at night because she's sad, and then they'll have to bring her back.'

The vicar puts his cup in the saucer and bends down. His nose is lumpy and red.

'I'm sure you're right, Andy,' he says, 'but did you know that the Russians filled the capsule with gas? They didn't know how to get the poor creature back to earth safely, so they killed it. What do you make of that, young man?'

The vicar has eyebrows like spiders' legs hanging over his eyes. I run away from the vicar up the stairs and take the rubber thing out of the tummy of Susie's piggy bank. Now I have farthings and pennies and sixpences to jingle.

Father stands with the other men, talking and moving his hands in the air a lot. The men listen to him and smile. He chops at the air with one hand and it must be the end of a story because the men all burst out laughing. One wipes his forehead with his hanky, puts his hand on Father's shoulder and laughs.

My neck is hot and sweaty so I take my tie off and put the elastic round my head to make a headdress and slide down the handrail of the steps from the French doors. When I reach the bottom one of the men standing next to Father claps and makes Indian whoops with his finger in his mouth. Father comes over and takes tight hold of my arm. He puts his face down near me. He is not smiling.

'You're not to behave like a hooligan, Andrew.'

I want everyone to go home now. I sit on the grass near Mummy and Honey. Mummy's shoes have twisty bits and gaps and only the end of her big toe shows.

No room for me on her lap.

People come to kiss Mummy goodbye and the men have black shiny shoes like Father's. Mummy's nurse friends come and stand round her and put their hands on her shoulders and say things in quiet voices:

'Let me take her for a while, it's so hot for the time of year.'

'They make you hot, don't they? Holding them against you in this weather.'

'Come inside; let's find you a cold drink, some ice.'

They take the white shawl and Elaine away from Mummy's lap. One of them puts her arm round Mummy's back. Mummy's face is wrong and she has tears going into her mouth. Mummy's nurse friend helps her up. Mummy leans against her and they go into the house.

They've all gone now. There are empty chairs and a rug on the grass. I pull off my shoes without undoing the laces. I pick bits of grass and put lots in my shoes. I take my socks off. I try to push a stick from the apple tree into the underneath of my feet. It makes a white dent and red all round it. Red. White. I find a littler stick and I can hold it between my toes and walk, but anybody can see it. Houdini had secret invisible places underneath his feet. He hid things there so that he could pick locks.

No one comes to see where I am. I throw the bigger stick for Honey to fetch. I shout 'Fetch!' She lifts up her head and puts it down again. I go nearer to the house. I sit on the red steps that go up to the French doors. I will be Harry Houdini the Handcuff King and handcuff myself to the railings and stay until it gets dark and everyone will say, 'Where is Andy, Andy, where are you?' and come looking. My handcuffs are upstairs.

There is a key in the door. I take it out and put it in my pocket. I will pick the lock. My stick fits into the lock but it won't turn. I twist it really hard and it sort of turns but it is only going round in the hole. It is not picking the lock. My stick has chips and scratches in it now.

A crash and noise from the kitchen, Father's voice shouting, 'THE BOTTOM LINE.' I throw my stick into the hedge and put the key back in the lock. I run into the house and push open the kitchen door and it is hot and people and noisy voices and faces and cups and saucers and plates and crusts everywhere. Auntie Jean is pointing her finger at Father. Hoggie wipes her hand across her forehead. Even with my hands over my ears I can't keep out the buzzing crossness. Two of Mummy's nurse friends are talking to each other in big voices. One of them has the white shawl over her shoulder and her hand is on Elaine's head. Grampy and Mummy are sitting down. They are looking at the blue table top and Grampy holds her hand. She has a handkerchief in the other hand. The words buzz buzz buzz over the top of Grampy's head and Mummy's head. My breath gets jumpy inside me. Grampy looks up and sees.

'There you are, my Treasure! Why don't we go for a walk?' He stands up and takes hold of my hand. 'We can take the dog down to the river.'

We stop in the hallway and Grampy looks down at my feet. 'Better get something for those first, had we not?'

He lets go of my hand and goes back into the kitchen. Crossness is still going round and round like the rollers on the wringer, squashing everything. He comes back with my wellies. The noise from the kitchen has stopped. I count, like for lightning and thunder. Grampy closes the front door and we go up the side path to get Honey from the back garden. When I get to twenty the loud voices start up again.

We walk all along the river and Grampy tells me that today Elaine is not quite all there under the white shawl. He tells me about Houdini's tricks and the freak shows with the fattest woman in the world, and all about how Houdini went to all the police stations in all the towns and said, 'Handcuff me and put the leg irons on,' and Houdini always escaped and was famous because he got into the newspapers. Except once when a bad man jammed the handcuffs shut on purpose.

Houdini made lots of money escaping from handcuffs and one day he went home to where his Mummy sat on a kitchen chair and he poured gold coins all over her lap.

Grampy and me walk over the bridge next to the railway line but there are no trains today, just the track going a long way away. We go up the spooky footpath in the cool between high fences and walls and through the allotments all the way to Grampy's house.

YOU STAND BY THE front gate. The muscles of your belly, slack after Elaine's birth, are tangled with tension, the sense that something awful is about to happen. Susie waves from her new seat on the Silver Cross as Jean manoeuvres the pram down the kerb to cross the road. Susie has a harness with metal clips to attach her to the seat's frame but still the whole arrangement seems precarious, perched high above the gleaming black body of the pram where Elaine lies, out of sight. You'd fussed, tucking her down with a blanket, fiddling with the angle of the sun canopy, until Jean put a hand on yours and said, 'Stop.' This is Jean's idea, after Andy ran away to your father's house yet again, this time in the middle of the night. She says you need some time with him, time without one or other of the babies constantly in your arms or on your lap. But today Andy is flushed and irritable. Perhaps he has a temperature. The mumps are doing the rounds.

You step into the cool of the larder with the butter dish in your hand and stand for a moment in the half light, listening to the distant rattle and pause, rattle and pause of a lawnmower: yet another summer afternoon.

Lying open on the kitchen table is a hard-backed note-book where you've set out, on blue-lined pages, lists of things to do.

Monday: washday, grocery shopping for the week.

Tuesday: turn out the dining room, ironing, polish the front step.

Wednesday: dust through house, rugs, baking.

Thursday:

Friday:

The twin tub stands in the middle of the kitchen floor, filled with damp washing that needs to be put through the wringer, and there's the lining of the new winter curtains to finish. But there's that weight of slowness, a silting. Some-times you just sit. You sit on the edge of the armchair as if you're about to get up and get on with something.

You count the stairs as you climb them. In Andy's bed-room, a red wigwam takes up most of the floor space and every night since his fifth birthday he's slept in there. His bow and arrows lie on the floor by the entrance. Through the tasselled door flaps, the space inside the tent is inviting, red and warm from the glow of the sun on the material. Andy's stroking the coloured feathers of his headdress from base to tip. He wriggles over to the back of the wigwam to make room.

You slip off your shoes, get down on hands and knees and crawl in. There's the smell of cheap, dyed cotton. No room to lie flat, so you tuck your legs up. Already the skin behind your knees is damp and slippery. He leans across you and pulls at the door flaps, trying to make them meet. The manufacturers have been economical with the fabric and it is flimsy, the hemmed edges flop apart again. You prop *Hiawatha* on your thighs and Andy snuggles close, thumb in his mouth. The top of his head is warm and biscuity.

You begin to read and his fingers on the feathers slow, then stop, so you ease the headdress from his head, lower the book on to the eiderdown and look up into the cone of the wigwam where the four long canes meet and poke through the cloth. The repetitive rhythm of *Hiawatha* laps at your mind:

> *dark behind it rose the forest,*
> *rose the black and gloomy pine-trees,*
> *rose the firs with cones upon them,*
> *bright before it beat the water.*

Your eyes have closed. The outside sounds of the June day buzz at your ears: the lawnmower a few gardens away; sparrows landing on the gutter. Then, the whoosh of car tyres, slick, glides you along, takes you with it, and you're back at St Mary's, years ago, it's raining, and you're hurrying from the nurses' home, shutting the door on the steamy, crowded kitchen: the clothes airer in front of the stove hung with stockings and suspenders; Hoggie at the ironing board again because she has a date and is trying to straighten her red frizz by ironing it through brown paper; Nurse Pierce, limp on a chair, just come in from her shift, her feet in a bowl of water. You almost run, would if it was permitted, across the forecourt towards the tall lighted windows of the hospital to push through the swing doors and be swept up by the current of routine and emergency before you even have time to remove your cloak. You're laughing and chattering with the other nurses as Mr Robertson, the consultant oncologist with a penchant for patterned bow ties, passes, raises his tufted eyebrows that point in different directions, says, 'Here's looking at you, kid,' because he thinks you look like Ingrid Bergman – and from behind a clipboard Matron shoots stern looks through the thick brown frames of her glasses.

And your Oxford lace-ups are marching down the corridor as your fingers pin your hat into your hair, your eyes glance at the watch swinging against your apron, you check the instruments fanned out, gleaming metal on white cloth, and the heat from the circle of lights above the operating table is on your face, fierce.

But it's the sun on your eyelids, glaring through the walls of the wigwam, that wakes you. You twist over, curled on your side, to face Andy and, as you do so, your breasts – swollen and tender, heavy with the milk Elaine doesn't drink – shift position.

Andy lies on his stomach, arms up on either side of his head, hair damp around his ears. He sleeps so soundly you could pick up a leg or an arm and let it down without him stirring. You run two fingertips across the top of his back, where his neck meets his shoulders and blond hairs lie against his skin. The hairs gather together, growing towards his spine. He's breathing through his mouth because one cheek is squashed against the pillow, pushing his lips apart. They are moist. You remember your nipples spurting milk in response to his cries. Sometimes your breasts would be full and tight as they are now and you would go to him, nudge him awake, desperate for the relief as he latched on and began to suck. Often, when his lips slid from your nipple as he fell asleep, he'd have a milky blister from sucking. You'd lower him into his pram and wheel him down the garden knowing that his contented sleep was entirely due to you. *You don't want to spoil him*, Michael had said.

If you were to offer him your full breast now, if you were to dab his bottom lip with the tip of your nipple, would he, in his sleep, begin to suck? You bend towards him, feeling the heat rise up from his skin, and put your lips on his back, between his shoulder blades. His breathing is steady.

You sit up. It's stuffy in here, the air like a sponge. You should make yourself get on with something while he's asleep. You crawl out of the wigwam and wander into the box room where it's cooler. The sewing machine on its small table is surrounded by piles of folded curtain material. The mending basket is overflowing.

You'll ask Michael if you can go down to The Siding earlier this summer. Jean could come with you to help with the three children; she loves the railway carriage house as much as you do. You'll feel better under the open skies, crunching over shingle banks, smelling the mudflats at low tide and sleeping to the suck and whisper of waves.

Early days, is what you'd say to a patient. Take it easy, give yourself time.

You have hours, day after day of time.

You should finish the winter curtains as quickly as possible because you've bought some material in the sales to make curtains for The Siding. In the end-of-roll box there were several oddments of a pale blue splashed with huge dark cornflowers, very cheap, and just right for the small windows of the railway carriages – four rows of them; a lot of sewing to do. The first thing you'll do when you get down there this summer is take down the pieces of limp towelling and sides-to-middle sheets. *Make do and mend.* You haven't told Michael about the cornflower material; you scrimped on the housekeeping.

The lining material is thinner than the green velvet that you have chosen for the winter curtains, and your guiding fingers can only just keep pace with the silver foot as it slips along the ironed seam. Even so, you want to press harder on the pedal, to keep pressing until the needle can no longer keep up, until its steady up and down is forced into a different rhythm, a more extravagant motion, one that no longer produces a row of tidy stitches.

Your hair is hot and heavy. You lift it with both hands, relishing the shift of air on your neck as you twist and divide the handfuls of hair into sections, folding them into the French roll you wore for nursing, pinned with three Kirby grips from your pocket.

Michael says the winter curtains for the house should go up in September, so you aim to have them ready before you go down to Sussex for the summer. He wants to save on the coal bill. The door that opens on to the garden doesn't fit well, and there is a cold draught once the fire is lit. He wants a curtain over the front door too.

The needle jerks. It snaps. You lift the foot, turn the seam over and find that the thread is tangled into a clump. The previous twelve inches or so of stitches have pulled the seam into wrinkles. It will have to be unpicked.

Michael has already had bristles fitted along the bottom of the back door, and metal strips around the door frame. You worried about Andy's fingers getting caught. *He'll only do it once*, Michael said.

Part Two

YOU CAN SEE MICHAEL'S face in the dressing-table mirror three times.

'She's almost four.'

His mouth is talking from three different angles. Triple. The word sounds precarious. And it doesn't seem possible that four years have passed since Elaine's birth.

'Soon she'll be too heavy for you to lift. A decision has to be made.' He bends towards his reflection and slides the knot of his tie up to his collar. The centre mirror tilts. A deft adjustment settles the knot into place, three times. '—take the expert advice we're given—'

His words topple like skittles; their falling clatter making you dizzy.

'—Elaine's awareness—M.D.—general well-being—future complications—'

The bedspread lies wrinkled on the floor.

C a n d l e

w i c k

Meanings dwindle into images; nonsense.

'—institutions—several highly recommended—beneficial—siblings—'

No.

You will tell him about yesterday. Slicing onions, Elaine

asleep in the carrycot, legs splayed open, her nose close to the curled fingers of one hand as if she was trying to breathe her own smell. Then, the doorbell, Elaine's eyes flying open, a little gasp.

You will tell him, now, and then this will stop. But you're half in, half out of bed, nightdress rucked under your thighs, words rolled up somewhere, like socks put away in a drawer.

'For all concerned—future—'

It was only yesterday. The doorbell rang again, an insistent buzz, and Elaine straightened her legs, beat them twice on the mattress, her eyes fixed on you. You'd thrown down the knife, wiped the smell of onions on to your apron and heaved Elaine up out of the carrycot.

'There are no other options.'

Take a breath. Speak now.

You're back, almost tipsy with it, yesterday, on the doorstep – smiling and stumbling a little, Elaine clasped against one shoulder – and the huge, tawny man in white painting overalls smiles back, the tips of his teeth showing through a bush of reddish beard. Something: a swoop in your blood. You had wanted to grasp hold of him, tell him. Elaine had heard the bell. You were certain. You wanted it to happen again. He could ring the doorbell again. Your eyes pricked from the onions. He put down his tool box and offered his hand.

It might happen again.

Michael pauses at the bedroom door. He's crisp and ordered, ready for the hospital. You smudge the tears from your face with the heel of your hand.

'We can't go on like this.' He gestures towards the contents of the room, the tasselled bedside lamps, the pink roses on the eiderdown, as if this is the unsatisfactory clutter of your marriage. 'You're exhausted.'

There's dust on the glass top of the dressing table, a pattern of spring flowers on the curtains: wisteria blue, the colour of Elaine's eyes.

You look back to him. 'No.'

'Well, someone has to do something, make a decision, soon.'

He closes the door. A distant rattle from a passing train. Anger scrapes in your stomach.

M.D. he always says, *M.D.* Why can't he say what he means? Why can't he just say, 'Mentally Deficient'?

You get up, walk through to the box room where Elaine is lying on her back, awake, but silent and still in the early morning light. Andy is curled, asleep on the floor beside her cot, wrapped in his eiderdown.

Later, you reach into the cupboard under the sink for Vim and a cloth. From behind the closed door of the dining room comes the muffled sound of movement: a ladder dragged across bare floorboards; the metallic ring of a wallpaper scraper. The broad, tawny-haired man has been in there for hours, since before you took the children to school. It's difficult to concentrate. Elaine is propped up with cushions in her usual place on a rug on the floor, but there's a charge to the air – someone else, not a child but an adult, in the house all day. You can't shake off the sense of his presence. You notice fragments of yourself: the angle of your wrist and gold watch; toes peeping out from cutaway shoes; bare legs beneath the flared skirt of your gaily patterned sundress.

It's warm for May; perhaps you could offer him a drink.

Outside the dining room you pause; listen. There's the shift of boots on gritty boards; a sigh. You knock on the door before opening it. The dining room is unrecognisable, a space heaped with dust sheets and paint pots, strips of wallpaper hanging from the walls. The brown tiled sur-round of the fireplace is surreal: order and pattern in the middle of the chaos. You sniff, feeling a sneeze at the back of your nose. The air smells of soot and glue.

'Some tea?' Your voice echoes in the uncarpeted room. 'And would you like to take your lunch in the kitchen?'

'Ay, if you're sure now.' His accent gives the words a different texture. You concentrate so as to catch the sepa-rate sounds and make sense of them. Scottish? Irish? He strides towards you, then halts, glancing down at his filthy boots. 'I'll take these off, will I not?'

He bends and his sudden dipping movement is startling – the bulk of him so close, his head down at your feet, his shoulder muscles swelling as he tugs at his shoelaces. You turn quickly to the kitchen.

He pads after you, the top part of his overalls hanging down from his waist. Underneath, stretched over his torso, is a faded cotton T-shirt that seems incongruous – a child's item of clothing. He's young, possibly ten years younger than you. Michael mentioned a few details when he ar-ranged for the redecoration. He's the son of a patient, a struggling artist living in a houseboat on the river. His name . . . is it Ian? The family is from somewhere north of Aberdeen.

There's a patch of sweat on his chest and coppery hair surges at the neck of his T-shirt. His hair is tousled and pale with plaster dust. He puts a hand up to it, and through a rip in the seam under the arm of his T-shirt you catch a glimpse of his underarm hair: thick, fluffy, almost blond.

'Ach, I'll mebbe step outside. Hae a wee dust doon.' He grins like a boy.

From her rug on the floor, Elaine whimpers. She's mis-erable today, her chin red and sore from the dribble. You put the tea towel and cutlery down on the draining board.

He comes in through the back door, asks if he can hold her and already he has his back to you, squatting down over the rug and moving a hand with fingers spread wide to catch Elaine's eye. She quietens, gazing up at him.

Reaching up to the cupboard for teacups and saucers, you watch as he puts his hands under Elaine's arms to lift her. He straightens, holding her out at arm's length as if gauging how best to hold a solid four-year-old child who has the wavering head of a newborn.

'She's . . .,' you begin, because Elaine will not be comfortable held like that, but he is speaking, '—such a bonny wee lass.' He holds her now with her stomach firm against his chest, one arm running up her back and a broad hand spread across her shoulder blades. Blond hairs gleam on his forearm. Elaine's head bobs at his shoulder, her neck straining.

You swirl boiling water round the teapot as he dandles Elaine around the kitchen, murmuring to her and showing her things over his shoulder. He points out the cupboard doors, swinging them open and closed, open and closed. He flaps the tea towels hanging from the airer, pulls the roller towel on the back door so that it rattles and the moving stripes of colour catch her eye. Her head stills. Whenever he stops walking he lifts one heel up and down in a rapid, repetitive rhythm that jiggles Elaine's body. She starts with her humming noise, a sort of musical groan in her throat that varies pitch with the vibrations of his movement. You stir the tea; the tension in your shoulders eases.

He stands, holding Elaine, jiggling, while he drinks his tea and that's when he tells you about his sixteen-year-old brother who lies on the settee for most of the day. He can't speak a single word.

'But he has a smile,' Ian says. 'A smile for his own breathing. Smiles ear to ear when you step into the room. You canny ask for more.'

Ian refuses to sit to eat his sandwiches, so you pass them to him one by one from the greaseproof paper bundle he's brought with him. He holds Elaine; she's quiet and relaxed. He asks questions, and you are talking, about the children, and then about nursing. You find yourself telling him about studying for your final exams at St Mary's, how cold the nursing home was. To keep warm, you and Pierce and Hoggie bought the cheapest tickets you could at Paddington Underground and travelled round and round the Inner Circle Line with your books. After the twelve-hour shifts on the wards, the lull of the train's rhythm and the warm air made you dozy. You pinched the skin on each others' arms to keep awake.

When Elaine falls asleep in his arms, he passes her over and you carry her out to the pram. You stretch the cat net over and think of the Mary's Penny you were awarded after four years of nursing training, its inscription, 'Whatever thy hand findeth to do, do it with thy might.' You were proud to be a nurse from St Mary's. Is that why you're still talking about it as if it were only yesterday? As Michael's wife you have no need to work the wards. And now that he's arranged for Mrs Hubbard to come and clean three times a week, the days have even less of a sense of purpose.

Running your hands through your hair, feeling your skull, you find it, the lump – small, hard – from the dressmaker's pin that anchored the nurse's cap to your head. Fanned folds of fine starched muslin were held in place with two white Kirby grips at the back and, at the front, the pin pushed through the underside of the starched band, its sharp point embedded into your scalp. 'It will,' Sister Tutor said, 'hold the cap in place, even in the storm of a surgeon's fury.' And once the hard round 'pea' had formed, the pin was no longer painful. The local hairdresser felt it. She met your eyes in the mirror and said, 'Another nurse from St Mary's?' Nodding sagely, she tapped her scissors on the back of your chair. 'Can always tell.'

By the time you step back into the kitchen, it's empty. Ian has returned to the dining room and the door is closed.

SUSIE IS FIVE. I need to teach her about knots and untying.

The garage doors rattle in the wind. On the concrete there's a wet patch where the rain blows in. Father's saws hang on nails, big saw down to little saw. By his vice is the tin of green jelly stuff for cleaning his hands. There's the smell of dirty metal and pine-tree sawdust and the dark brown stuff Father paints on the garden fences every summer. I'm not allowed in here by myself.

Mummy's peg basket is by the door, next to her wellies. And the bundle that is the new washing line. It's tied in loops.

I open the door leading back into the house, turning the handle slowly, peering round like they do in films, to check if anyone's about. The painting man has finished his cup of tea and gone back into the dining room. I think about going to see him but now I have the washing line. Across the hallway in the kitchen I see Mummy's back and her arms lift and fall because she's washing jumpers at the sink. She is singing 'la la lah' with the radio. On the floor, Elaine is propped up with lots of cushions. She's half-sitting, half-lying, her chin right down on her bib. The bib stops dribble soaking into her clothes and making her chest sore, but it makes her chin sore instead. I waggle the washing line at her

74

and put a finger to my lips so that she knows it's a secret. Elaine wobbles her body a little bit from side to side a couple of times. Elaine is four now but she wobbles because she's fat like a Jelly Baby, much fatter than me or Susie, that's why Jelly is my special name for her. I wave to Jelly and do our Secret Sign, before I tiptoe up the stairs.

Susie has my old wigwam in her bedroom. The sides have got too short for the poles and I can see her ankles and slippers moving about inside. She's talking to her dolls. I stick my head in through the flaps.

'Look what I found.' I flick the washing line like a whip to shake out the kinks.

Susie is putting her golliwog in a dress Elaine has got too big for. It looks very stupid. She's undone the plaits on her Indian headdress and the black hair is all in crinkles round her ears.

'Go away.'

'How about I put all the animals in a stockade for you?'

She looks at the new washing line on the floor. 'All right.' She closes the flaps of the wigwam again.

There are three teddies and a big blue elephant and Eeyore to tie up. Then there's Susie's new hobby horse which was a present from a patient. Susie's hobby horse doesn't look like a real horse. Its eyes and mane are painted on to its wooden head. My hobby horse is furry and grey and has real glass eyes and a real woolly mane that shakes about. Mummy made it out of Father's old grey dressing gown. I rub at the painted eyes on Susie's hobby horse with my finger and pull on its leather harness. It would come off if I had some scissors or Hugh's penknife. Susie's horse could have the red dressing-gown cord from my horse instead.

Grampy says the Fiador Knot is the cowboy's best emergency bridle, but it's hard to do without two cords of different colours and I can't cut the washing line. So I make Harness Loops for each animal, joining them all together, then I crawl back into the wigwam.

Susie has wrapped Looby Lou in a shawl and is rocking her to and fro in her arms. 'Shhh, Andy. Sshhh!' She puts a finger to her mouth. 'It's night time.'

'You need to know some knots, don't you? To keep the animals safe from rustlers.'

'Tell Big Doll. I'm the Mummy. Big Doll can be the animal looker-afterer. She can stay out all night.'

Susie does not like Big Doll. Big Doll came from another one of Father's patients. The patient saw Mummy and Susie at the surgery once and said to Father, 'What an *adorable* child.'

Father lifted Susie on to his lap at teatime and stroked her hair and said to her, 'Do you know you are adorable, Susie? Someone else apart from me thinks you're adorable. Mrs Reeves thinks: *A, you're adorable, B, you're so beautiful, C, you're a cutie full of charm . . .*' and he sang the whole song.

Big Doll came in a huge box on Christmas Eve when the tea trolley was in the sitting room and the fire was lit. Father answered the door. Patients are supposed to see him at the surgery, not at home. It was Mrs Reeves and she said, 'Merry Christmas, Michael,' and didn't call him Doctor.

Big Doll has hard arms and legs and she walks and talks. In her back she has a string with a ring on it to pull. 'I want my mummy,' she says, and, 'Is it time for bed?' Her hair is orange and has a funny smell. Every bedtime Susie makes Mummy put her out on the landing.

I fetch Big Doll from the landing. Big Doll can only stand and walk, she can't sit down. Susie has poked in one of her eyes and it does not open now. I tie a Jack Ketch's Collar around Big Doll's neck and stand her in the stockade with the other animals. Her fingers stick out straight.

I make another running noose. Now I'll teach Susie how to untie a Jack Ketch's Collar. Jack Ketch was a hangman, but not a very good one. I crawl back into the wigwam. 'Just try this on.'

She holds out her wrist.

'No, nit twit.' I put the running noose over her head and her headdress gets knocked crooked.

'No,' she says, 'take it off.'

'Sit still. Sit *still*!'

The black hair from her headdress gets in the way and her face is all red and cross. She's turning her head this way and that and pulling with her fingers at the washing line around her neck. 'It's too tight, Andy,' she says, 'too tight! It *hurts*.' Her fingers pull at my fingers.

'It's nearly done.'

'Noooo!' She stamps her foot. 'I don't like it.'

She's wriggling and slapping at my hands. She's very silly.

'SIT STILL! SIT STILL!' I hold her ankles, she falls over and my teeth press hard together. There's a hot fizz in my chest that tells me I can hurt her.

She's kicking and yelling, 'I'm telling!' She gets up and runs out of the room, the washing line trailing behind her down the stairs. All the teddies and Eeyore and Big Doll and everything get pulled across the floor because they're all joined together with the washing line. She spoils everything. I kick the wigwam pole.

'Mummy! Mummy!' Susie screams.

Thump and stop, thump and stop – her feet go down the stairs one at a time. She can go down them properly but today she's being a cry-baby and making a fuss. I sit on the yellow-and-black carpet in her room and listen. There's the painting man's voice and Mummy's laugh. After a while, Mummy's footsteps come slowly up the stairs. The smell of cigarette smoke comes into the bedroom with her.

'Susie's so silly. I was showing her how to undo it.'

But Mummy's face is boiling red and she slaps my leg. It doesn't hurt.

She puts her face next to mine and says in a very quiet voice, 'Don't you ever, ever fool around with that washing line again. What on earth? Round her neck?'

She snatches Grampy's book on knots, ties and splices up from the floor. 'I'm taking this away until you're more sensible, Andrew.' She shuts the bedroom door and is gone.

I shuffle on my bottom until I am wedged in the corner between Susie's bedroom door and the side of her white painted wardrobe. If anyone comes I will be hidden. I sit with my chin on my knees. Downstairs, the television goes on. I hear Mummy call out from the kitchen for Susie. Then she's talking. The painter must be having tea in the kitchen again. I put my ear down to the floorboards to listen and that's when I see Mummy's lost thistle brooch on the floor under Susie's chest of drawers, right back by the skirting board.

Yesterday, when Mummy put her coat on to go to the shops she saw her favourite brooch was missing and she put her hands over her face and sat on the bottom step and cried real tears.

I reach under the chest of drawers and put my fingers around the brooch. It's hard and scratchy in my hand. On Susie's chest of drawers is a photo with Mummy smiling. Auntie Jean took it ages ago, before she had the Ilford. The photo is just me and Mummy sitting on the hospital blanket next to a breakwater. Susie and Elaine are not born yet. In the picture, Mummy is doing Cheers! with the mug from the top of her thermos.

Yesterday, after Mummy saw her brooch was gone, she went out into the garden for a breath of fresh air. It was raining but she went out all the same and stood by the rhododendron bushes to see the buds coming. When she came back in, the rain was in her hair like drops in a spider's web. I put my hands in her hair. It was soft and wet.

THE DAYLIGHT HAS almost gone by the time I wake up. I'm on the sofa. My neck's stiff and my throat dry.

At first I curse Susie for taking the last of the water, but then see the empty plastic bottles scattered around with the boys' buckets on the grass. I try the taps again and check the mains, but finally resign myself to dying of thirst or traipsing next door for water.

Lights are on, but there's no answer when I ring the bell, nor when I rap on the door. Some flinty stones, sharp-edged, are piled to one side of the step and an assortment of cockle and razor shells fills an aluminium bucket. Someone has hung pebbles on lengths of string in the porch. I start to count but give up when I get to thirty.

Turning away, I catch sight of a sea-bleached branch stuck, upright, into the earth and hung with an assortment of flip flops and jelly shoes. Some adult, some child-sized. All lost. The once bright plastic and rubber has been faded by sun and salt. A sign, white paint on a piece of scaffolding plank, says: 'The Jelly Tree'. The hairs on my forearms rise and I glance back at the windows of the house. Instead of being set at right angles to each other as at The Siding, the two railway carriages are parallel and joined with a wooden structure that creates a large living area. From here, I can see right through the house and out the other side. The window on the far side, the seaward side, gives a glimpse of dark sea and sky. And there's a shape. Not moving. It looks like the outline of a leg; a pointed foot. I'll get a better look from the beach side.

When I get there, a woman is crouching on the decking. She's wearing dirty white overalls and is holding a hose. Even in the half light I can see she's in a trance, gazing at water coming out of the hose and whatever the water is falling on to. She has a long plait over one shoulder that swings as she stoops. The end of the plait is darker, perhaps wet. Her forearms are splattered with what looks like mud. She's oblivious to my presence. She stands upright – she's tall – and heads off round to the other side of the house, striding with ease over the pebbles even though her feet are bare.

I hurry up to the decking to see what was holding her attention and find a head. A clay head. The hose is still running. I pick it up and hold it over the head. Water courses over the swerves of hair, slowing into twisting ribbons and smaller rivulets that spread before they spill on to the wooden decking. I'm kneeling down to get a closer look when the water stops.

Scarlet toenails appear on the wet boards. I straighten up. Her eyes are snapping dark, almost black. She opens her mouth to speak, and it's not difficult to see from the lift of her chin and the shock-ready turn of her back, that her fury is barely suppressed. I want to touch her. I want to prevent whatever it is she's about to say. I reach for one of her hands. But she's startled, I've gauged it wrong. She twists back. The swell of her muscle under my palm tells me I'm gripping her upper arm. I drop my hands hurriedly.

'This,' but my voice cracks, 'is really good.' I can't read her expression. There's a smudge of clay on her forehead. She's a lot older than I thought at first and she's shaking.

I squat down on all fours again, admiring the head. 'You must be pleased.' I try smiling up at her, but she doesn't look at all pleased. She's breathing hard, muscular arms folded across her chest. She has no bra on under the thin T-shirt.

'Need help?' She brushes a windblown strand of hair from her lips.

My attempt at enthusiasm has not won her over. She rubs her upper arms. Like me, she's not dressed to be outside in this temperature.

'Oh God, I'm sorry.' I stand and offer my hand formally. 'Andrew.'

She flicks the plait over her shoulder and for a moment I think she's so pissed off she's going to ignore my hand, but then her handshake is strong and dry and she says, 'Sarah,' without smiling. Her eyes are that pale blue-green that makes the pupils darkly noticeable.

I start again. 'Sorry to disturb you. I can see you're busy. But – I'm from next door. Can't get my water to work.'

She doesn't like me saying I'm from next door, her pupils have shrunk.

'Is this your place? They certainly built these railway carriages to last.' Talking is never my strong point.

'Ah, no – not mine exactly.' A response at last. 'I just rent it. Did you want to fill your buckets?'

She's going to get rid of me as fast as she can, that much is clear.

'Yes, please. That'd be great.'

She hesitates and I realise she probably doesn't want to leave me with the head while she goes to turn on the hose.

'Where's the tap? Round the side?'

'Yes, yes. Round there.' She points.

I pick up my buckets.

When I get back with the buckets filled, she's gone inside. And taken the head.

YOU TURN THE MATCHBOX over and over on the bench. Wood pigeons murmur, sparrows chirp and flutter under the eaves. Smoke from your cigarette drifts across the garden.

Jean had waved the packet at you. 'Go on, take them,' she said. 'Take them all! They'll help you think while you're walking the dog.' You took two. There's a chance Michael won't smell anything if you smoke them outside.

At your feet, Honey slobbers and gnaws at a chew, head to one side, teeth bared. A blue Basildon Bond envelope lies on your lap: a letter for you this morning from Pierce. She's sent a photograph. She poses in uniform, chin lifted, jaunty, under the circular light of an empty operating theatre, one arm leaning on the operating table, the other hand on her hip. A big grin on her face because she's Theatre Sister now.

What will you write back?

Last night at the hospital dinner dance you sat with Michael at the top table with the other consultants and their wives. The Senior Obstetrician, eyes like beads behind his round spectacles, pressed his thigh against yours while his wife, opposite, talked about choosing between a frilled or a box-pleated hem for the loose cover she was making for her settee. The stiff lace on your gown chafed the under side of your upper arms.

But this is not what you're supposed to be thinking about.

Mrs Hubbard's key scrapes at the door.

'For God's sake get yourself out of the house for an hour or two while that woman's here. That's why Michael hired her,' Jean had said as she left with Elaine.

You tread the cigarette into the lawn and get up to prepare a tea tray for Mrs Hubbard with the Royal Albert china, silver sugar bowl and tongs, the Nice biscuits. In the hall, floral overall draped loosely across her bony front, Mrs Hubbard nods as she hangs up her coat. Seconds later she has disappeared to the sitting room to clear the grate.

You stand in front of the sink and stare at the cracks in the green block of Fairy soap. Think, think about the notebook Jean found hidden under the mattress of the bed where Andy sleeps when he stays with her.

The breakfast bowls plop, one by one, into the bubbles and slide below the surface.

Michael keeps on about sending Elaine away. Jean, and even Hoggie, seem to agree. 'You'd all get your lives back,' is what Jean has said. Everyone acts as though your desire to keep Elaine at home is simple selfishness.

You make your fingers loosen their grip, watch the wooden handle of the washing-up brush slip into the bubbles and out of sight.

They say Elaine will not know the difference, will not know where she is. And yet, when she was a baby, a doctor said she'd know the smell of your breast. Not the milk, but your skin. Experiments have shown a baby will turn towards a pad that has been next to the mother's breast, rather than to one on to which the mother has expressed her milk. 'But it's not just Elaine you need to think about, is it?' Hoggie said last night, a hand on your wrist. 'It's the whole family.'

Birdsong comes in through the open back door. You dry your hands, tug at the ties of your apron; dump it on the draining board. You pick up the notebook, hold it to your breast and walk out of the back door, leaving it open. Honey pads behind. You head for the river.

The notepad is tatty, its cardboard cover creased and soft with use. 'TOP SECRET' it says in red ink, underlined three times with black. On the first few pages Andy has written lists of questions, the answers written upside down at the bottom of each page, like clues for a crossword puzzle. Every question has something to do with rope.

The pages of the notepad are brittle as dead leaves and the pencil lines have scored hollows and ridges in the paper. Towards the back, there's page after page with drawings of gallows in various stages of completion. One has a pin man hanging, the circle for his head drooping to one side. He looks dead, or dying. Seeing it, you'd remembered the incident with Susie and your scalp tightened.

'Just look at this,' Jean said, showing you a page with six dashes, with the first letter, A, filled in. *Clue: Stress placed on rope due to increasing the velocity of the load. Answer: Abrasion resistance (A).*

She flicked more pages. 'It's his name, he's spelling out his name, over and over again. *Double Braid. D. A very strong and flexible rope that doesn't hockle.* What does "hockle" mean? – *doesn't hockle, kink or rotate under a load.* It's from that big book of Dad's, isn't it? On knots?'

'What, *Ashley*'s?'

'Look: *Devil's Rope.* What's that?'

'No idea.'

The dashes and drawings, surely – you think now – they're just a version of that word game, hangman. You'd wanted Jean to stop flicking, to hand the notebook over. Playing it down in case she mentioned something to Michael, you said, 'Andy only knows a lot about rope and knots because he spends time with Dad.'

A match flared with the smell of sulphur as Jean lit up. Her words were distorted when she continued, cigarette slanted between her lips. 'Wake up and smell the daisies! Why does Andy spend all his time at Dad's? Because you're too busy with Elaine!'

'Perhaps he has too much time on his own at your house!'

Jean exhaled. 'Because he hid it there? But, OK, I'll talk to him about it.'

'No,' you told her, finally taking hold of the notebook. 'It's all right. I'll do that.'

Now, you've started to shake again. Not because of the detail of the hangman pictures, the lists of words and terms, but because your son is nine and you have lost touch with the working of his mind.

You sit down on the sloping river bank. From here the bottom is invisible, even at the edges. The water is brown and sluggish, its algal smell trapped by the high banks and trees on either side.

Barbed wire; Devil's Rope is another name for barbed wire.

At the back of the notebook are more drawings with underlined headings; two or three pages of what look like whips. The slapping curve of the pencil lines reminds you of the circus last year. You took Andy and Susie, and watched elephants, plumed feathers on their foreheads, heave themselves on to their hind legs to balance on a red painted circle while whips swooped and snaked, never quite touching their wrinkled hides. And the lion tamer, flamboyant in red jacket and tight trousers, cracked his whip, sawdust flying up into the air at the bars of the cage where the lion plodded. The lion yawned; strings of saliva glistening. Its mane was matted. This year you had ignored the circus posters.

Fumbling in the pocket of your sundress for the last cigarette, you realise you've left the house with no handbag. No key to get back in. No money. As you pull smoke deep into your lungs, your mind spins as if you've had a sherry or two. A gust of lightness makes your heart beat faster. *Run,* your limbs say, tingling, *keep running.*

You run. Speed up. Heading for the houseboats, the jolt and jar of your feet on the sun-baked towpath reverberating through your knees, hips, lungs. Honey leaps ahead and back, jumping up, tongue curling out, her hot breath on your face.

From one of the houseboats a man waves and calls out. You stop, breathing hard. Ian's shirt, unbuttoned, flaps in a breeze lifting up from the water, the buckle on his belt catching the light. The hair on his abdomen – blond, growing upwards in lines and eddies, swirling over his chest – lies flat against his skin. You stoop, hands on thighs, the shock of seeing him catching at the breath in your throat, although it's why you're here.

You brush invisible grass from your sundress. Honey sniffs and pauses her way through the undergrowth as Ian buttons up his shirt and suggests a cup of tea. There's the smell of bacon frying. Through gaps in the gangplank, the brown river slides by. Dandelion clocks stick and drift on the water.

The space you step into is tiny, and rocks as he steps down behind you, ducking through the doorway. The ceiling is low – he has to stoop a little – but the space is bright with the sun pouring in through windows on three sides and the ripples of light on the ceiling, reflections from the water. He strides across the floor into a little kitchenette, wiping his hands on an old cloth. His fingers have blond hairs on either side of the knuckle. There's the bacon, and something else: white spirit, or turpentine. He fills the tiny cabin room – his height, his shoulders, the exuberant bush of his beard – glancing your way often as he stands by the small stove frying his bacon and eggs. His eyes are not the washed-out blue you'd expect with his colouring, but a curious shade of clear golden brown, like Demerara sugar. Perhaps it's more common in Scotland. Blond lashes grow in triangular clumps at the outer corners of his eyes, giving them a languid look, dreamy. Come-to-bed-eyes, Jean would call them.

He's offering you bacon. You shake your head and ask for just tea, wondering how to explain why you're here, but he behaves as if you were expected, smiling and asking about the children, about Elaine.

And so it pours from you: levering Susie's fingers from your arm one by one as she screams because she's being left at the school gates while Elaine goes home with you. At bedtime, she'll turn away and insist on Michael reading to her, as some sort of retaliation or punishment – or so it feels. One day you caught her pinching the flesh of Elaine's upper arm. And then you tell him about finding Andy, night after night, lying next to Elaine, the cot side pulled down, his mouth to her ear. Andy says Elaine's bad dreams wake him. In the mornings his eyes are bruised with exhaustion.

'He's like a dog, guarding her. I'm sure he's overheard us talking about sending her away.'

Water laps and plops while your words spill over one another, a torrent, and you need a handkerchief but have no handbag, nothing. You look away, disoriented by liquid sounds and movement in the enclosed space that dances with dust motes on streaming rays of light. The splashes of crimson paint on the floor; the copper strands in his hair and the white line across the back of his neck where his hair's been cut shorter; his beard with its ginger glints. A dog is barking, on and on.

Sounds float. Your ears hum; a fog of silence. The paint-splashed floor zooms upwards.

He's caught you, supporting you in his arms, your head resting on his chest where hair pushes against the fabric of his shirt and your cheek. There's a smell of skin and something oily. His shirt is damp. Sweat, your tears, you can't tell.

He yanks off the filthy dust sheet covering a sofa, one arm still around you, the swell of his biceps at your ribs.

'Here.'

Your mind is cotton wool, his face so close you can see the pores with the blond hairs sprouting, the way they glisten. He lies you down and lifts your legs up on to the sofa. Your head falls back and your eyes close.

'I'll away fetch some water.'

He brings water and goes away again.

He comes back with his plate of eggs and bacon and sits cross-legged on the floor beside the sofa.

He talks a little about his childhood and his brother, then about his painting, his voice low and deep. The vibration's there but you can't make out words. Your arm's hanging down, loosely, and now and then you feel the brush of his upper arm as he lifts the fork to his mouth, the rough warmth of the hairs – or the promise of it. You wait for it, that promise of warmth, substance slowly returning to your limbs. Finally you sit up and straighten your sundress. You're ravenous. He passes half a slice of buttered brown bread from his plate and you eat. A dog is barking itself into a frenzy on the bank.

Honey! You leap to your feet.

I'VE BEEN MESSING WITH rope from the shed and forgotten about eating. Now I'm starving, halfway through opening a tin of sardines from Susie's box of supplies, when thunder cracks overhead. The lightning is almost simultaneous and the lights go out. A pause – silence – before the downpour unleashes. In the darkness, I place the tin on the draining board and feel for the curve of the peeled back lid. Once I've located the sharp edges with my finger tips, I plunge thumb and forefinger into the slippery mess of the contents. Can't see what it is, but it's in my mouth anyway: a small chunk of fish.

I fumble in the dark for Susie's torch on the kitchen window sill. Momentarily, there's a wavering light. Then it's out. I kick the kitchen unit.

Rain strikes the roof, vicious as the thwack of arrows. A gutter must be blocked because water courses down from somewhere and smacks on to the concrete path. Another thunder crack and glass vibrates in the window frames. The kitchen is lit by a flash of lightning. In that split second I catch sight of the opened sardine tin on the draining board and, returned to darkness, feel gingerly for the fragile pieces of fish, putting them straight into my mouth.

The rain's volume is disorienting. I grope my way back to the sofa, burrow down into my sleeping bag and bury my head.

My hands reek of sardines. A spring coils into my back and hunger growls in my stomach. Rain crushes the room with its crescendo, flinging at the windows, pelting the roof, whipping the walls: a whirlpool of swirling sound dragging me down.

Breathe. Breathe slowly.

But I'm drowning in it: choking and coughing. Coughing until I'm gasping and retching. My throat constricts. Panic slams through me like acceleration stress, that sudden moment when tall buildings tip, the sky swoops and the slap of the ropes ceases as they pull taut. I am swaddled in Houdini's straitjacket, its padded bulk of stale madness, winched higher as the pulleys rattle and squeak. Ten storeys up, I hang.

Sweating, I throw off the sleeping bag. Sit upright on the edge of the sofa. On the floor at my feet is the old rope from the shed, now in several sections. In places, the heart was grey. It needed cutting out. I grab a fraying end. Hold it to my face and inhale its mustiness. OK now – deep, slow breaths.

Because the rope has been neglected, its end has become untwisted. I try to consider which ornamental knot I could work to the strands, try to think about back-splicing, or whipping the ends with twine.

But it's no use. The rain's presence is overwhelming, flooding my head. My fingers pick weakly at the rope. I give up. Sit on my shaking hands and feel the bulk and tension of my thigh muscles. Stare at the rope on the floor. Rope: its strength. Strands twisted in opposite directions. I think of the arm of the woman next door, the swell of her muscle as I gripped it, her shock-ready stance. The curling tip of the long plait reaching her buttocks and the way she tossed it over her shoulder, her nipples pricking and tight in the cold.

I'm drenched in the few paces it takes for me to dash to her door, and then she takes her time. She opens the door a crack and peeps out, holding up a metal lantern with a nightlight wavering inside. The wind snuffs it out.

'Bugger!' She's muttering and fiddling with a lighter.

I shield my face from the rain, holding up an arm.

'I'm on the scrounge again,' I shout against the wind's gusts. Rain snakes down the back of my neck. 'I've no candles. A torch—' I hold Susie's torch up as proof, of something '— no batteries.' My sodden hair slaps like seaweed.

'You'd better come in.' A hoarse voice, almost masculine; she must have smoked a good many fags in her time. 'I'm getting sick of this,' she adds.

It takes a split second to work out she's talking about the power cuts, not me. I hope. I follow her through another door and we're in the main room that fills the space between two parallel railway carriages.

'This is the third power cut in the last fortnight. The novelty wears off.' Her voice and our footsteps echo. The room is vast and the floorboards are bare. Light blazes from several candles in a huge candelabrum that hangs on a long black chain from the high pitch of the roof. No ceiling. All pine beams and planks. Hollow, like a drum, it magnifies the pounding of the waves and the sliding of the shingle. But I can't hear the rain.

'Wow.'

She's lighting a roll-up. 'Ikea,' she says sideways, through clenched lips, and nods upwards.

'Ikea?'

She exhales, and smoke billows out like a sigh. 'The candelabrum.' She nods, as if that explains everything.

It's a workroom. Clay-splattered sheets are draped around the room; plastic and newspaper litter the floor. The shelves hold clay heads, some life size, some tiny, hands in various positions, a foot, an assortment of junk. There's a child's jelly shoe. In one corner a human form, life sized, is shaped in chicken wire. I turn towards the black expanse of uncurtained window that's melting with rain. The shock is electric: in front of the window, a naked woman is diving, her limbs outstretched, her face hidden.

'Don't touch!'

As if I'm a child.

'Of course not.'

The sculpture is a presence, a pause of muscle and motion that draws the eye.

Sarah moves so that she is between me and the sculpture. She stands, back towards me, legs straight, apart, one hand buried deep in the pocket of her jeans. She's chewing the inside of her lip. The rope of hair hangs down to her buttocks. Some has escaped the plait and curls away in wild corkscrews. There are streaks of grey. I'm not good at women's ages, but she's older than me and that's reassuring. Chances are she won't want looking after.

She steps forward, and the hand with the cigarette hovers over the soles of the woman's feet. 'The water source will be here somewhere, in between her toes.'

The startling effect of pause and motion will be heightened with water flowing over it.

Still gazing at the diving woman, Sarah picks up an almost empty glass of red wine from a wooden tea chest and drains it with one swig. Then remembers I'm there. 'Oh – want one?' She holds fag up in one hand, glass in the other.

'Thanks. Wine'd be good.'

After a quick search, she finds another glass on a shelf beside a smooth, curving sculpture that makes me think of a lasso. She inspects the glass and wipes the rim on her T-shirt. Wine glugs from the bottle. It's a very large, blue glass, thick and heavy with air bubbles trapped in the glass. Very cheap or very expensive, it's hard to say, but I like its weight in my hand.

'The head's not finished.' She refills her own glass and turns back to the diving woman.

Again, I notice the set of Sarah's shoulders, the muscles in her upper arms, her bare feet. She's strong, wiry. The joint of her big toe protrudes, giving her feet a gnarled look. There's a silver band around one middle toe. I knock back half a glass of red. Feel better.

'I want the water to run over her heels, down her legs, over her bum, back and shoulders,' she swoops with her hand, 'and then over her head. And I want her to have long hair.'

The diving woman has Sarah's feet, but more bony, and larger than life.

'But,' Sarah continues, 'the hair's a real bugger. I want tumbling locks, the water to swirl, not pour or trickle.' A little red wine sploshes from her glass as she gesticulates. She must've had more than one already. 'Want a towel?'

I'm startled at her change of tack. She's staring at my chest. Water from my sodden hair has spread across my T-shirt. Halfway down my back, there's the cling of wet material. I bend down towards the floor, scooping a mass of dripping hair forwards over my head. 'I could model for you,' I joke from between my legs.

'Actually . . .' Her feet, sturdy, wide, come close on the bare boards. The red varnish is chipped. 'Actually, you know – you could. Your hair's just about long enough. A photo . . .'

Her fingertips graze my scalp as she lifts sections of my hair between her hands and lets it fall.

'And thick enough,' she adds. The bones in her feet flex and ripple as her weight shifts. 'Sorry, I'll get that towel.'

I lift my head. She's gone. I want to touch the diving woman, run a hand over the curve of her lower back and buttocks, but instead I pull off the wet T-shirt and sit cross-legged on the floorboards facing her. The room is filled with the sound of shingle hauled forward and back.

I down my wine and help myself to the remains of the bottle. Sarah's fag rests where she's left it balanced on the ashtray; smoke wafts in slow curls.

YOU HAVE MADE LEMONADE and shortbread this afternoon, you tell Ian, peeping around the dining-room door. He has his back to you, crouching with the dustpan, and he wipes a hand across his forehead, his face preoccupied and distant for a moment, his mind elsewhere.

Today has been so hot, you say, opening the door wider, he really should have a cool drink before he leaves – maybe in the garden? His eyes seem to register you standing in the doorway, and he smiles.

You smile back, prompting him. 'Yes?'

The jug, as you carry it out to the garden, is slippery with condensation. Ian's lying on his back, sprawled like a lion on the grass, the vulnerable pale underside of his arms exposed. Ice clinks. He sits up, stretching, takes the glass from you and puts his lips straight to it. His mouth, framed by moustache and beard, is half hidden. You search for his mouth when he speaks, watching for his lower lip. He downs the lemonade in one and runs a hand over his beard.

'I'll be away hame,' he says, looking at his wristwatch.

The tightening of disappointment is fleeting because your watch tells you the same, Ian's usually gone by now. The children should be home from school. Often they're back in time for Andy to rush straight upstairs to change out of his uniform and disappear into the dining room. While Ian cleans his brushes, he gives Andy a sheet of sandpaper to use on the skirting board or window frames, or stands behind him at the wallpaper table, guiding Andy's hand as he spreads the glue in sweeps. As these images pass through your mind, time hovers. You should really be loading Elaine into the pram, walking down to the bus stop to see where the children have got to. Ian should be wheeling his bicycle down the front path. Neither of you moves. A butterfly lands on the buddleia. Then from the kitchen comes a burst of noise as the children arrive, the two of them bundling in through the back door, arguing, and they're out through the French doors, shedding bags and shoes and blazers across the lawn, stirring up the air.

Susie is wailing and her hand goes out for a piece of shortbread from the plate as she clambers on to your lap. Her forehead is sticky with heat.

'You're a bit late today. Where've you been?'

Andy fishes a book out of his satchel. 'Just down to Grampy's. Look what he got me!' Although he's holding the book up for you to see, he's sidling up to Ian, who's still sitting on the grass, arms looped around his knees. 'There's even photos. Loads.'

Andy sits down and wriggles close to Ian, leaning into his arm with a shoulder until he's snuggled against Ian's bulk. A fortnight ago, Ian was a stranger. Susie still keeps her distance, round-eyed at his size, his beard, staring at him over the rim of her mug of lemonade. She's confided to you at night that he might be the giant from the top of the beanstalk.

'That's Houdini's Suspended Straitjacket Escape.' Andy points at a page. His finger is stained with blue Quink.

'Tha's Houdini?' Ian says, dipping his head to the glossy black-and-white page.

From where you're sitting, you can just make out hats, hundreds of bowler hats and trilbies filling the street between two rows of tall buildings.

'Will ye leuk at this!' Ian holds the book up for you.

There are ropes and pulleys. A bundle hangs from the side of one of the tall buildings, high above the upturned faces. You peer at the bundle. Yes, it's a human form, upside down, wrists tied behind. The hairs on the back of your neck prickle. You imagine the rush of blood to the head, the grind of wrist and ankle bones. There's white handwriting across the photograph: *Straight jacket escape*. You laugh, handing the book back to Ian. 'Someone can't spell straitjacket.'

It's Andy that takes the book from you, smoothing the page with the palm of his hand. 'Grampy got it from the library for me.'

'Lucky old you! How is he today? Did he give you a drink?'

'Yes.'

Ian looks at his watch.

'How's your brother?' A clumsy attempt to distract him from the time, keep him here in the hot garden with the smell of creosote rising up from the fence.

'I'm awa the noo tae pay him a visit. Take him to the pairk.'

'To see the horses?' Andy's face lights up.

'Ay, the horses. Ye cud come. Whit wid ye say tae that?'

Already Andy is on his feet.

'Andrew, no, you've just got in. It's far too hot.' Your voice trails off because Susie slides from your lap, stripy summer dress riding up over her bottom.

'And me,' she says.

Three expectant faces look at you.

Ian pushes the wheelchair, while you have Elaine in the pushchair with the canopy to give her some shade. Other couples in the park have small babies in perambulators and pushchairs.

Andy and Susie race in and out of the rhododendron bushes playing hide and seek as Ian explains that he takes his brother out two or three times a week. His mother, who is quite elderly, can have a nap, or just put her feet up.

Jamie stares at the sky, hands plucking at his trousers, his face still at last. When you first arrived at Ian's parents' house and went into the sitting room where he lay on a sofa, you'd been shocked to see Jamie was a man, not the boy you'd imagined. Only sixteen but already broad-shouldered, like Ian, with muscular, hairy arms. His jaw, working furiously as soon as Ian stepped in the room, was dark with a five o'clock shadow. His tongue twisted and toiled, his mouth opening and closing and stretching into a grin, as he grunted and yelped in greeting. Appalled, you'd halted in the doorway with the children, struggling to regain control of your emotions as Ian embraced his brother.

You stop by the pond and pull out the bread. Ducks appear, flapping and quacking, from all directions. Some stagger out of the water and putter at your feet with their beaks.

Heat rises from the tarmac path. It won't be long before Susie and Andy demand a drink or an ice cream. Jamie's head rolls as if too heavy for his neck, but he rests his chin on his chest and carefully cups his hands together as you give him some torn-up bread. As he flings the bread towards the ducks with both hands, crumbs and chunks scatter on his lap. When the bread is gone, you stroll together around the boating lake, where the boats are bottoms up because it's getting near to closing time for the day. One or two of the boats need repainting. The ticket hut is already shuttered and bolted. The park is emptying out now, people moving towards the exits. Soon the big iron gates will be locked.

As you walk on, past the striped bowling green, past the tennis courts where people are zipping racquets into covers and collecting up balls, and past the crowds of damp-haired children smelling of chlorine gathered at the entrance to the open-air swimming pool, Jamie hums and points and rocks his head. Ian bends down to him every now and then. Andy and Susie run around the empty bandstand ahead and duck down, ready to leap out when you walk past. The sky is blue, cloudless.

'Real June weather today.' You want to break the silence.

Ian stops, cranes his head backwards, looking up at the sky. Below his beard the hair on his neck grows upwards, like lush grass against the foot of a fencepost. His Adam's apple slides when he speaks. 'Gey near noo. One of Jamie's favourite places.' He points to the top of a Witch's Hat roundabout a little further on, just visible above the shrubs. He looks ahead and walks quickly. 'I hae a commission – weans in a playground, for a charity Christmas card, to go on sale next year.'

'Goodness.' You do a little skip to keep up with Ian and the wheelchair. 'How wonderful!'

'Only a commission.'

'Yes, but . . .'

As you round the bushes, Susie and Andy are already there, fingers and noses through the wire mesh fence, eyes on the two rows of rocking horses. There are about fifteen in the enclosure, their painted flanks gleaming in the sun. These are not traditional rocking horses, legs tidied into symmetrical curves, but individually carved. Every leg has been given a different angle, stretch or lift or flick of a hoof. The horses are assorted sizes, some piebald, some brown or black, some white. They're beautiful.

Jamie is gurning again at the sight of the riderless horses, his face contorted with smiles. The playground is empty, no other children anywhere to be seen.

'I'd love to know who made them.' You gaze through the fence. 'They've been crafted so lovingly.'

'Ay.' Ian puts the brake on the wheelchair and rattles the gate to the enclosure. 'Do ye no think we should mebbe try to get in?'

'Oh. Is Jamie all right?'

'He's no complaining.'

Jamie's face moves between grimace to grin, his tongue twisting as he nods vigorously. Elaine stares ahead placidly. You push a damp curl from her face. 'Look at the lovely horses, sweetheart.'

'Mummy, it's shut, it's shut,' Susie whines. The gate is padlocked. Andy has a toe in the wire mesh ready to attempt to climb the six-foot fence, waiting for a signal from Ian.

Ian lifts the padlock, twists the metal hoop and it drops open. 'There we are noo!'

The children cheer and barge through. Ian manoeuvres Jamie's wheelchair through the narrow gateway. Jamie's grin is lopsided, gummy, but the sparkle in his eyes gives you a jolt; it's the first time you've looked him in the eye.

'Look see!' Ian says, a hand on your arm. 'Close your eyes and open them – they're galloping.' He laughs and whistles 'Hop-along Cassidy' as he walks down the row, running his hand over the horses' rumps.

You put a hand on the arching neck of the largest black horse and stroke the horsehair mane. The eyes are glass, shining and dark, with both pupil and iris. 'Are you going to paint these?'

'For starters, I'm gonny ride one.' He's gathered the leather reins of one horse into his large hand. His fingers still have white paint on them.

'What?'

Andy and Susie are already shrieking and waving, rocking to and fro.

'Think I'm jesting?' He strides back up the row towards you, putting the palm of his hand under each horse's nostrils as if they are breathing creatures, his face glowing as if he's caught the sun. 'I havnae ridden a real one. You?'

You shake your head.

He comes to where you're standing by the big black horse. 'This one's biggest. It'll take my weight, for sure. For sure.' He grips the worn leather saddle with both hands and glances over his shoulder. There's no one around. 'Aye, gie it a whirl!'

He grunts as he mounts. 'Come on!' His voice holds such urgency that, before you know it, your foot's in the stirrup and you've thrown a leg over a horse's back. The horse responds to the forward thrust of your hips; you and Ian move forward and back in unison. You smile at his smile, the exhilaration and the children's ecstatic whoops. Jamie's head nods to and fro with the movement, smiling broadly, his eyes wide beneath raised eyebrows. He whoops too, lifting a hand. Elaine sits motionless in the pushchair, her face shaded, but her eyes slide, following you, forward and back.

Ian shouts to Jamie, 'Will you take a look at us!' Jamie lifts his twisted hands from his lap and carefully brings them together and apart again. He's clapping. 'Uh Huh! Uh Huh! Uh Huh!' he repeats with each clap. But it brings a lump to your throat when you look back at Elaine, silent, her face devoid of emotion.

Ian throws his head back, laughing again. 'A posse!'

'We're a posse!' Susie and Andy shout. 'Yahoo!'

You lean back too, blinking back tears. The sky is open and blue. Yes, you think to yourself, a posse.

You will save this memory, preserve it clear as crab apple jelly so that you can look back and wonder at your childish excitement, the blue brilliance of the June sky.

I LOOK AT MY new Timex wristwatch. There's time to go and
see Grampy on the way home from school. I take Susie's
satchel and pick up her hand to make her walk faster.

Grampy's house smells of kippers today. So do his hands.
Grampy's fingers are big and lumpy. There is dirt from
gardening down behind his fingernails. He makes *sss-sss-sss*
noises between his teeth while he's winding the seaming
twine around the rope.

'Do you see?' he says, and holds the end of the rope up
for me to look at the whipping turns. Then he shows me the
other end of the rope, with the strands coming undone so
that the rope is fuzzy instead of smooth.

'This,' he waves the untwisted end under my nose, 'this is
what happens if ropes or cables are left with their ends
uncared for. They become unmanageable. So, my Treasure,
which knot could we use on this end?'

I scratch my heel and pretend to think hard about his
question but I decided, as soon as I saw it was a four-
stranded rope, I would show Grampy I can do a Royal
Crown by myself.

'Can I do a Royal Crown?'

'Mmm. We'll see whether you can or whether you can't,
shall we?' Grampy hands me the ball of waxed seaming

twine and sits back with his arms crossed over his chest and his hands tucked into his armpits.

Susie comes in from the garden with a daisy. She gives it to Grampy and then holds her arms up to be lifted on to Grampy's lap. She leans her head against his chest and sucks her thumb.

Grampy holds up the daisy and swirls it between his finger and thumb. 'If you can find me a few more of these, duck, I might be able to make you a daisy chain.'

Susie takes her thumb out of her mouth and smiles and nods as she slides off his lap and runs back outside. It's just me and Grampy, which is best. I check my new Timex again. Ten more minutes or Mummy will start to worry.

Back home, I stand in just my underpants in front of the wardrobe mirror in Mummy's room. I have my handcuffs on, like Houdini in the photograph on page 24 of Grampy's book. Houdini has loads more muscle. In the mirror my legs are white and thin. There is Elastoplast on one knee. My hair is a bit the same as Houdini's, sort of thick and wavy and with a parting to one side, but otherwise I don't look much like him yet. I squeeze the muscles in my legs really hard. My kneecaps move up.

In the photograph, Houdini is behind bars like a prison door, but they are not real bars. The bars, Grampy told me, have been drawn on with a pen. The photograph is a fake, a make-pretend picture of Houdini in a cage. Even Houdini's swimming trunks are drawn on.

Houdini's name wasn't really Harry Houdini. It was Erich Weiss. His old name sounds wrong.

When I can swim a length of the swimming pool by myself, I will get a yellow cloth band for Mummy to sew on to my swimming trunks. I've already got a white one for swimming a width. There are other things I must learn if I am going to be an escapologist, like holding my breath for a long time and treading water.

Houdini was very good at treading water without using his hands to help keep him afloat. He needed his hands to untie the knots under water. He could hold his breath under water for three minutes. I practise this part in the bath. I push the bolt on the bathroom door across and put my new Timex on the edge of the bath. My ribs go up and my tummy sucks in and I practise untying knots with my hands under water, holding my breath.

Mummy raps on the door. 'Andy, do hurry up in there. It's time for Susie's bath.'

Houdini practised all the time to get good. He knew about lots of knots. And my book says he listened for The Voice. It was only in his head. But he never jumped off a bridge or went under water until he heard The Voice. I want to know if The Voice was big and loud, or soft and quiet.

With my black wax crayon I draw thick bars on the wardrobe mirror. Grampy tells me that in ancient times, the art of knot tying was held in great esteem because knots kept treasures safe.

RUBBING FLOUR AND SUGAR and margarine for tonight's rhubarb crumble between your fingertips, you decide to bake rock buns, something different to offer Ian tomorrow.

Showery rain hits the kitchen window like gravel and Michael's key turns in the lock. While he's in the hall shaking the water off his mackintosh, you slip Andy's TOP SECRET notepad back into the drawer under the tea towels. The potatoes have just come to the boil. You're reaching for the matches to light the gas under the peas, have the match ready, about to strike it, when Michael turns swiftly in the kitchen doorway and closes the door. He leans back against it, knocking the peg bag from its hook.

'What . . .?'

A muscle is working in his jaw. There's something . . .

'It's Andrew.' Michael's back is pressed against the door. 'Don't go out there.'

'Michael, I . . .' Your hand, still holding the match, shakes. Focus on sliding the match box open and laying the match beside the others, the round brown heads clustered neatly together. Close the box. Place it beside Susie's empty glass. Take a breath.

'Michael, you're being very melodramatic. What on earth's going on?'

Another step and you reach for the door handle. Michael grabs your wrist, pulling your body to his. You can smell hospital on him, stale antiseptic. His eyes flick from side to side as he looks into yours, his pupils like pinpricks.

'Andrew's playing some damn fool trick, hanging himself upside down from the banisters.'

As if lit by a flash bulb, you see it: the black-and-white image of Houdini wrapped in a straitjacket, hanging from his ankles above a street thronged with hats and upturned faces.

'No!'

Michael has his arms across your back, his mouth at your ear, hissing, 'You mustn't. Ignore it. Think about why he does these things!'

'My God, Michael!' Every muscle is straining. 'He could kill himself.' Willing your body free from Michael's hold – teeth clenched – grunts of exertion come from deep in your throat. He's got both your wrists now, and holds them at shoulder height so your arms cannot move. The lid over the potatoes rattles; water spurts out, hissing on the hot stove. Michael's body is rigid, his neck flushed and swollen against the collar and tie tight at his throat, his breathing hot against the side of your face. He's so much stronger than you are.

Your body flops, your head droops, eyes following the line of the crease in Michael's trousers down to his polished shoes, dark with damp. Beyond the shut kitchen door, Andy hangs in the hallway, a rope around his ankles. Arms limp now, you sway a little, towards Michael's chest. His shirt is coming untucked. He licks his lips and begins to lower your arms, his fingers loosening their grasp on your wrists. He frees one wrist to sweep the flop of hair from his eyes and that's when you bring your knee up, hard, into his groin so that he groans and bends double, staggering forward just enough to let you pull the door open a little and wriggle past him into the hallway.

Andy is hauling himself hand over hand back up a rope that's tied to the banisters. He can't use his feet to take his weight, because they're tied together at the ankles.

'Andy!'

You run up to the half landing and lean over the handrail to grasp the rope and heave him up. Once the weight of the top half of his body is over the handrail his legs slither over and he falls into you. You both end up on the floor. You wrap your arms around his shoulders and rock. Andy rubs the palms of his hands. From the kitchen comes a strong smell of burning; the potatoes must be sticking. You're just about to call out to Michael when you hear an almighty clang. Something metallic rolls: a saucepan lid. The back door slams. The painting of the ship at sea above your head rocks on its wires. Susie appears in the sitting-room doorway, thumb in mouth, and looks up at you both.

At first Andy resists your enclosing arms, rubbing his ankles and then his palms again, but you hold him, rocking to and fro, to and fro, until your heart slows down and you can get to your feet.

Michael has flung the potato pan into the sink with such force bits of potato are spattered over the floor, the walls and the curtains. You fill the bucket and mop the floor, squeeze out a cloth, dab at the curtains and wipe drying lumps from the Formica surfaces. By the time you've finished, both children are at the kitchen table squabbling over crayons and you must feed them before they are too tired to eat.

Once they are in bed you take the notepad from its hiding place under the tea towels and rip it apart, feeding page after page to the boiler. Bone weary, you dial her number and, even as you begin to recount the evening's events, you know Hoggie will get on her bicycle and be with you before ten minutes have passed.

At the front door, her mass of red hair is haloed by the setting sun and the relief reduces you to tears. She puts her arms round you, hugs you close, palms rubbing your back in comforting circles. You talk into the red hair. It smells faintly of the hospital kitchens.

'I'm worried he will have gone to Dad's. He was so – furious. And he'll blame Dad for this whole Houdini thing. And . . . do you think I hurt him badly?'

'Go.' She gives your back a final dismissive pat. 'Go and find him. I'll stay here with the children.'

Because you've forgotten to lift before you push, your father's metal front gate grinds to a halt on the uneven crazy paving slabs. You struggle frantically to force it wide enough to squeeze through. The house is quiet – no lights blazing, no raised voices clamouring through the open windows. You're wrong; Michael hasn't come here after all.

Honeysuckle, damp after the rain, scents the dusk. Of course your father won't be in the house, he'll be in the greenhouse. You hurry down the side passage, past the open back door and down the narrow garden path between the glossy hebe bushes, where your pace slows because the masses of purple flowers are so fragrant tonight that the desire to stand still and breathe their perfume into your body is almost overwhelming. But you make yourself keep going, following the narrow path down between the apple trees towards the old greenhouse.

As you approach, although it is almost dark, you see them together in the greenhouse: your father, dishevelled, a trowel held loosely in one hand, leaning against the wide shelves he has built for his seedling trays as he looks down at Michael, who sits on an upturned box, his back to you. Everything about the contours of Michael's body – his shoulders, his head, his hands – is limp and bowed. Neither of them seems to be talking. The intimacy of the scene is so unexpected it brings you to a halt, one hand resting on the rough concrete edge of the ugly birdbath your mother bought when they first moved to this house. The words on the pedestal – 'You are nearer God's heart in a garden, Than anywhere else on Earth' – you've always considered trite and sentimental but now, in this moment, you almost feel the weight of meaning they might carry.

You step forward; they both hear your footfall and turn. Michael gets to his feet abruptly, hesitates at the greenhouse door and then strides off further down the garden towards the raspberry canes. For a moment his shirt is white against the dusk, before he disappears from sight.

In the greenhouse, you perch on the upturned box Michael has just left. His tie lies on the ground at your feet. You bury your face in your hands. Your father moves away down the greenhouse. There's the slosh of water in the watering can, the fine spray of water on leaves.

After a while his footsteps come close again, and his hand is on your shoulder. 'This home in Sussex, have you paid a visit? Had a look? Michael says they specialise in caring for children like Elaine.'

'Children like Elaine?'

Anger tightens your throat again. It's the word 'home'. Your father is as bad as Michael, can hardly bear to look at her. His mother, your grandmother, a country midwife in Yorkshire, told him stories, stories that he repeated to you recently, of babies born and put straight on to the fire, 'For the best', because they were deformed. You'd stared at him, horrified. 'But Dad, Elaine's not deformed,' you'd shouted.

'Look at her, Dad. Look!' Pulling him over to the rug where Elaine lay, her wisteria-blue eyes staring up at the ceiling. 'She's perfect! Physically, she's perfect!'

You swallow and look down at Michael's discarded tie. 'Some of them in that place are monsters, Dad. One little boy crouches under the table and growls like a dog. He bites too.'

'Well,' he takes his hand from your shoulder, 'there's others in the family you need to look to, duck. She's using you all up.'

You think of Houdini and the straitjacket picture and feel your father should be taking some of the blame for what has happened tonight, not handing out advice.

'Dad –'

'Andy talks to me, duck. He imagines things. He needs more of you. And Michael . . .' He turns away to the tap and begins to refill the watering can.

'And Michael?' you prompt.

'Michael is beside himself with worry.'

'What's he said?'

'Well,' he pauses to fiddle with the sprinkler rose on the spout of the watering can.

'Well what, Dad?'

'He seems to think Andy's reacting in an extreme way to . . .'

'Did Michael tell you how he himself reacted?'

'Perhaps if it's just a temporary arrangement that you make,' he seems not to have heard, 'for Elaine. Just to see how things go.'

Exasperated, you stand up, but something about your father's patient expression as he waits for you to respond to what he has said cuts through the tension in your chest and it's as though you're letting go of something, because perhaps he's right after all, perhaps everyone else is right after all and there's no point fighting the inevitable any longer. You're failing.

He bends to examine a tray of cornflowers, tweaks out a spindly seedling and drops it on to the shelf. He runs his fingers lightly over the tops of the silvery-green leaves and pinches out another stunted plant. Lying on the rough wood, the tiny discarded seedlings appear to wither almost immediately.

Michael's sudden movement at the greenhouse door makes you jump.

'There's a robin caught,' he pants, not quite looking at you, 'just flown into the nets. I need some scissors.'

Your father holds up a Stanley knife. 'Shall I do it?'

Michael shakes his head. 'I'll have a go.'

As a child you hated the yards of black netting that shrouded your father's precious raspberry canes. Leaning out of your bedroom window, you could see the dark swathes of it at the bottom of the garden. You'd hear the flap and squawk of a trapped bird and hurtle downstairs, screeching for your father. Once, sent to pick raspberries for supper, you'd lifted aside the net to find a dead blackbird tangled close to your hand, its claws curled, the one visible eye a slit.

You follow Michael down the garden. The bird is hanging, twisted, an exhausted bundle in the netting. As the two of you approach, it struggles in panic and the black thread digs deeper into the feathers at its neck. Murmuring, Michael wraps one hand around the bird, firmly enfolding its wings against its body, but the robin strains its head in terror, beak open. You see the stiff tongue moving, making no sound. Michael hands you the Stanley knife and carefully lifts the thread from the bird's neck for you to cut through. The wings are not too badly tangled, but nevertheless Michael has to use his other hand to gently lift and spread the wing for you to be able to cut the thread underneath. Once it's free, the robin almost falls from Michael's hand and flutters down to the ground, hunched and wary, under the laurel hedge.

Moving slowly, you wander together back to the greenhouse. The kitchen light is on now and your father is moving about inside.

In the greenhouse, Michael picks up his tie and takes one of your hands in both of his. 'I don't know what to do.' He sighs. You have never seen Michael like this, at a loss. 'Perhaps we all just need some breathing space.'

You recall the dusky fragrance of earlier and inhale, but the greenhouse air is too warm and damp, heavy with the cloying smell of soil.

Taking your hand from his, you move to the open door, your back to him. 'I don't know what I think any more.'

'You could take the children down to The Siding for a week or two, before we decide. Give yourself some time. Perhaps Jean could keep you company?'

You hold your upper arms and rub them, though you are not cold. There's no escaping this decision, much as your mind shies away from choosing. Endless postponement is no answer; everything and everyone is in limbo. If only there was someone who could tell you, with conviction, what to do. Like the Ward Sister at St Mary's. Although she was a tyrant, she knew how to tell people what to do. Once, during visiting hours, she made you clean and oil the castors of the beds. Another time she called you back just as you were going off duty after a night shift, so tired you could hardly put one foot in front of the other. Your feet throbbed. She picked up a dirty hypodermic syringe and showed you how to sterilise the barrel, ready for the precious penicillin. Then she left you to it. Your hand shook as you reached for the first stainless-steel syringe from the pile on the tray, but you drew the boiling oil up, slowly, into the barrel. It was dawn by the time you'd finished, a neat row of sterilised syringes on the trolley.

'About Elaine . . .' you say, finally.

'It's hard,' Michael interrupts. 'No one is any good at making difficult decisions.'

Your father's shovel is stuck into the yellowing grass and rotting stems of the compost heap. You imagine the heat generated by the decomposition deep inside. If you go to The Siding for a couple of weeks, as Michael has suggested, by the time you return, Ian will have finished the redecoration in the dining room. He will have gone.

'But,' your voice is firm, disembodied, 'yes, I'll take them to The Siding – before we make any final decisions. Andrew loves it there. We all do.'

IN SARAH'S BED, much later, I'm battling to wake. My ears buzz. Every slip into unconsciousness holds me under a white-water blur of images: slanting, high, barred windows; the snarl of lions' head knockers. Limbs like treacle, I gasp for air against the drag of undertow. Elaine's porcelain skin, her unblinking eyes, clouded like the prize marble I once had.

Finally I surface properly, fighting with the duvet, exhausted. Sarah sleeps on undisturbed, arms flung out across the pillows. I slip out of bed without waking her.

Back at The Siding, chill moonlight lights the curve of the ceiling, the splintery wooden walls, the criss-crossed rope shelves in my Pullman carriage bedroom. My feet and shins tangle with the metal bar across the foot end of the narrow child's bed. Thunder rumbles in the distance as the storm moves along the coast. Although sleep seems unlikely, I plummet into another nightmare. I'm trapped in the wardrobe in my parents' bedroom. Hanging furs caress my face. Jerking awake again, heart flipping, I throw open the sleeping bag and curse the wine. Too jittery to remain horizontal, I get up, make coffee and take it outside. Shingle glistens in the moonlight, but it's stopped raining. I sit on the veranda's edge, hunched into the sleeping bag, and sip strong black coffee. Every now and then, I get up to make more, grateful that the electricity has returned. The hammock now hangs between two concrete pillars of the veranda. I could bundle myself into it but I don't want to fall back into sleep. Images from my dreams crackle with energy.

At last it gets lighter. I guess it must be after seven now. The sky is white, becoming bluer in the east as the sun rises. No clouds. No rain. The sea spinach smells strong today, salt-burned in the gales. My teeth clunk on the mug – there's a tremor in my hands. I'm not sure how much of Sarah's Shiraz I drank last night on an empty stomach. I drain my coffee and get to my feet: time to do something.

The length of worn shroud-laid rope from the shed is on the floor by the sofa. Yesterday I cut away a couple of the damaged areas. The rope looks as though it may have spent some time in the sea, so it seems appropriate to use the kind of multi-strand bend sailors used in the past to make emergency repairs to hemp rigging: French Shroud Knots to join the fragments. I'll finish off with grafting to make a strong, handsome finish.

Most of the equipment I need is in my rucksack. I spread it all out on the table. Rigger's knife, long-billed pliers, packing needles, flexible wire needles, twine, black thread, beeswax, pantograph, tracing paper. I begin by seizing and opening the two rope ends. Marrying them together, I hold the structure vertically and wall the upstanding set of ends to the right. Turn the whole thing end for end and wall the new upper ends. Finally, I draw it snug.

But it's no good. My mind whirs, my hands shake. I need to get outside.

The window glass is covered with salt and what look like tiny strands of plant debris. I can barely make out the shingle banks beyond. Salt crystals stuck on the glass glitter in the sun. Behind them, blue sky. I have seen so little of it recently. Today the blue is partially hidden by the overhang of the veranda where a section hangs down, rotten. Loose felt flaps in the breeze.

I get the rickety kitchen chair. It wobbles, might cave in under my weight, but I can reach the rotten plywood. One wrench; a crack. The wood falls lower. The axe from the coal bunker will do it.

A few blows. Felt rips, plywood splinters. Soon, most of the veranda roof lies on the ground below. Above me arches the elation of a scoop of blue. That colour. In Crete, blue is everywhere. Snatches of sky pulled down into everyday life. Blue railings on the terraces of tavernas and spills of blue paint on the uneven paving; faded blue-and-white check tablecloths; a blue jug filled with Vasilis's home-made wine; blue doors and window frames against whitewashed walls.

No clouds. The sky is empty of motion. I want movement. We had a painting when I was a child. It hung halfway up the stairs. A square-rigged ship, sails billowing in a storm-tossed ocean under swollen skies. It's that suggestion of time and distance I need; sails against sky. Canvas – the old tent. I'll rip it up. Hang some strips of canvas. Maybe use the rope once the Shroud Knots are grafted. Work some pairs of Star Knots, perhaps a solid sinnet too. Back in Crete, that's what I'd planned, to try *Ashley*'s sixty-one-strand pentalpha. I'll need the pantograph. The pentalpha is a complex sinnet, star-shaped in cross section. Perfect, if I can do it. A bit of research and preparation is required. I'll need *Ashley*'s instructions and diagrams.

I carry the kitchen chair back inside.

First, some sort of table will be necessary to hold the strands in place as I work. The old washing basket in the shed – I could use the circular base of that, the wicker's rotten anyway. There must be a broomstick I can use for legs, some inch brads or nails somewhere.

I rummage about in the shed. In the far corner, I glimpse a metal frame with wheels. A carrycot. Elaine's carrycot. What the bloody hell's that doing here? Somebody has loaded it with chunks of driftwood. The hardboard shows through rips in the plastic covering. I lurch through the piles of junk. Get that wood out, I hear someone mutter, GET THAT BLOODY WOOD OUT!

JELLY MAKES A SIGHING noise, a little whimper, like Honey when she wants to go for a walk.

'They'll be back soon, Jelly. Don't be sad.'

I shiggle her carrycot to make the eebie jeebies go away.

The sea's right out, thin and flat. No one else on the sand but me and Jelly and Honey on the edge of the pebbles, and a man digging for lugworms a long way away. When Mummy and Susie come back with the ice creams, I'm going to make an enormous sandcastle with my new spade.

I'm leaving you in charge, Andrew, Mummy said, holding Susie's hand.

Honey chomps and slobbers on a bit of wood. She's wet, the fur on her legs and on her tummy all dark and stuck together like little feathers. She's got her head on one side, chewing, the piece of wood pushed right up into the corner of her mouth, her black lips stretching back to show her gums. Her teeth are long and pointy.

Jelly's whining gets louder. She wriggles on her back as if she's itchy. Her head's right at the top and her feet are right at the bottom of the carrycot. She's much too big and fat for it. Even though she's four, she hasn't stopped being a baby. She cries a lot.

When I was nearly four, Susie was born and I helped

Mummy with things like passing Johnson's Baby Powder and lining up the cotton buds. I wonder if Jelly will always be a baby and what it will be like when she's the same size as a grown-up and I have to call her Elaine, her real name.

I lie on my back to see the same as she sees. Wind blows white bits of cloud across the sky. I practise my whistling. Grampy says whistling is the Devil's music. It might call up a storm or a death by drowning.

Jelly has stopped wriggling. I blow some spit bubbles for her, but she's not watching. 'Now, Jelly,' I lean right over her, my shadow big and dark, 'I've made you a pool and now I'm going to make drip people next to it. Or shall I write your name in the sand?'

We talk to Jelly in questions, same as when we say to Honey, do you want to Fetch? And Honey fetches her special tennis ball with no fur left. Or, do you want a choccy-drop? And she stands by the larder door.

I put a finger on the place where Jelly's neck joins her chest and stroke the little dip there. Her skin is soft and white. I whisper my question right into her ear, 'Which would you like, Jelly?'

Her head goes from side to side. She's staring at the tassels on the carrycot canopy. I take a deep breath in and blow them, puffing out my cheeks like the wind.

Mummy and Susie are a very long time.

Honey stops chomping. She drops her stick on the pebbles and nudges it, looking sideways at me. Then she sniffs at the stick, wrinkling up her nose to show her teeth. She gives one bark.

I know what she wants, but I'm pretending I don't.

Honey jumps up, brings her stick over and drops it on the pebbles by my feet. Her nose touches my ankle. Wind blows, cold on the wetness. She looks at the stick; me; the stick. Her eyebrows twitch.

I pick up a pebble and roll it in my hand. I watch the lugworm man digging his hole.

Honey pushes at my arm with her nose, her pink tongue curling out to give me a lick. She rests her chin on me and looks sad. I put my arms around her and rub her seaweedy fur. On the top of her head where the fur is thin, I can feel her skull.

Suddenly she's up. She leaps around her stick, crouching down and bouncing up, pebbles flying everywhere. The stick's all slimy with slobber when I grab it and run, run on to the hard sand. Honey – chasing, crazy – overtakes me, her body curled like a ball, a bundle of legs, as she gallops towards the sea, skids around and comes back. Another skid and sand sprays up as she turns and gallops off again, her ears blown inside out by the wind.

I fling the stick as hard as I can. Honey races past the man's lugworm bucket. He stops digging and watches the sand fly. He holds a hand above his eyes to look at me, then at Elaine's carrycot on the edge of the pebbles.

I go back.

Jelly's eyes are closed now, her mouth open. *She's not all there, Andrew.* I put my face right down to hers, but all I can smell is the hot plastic of the sides of the carrycot.

I don't like strangers looking at Jelly.

I'm going to write her real name in the sand with my new spade.

On Saturday night, Auntie Jean and Mummy talked about Elaine when I was in bed. They thought I couldn't hear. Mummy was crying again. They said about her going away into a Home, and I thought of Gladys at school who has warts on her fingers and smells like left-over gravy. She lives at the Barnardo's Home. We whisper 'Fleabags' be-hind our hands. I'd rather be dead than be like Gladys.

My new spade is red metal with a wooden handle. It's got a sharp edge that cuts through the sand. Susie has my old spade. It's small and rubbery with swirls of red and blue and green like plasticine colours rolled together.

I carve an E in the sand, five paces high and three paces wide. By the time I've drawn the bottom line of the E, the top line has gone blurry, rubbing itself out. I stand and paddle my feet up and down, up and down on the sand to make sinking sand. Real sinking sand comes when you're not expecting it and suddenly you're up to your ankles in slime. Sometimes there are hard bits under your feet, the bones of people who've drowned. I paddle more. My feet sink lower and lower until cold sand rings my ankles and my feet are deep under heavy wetness. Now Elaine's 'E' has melted back into the sand.

The man digging for lugworms has thrown Honey's stick for her but she brings it back to me. He starts digging a new round hole. My hole has nearly filled up with sand and water again so I kneel over and use my arms to heave out more sand. It slides all over my bare legs. When I take my soggy jumper off, the chilly wind gives me goose bumps.

I make my hole deeper, but water and sand come back to fill it. I have to be much faster. The metal disc with Honey's name on it jingles on her collar as she jumps and leaps all around me. She starts to dig with me, her paws flying. Sand sprays up between her back legs. I copy her, cupping my hands, chucking sand between my legs; panting.

If Elaine is not all here, like Mummy says to people, there must be a part of her that is somewhere else. Like Grampy says Granny is in a better place. Really, she's dead. I know, because we visit her headstone in the graveyard and leave her favourite flowers there. But Grampy talks to her and blows a goodbye kiss.

Elaine starts again with her whimpers. I feel sorry that she just lies in the carrycot and can't get out and play with us in the sand so I shiggle the sides of the carrycot a bit more to try and make her laugh. She doesn't do her giggle much any more, even when I lick the bottoms of her feet. Mummy says she's sore somewhere, they don't know where. I think they mean in her head. She wears nappies still, so perhaps it's them that make her sore. Or perhaps she's hungry because she only has milk from a bottle or sometimes mushed-up food. No nice food like chocolate, or even Parma violets which are only little. I thought she'd like them.

Now she's crying and coughing with a sound like she's going to be sick. I still can't see Mummy and Susie coming back from the ice-cream van. I push the canopy back and see that Elaine's head is squashed right up at the top of the carrycot and her hair is stuck down and wet with sweat. I put my hands under her arms and try to sit her up. She's heavy and very wobbly. She can't sit up by herself yet.

She takes a deep breath in. Her face goes red. She opens her mouth wide and screams. I lay her down again.

I'll have to wash the sand off. She's different from me and doesn't like the feel of sand on her skin, which I do know already so I wish I hadn't touched her with my sandy hands. I lick one of her fat feet and explain how to make sand go soft by pressing down so that the water comes through, or by squeezing the sand in your fist. That's how to make drip people, I tell her, but her mouth is big and wet and red with screaming.

Honey has gone for a swim. Her head is a dot in the water.

Elaine doesn't stop screaming even when I play Boo! over the side of the carrycot.

The man digging holes is looking again.

I'll fetch some nice clear water in the bucket to wash the sand off her and stop her being so hot and cross. I tip Susie's slipper shells out of the bucket. I'll have to run because I'm not supposed to leave Elaine. I'm in charge. The tide is far out, the sea a grey line.

Honey comes back from the sea and starts shaking her head from side to side. I grab her collar and drag her away from Elaine just as she starts to twist her whole body faster and faster and seawater droplets fly out, spreading everywhere and spattering me.

Now Honey's here, I can go. I spread my towel on the sand. Elaine is heavy, but I just manage to lift her out of the carrycot. I lay her on her back. She stops crying and gasps a little bit, screwing up her eyes because the sky is big and bright even though the sun keeps going behind the clouds. She stops crying and kicks her legs like she's happy.

The bucket is full to the brim but water sloshes out when I run, so I have to go back to fill it up again. This time I walk, watching the water in the bucket, my legs moving straight and hard. Ripples of sand press into my feet. Splashes of water spill and leave dark patches on my salty-white skin.

I'm on to the flat sand now. Honey is trotting in a circle round and round Elaine and I can see Mummy walking across the pebbles with the ice creams, taking huge steps because she doesn't want them to melt. Susie is left behind. She stops and shakes her head, holds up her arms. What a cry baby.

Elaine is probably even more sandy now because I can see that she has rolled over on to her tummy to play on the heap of wet sand by my pool. I am pleased that she has done that. Honey stops going round and round and sits down next to her. She points her nose in the air and starts to bark, loud short barks.

The lugworm man throws down his spade and he's running past me, his hands pumping like he's trying to win a race.

Mummy reaches my pool and, for a second, she stands very straight. My tummy slops downwards. The ice creams fall out of her hands on to the sand. Honey dips her nose to them. Mummy scoops Elaine up and wraps her arms round her. Mummy lifts her face up to the sky and her mouth is in a big O with a high sound that doesn't stop.

Part Three

I STRIP OFF MY sweatshirt, tug my T-shirt over my head. I'm fired up, working on the table that'll hold all the strands in place as I work the sinnet. My brain's tight as a wire, hands busy with hammer and brads, the counterweight bag of BB shot, the seven-inch wire spikes to weight the sixty-one bobbins. I'm just about to begin driving inch brads into the places I've marked on a paper disc, drawn up with reference to *Ashley*'s and attached to the table top, when there's a rap at the front door.

I hold the hammer, listening. Outside the sun-room window, above the veranda, strips of canvas from the old tent arch and billow. Perhaps whoever it is will go away.

Another rap; then nothing.

Sarah arrives at the back window of the sun room. She has flowers in a cone of paper and stands there for a minute looking up at the canvas, unaware of my presence behind the salted glass. Or so I think, until she puts down the flowers and begins, laboriously, to write something with her finger on the salt.

OPEN UP GRUMPY OLD SOD

She looks quizzical for a second or two, then puts a line through 'OLD' and writes 'YUNG'. So she knows I'm here.

If I don't open up, it'll be another relationship ended before it's started. Women read rejection into everything.

'Here!' she says when I finally open the door of the sun room. She clocks my bare chest, raising an eyebrow as she shoves the cone of paper at me and gestures upwards to the canvas. 'Looks great. It reminds me of something.'

The flowers, white freesias, are up against my chest and the fragrance is overwhelmingly tender.

'Don't you like flowers?'

I haven't yet taken hold of them.

'What's the matter? Touch a nerve? Is it the white?' Her words fire out in rapid bursts, an interrogation.

She can't possibly know. We've spent only a few hours together; some drunken fucking, not much talking. 'Thanks. I needed that,' was all she'd said afterwards, fiddling with Rizla papers and tobacco. 'Give me a knock next time you need shelter from a storm.' Made me laugh.

'Some people don't like white,' she goes on, a hand over her eyes because the sun is so bright. And I wonder if that's true, why she would say that. White is the christening shawl, Elaine not quite visible on my mother's lap. My mother's hand on the kitchen table, clenched around a handkerchief.

'It's not the white.' I take the freesias from her. 'Thanks. I'll put them in water.'

She doesn't follow me into the kitchen but stays outside, staring up at the canvas.

'Chatwin!' She's triumphant, when I return.

I join her under the slapping canvas and look up. Chatwin? My face must reveal my ignorance.

'*Bruce*.' She's emphatic.

There are glimpses of blue as the canvas soars and dips.

'Yes,' she says. 'His photographs. Not from Patagonia – from Nepal? I'll have to look it up. He does the same thing – fragments of cloth against a sky.'

'Never heard of him.'

'No? He was a travel writer, dead now. You've never read . . .? It's his photographs I love. All that old wood – ancient doors and packing cases. I've got a book. I'll show you.' She looks at her watch. 'Must dash now: tango. Taxi's waiting. The flowers are to say thanks. For your hair. Photo's great.' She jerks a thumb upwards. 'I'd like a picture of this too sometime.'

It's not finished and it won't work as a fixed image in only two dimensions, but I don't say this.

'Hmmm – yes.' She hesitates a moment longer, looking up. 'OK. See you?'

I nod.

A wave and she's off.

Drying sweat chills my bare skin. Two minutes' interruption is worse than two hours'. The canvas smacks. Clutter is littering my head again.

THE THICK FOG CARRIES the algal smell of the river: nasty driving weather. In the few paces between car and shop, your face is damp.

You push open the door and the bell tings. Dead leaves scuttle. When it was that summer was finally finished you can't recall.

As your eyes adjust to the gloom, you see someone waiting at the counter and your heart smatters at your ribs like a trapped bird. You haven't seen him for such a long time. He seems like someone from your distant past. You stop, steady yourself by studying the tins of Vim and boxes of cleaning paste stacked on cluttered shelves just inside the door.

Oxo
Surf
Fairy soap

Mr Coyne rings up a total. 'That'll be five pounds, two shillings and sixpence, thanking you,' he sings out cheerfully.

You hear the rubbery slop and shuffle of his boots on the floorboards as Ian strides across the shop in his enormous wellingtons.

'Guid tae see ye.' 'Good morning.' You and he speak together. His laugh vibrates the space inside you.

'How are you?'

'Fine, an yersel?'

'Perhaps . . .?' You nod toward Mr Coyne who is peering expectantly over his half-moon spectacles.

'Oh, no hurry today,' Mr Coyne says. 'Quiet day, is Wednesday. You two take your time.' He reaches up to a switch and the fluorescent tube above spats into life. His glasses glint as he pushes them on to his balding head. 'But come in properly, love, and shut the door. Keep that damp air out.'

You close the door and, swinging round, almost collide with Ian, standing so very close and still. Adrenalin leaps like fear in your throat, something in your core shivering and alert to the height and breadth of him, a mere few inches from you. He's so much broader than you remember. You lower your head, pretending to rummage in your handbag for a shopping list.

There must be words that will place him safely into the role of odd-job man, a decorator that you and Michael employ occasionally; the son of one of Michael's patients; a youth, but your mind founders. He's likely to have heard about Elaine, so you must be ready to steer the conversation in the right direction. You're getting better at that, fending off enquiries.

Mr Coyne leans on the counter and realigns the collecting box for the Spastic Society by the till. He folds his arms, magpie-eyed.

'My husband and I—'

Ian's head lifts a fraction and harsh light from the fluorescent tube rests in a bar across his face. His cheek and brow bones are prominent, so too is the bridge of his nose, which looks as though it may have been broken, giving his face a fierceness that reminds you of a boxer's face you once stitched – the same visible strength in the arrangement of bone and muscle, the line of the brow. A raw masculinity. You'd put your forefinger under the boxer's chin, lifting his face to the light to stitch it. The graze of the bruised, stubble-pricked skin against your fingertip, contrasting with your own skin's milky-white smoothness, had made you yearn for the roughness of sex, its urgency.

Blushing, you concentrate on the simple act of tugging at the leather fingers of your glove to loosen it. 'My husband and I were very pleased with the work you did for us during the summer.'

The glove is off.

'We're wondering about the bathroom.'

Ian's sheepskin jacket smells of apples and bonfire smoke, of autumn.

'Would you perhaps be interested in giving us an estimate?'

He runs a hand downwards over his beard. You wonder, if you reached a palm to its springy warmth, what it would feel like. The blond hairs below his knuckles gleam in the light. He's stopped smiling. 'When did ye hae in mind?' He's polite.

This close, in the white glare of the fluorescent light, you notice again how long-lashed his eyes are, the lashes so thick they clump together, as if wet. It's almost impossible to wrench your gaze away. Focus on the other glove.

'Let me see, shall we say next Friday?'

He slaps the back pockets of his trousers. 'Ach! Diary's in the boat. I'll be needing to telephone and confirm.'

'Thank you.' You and Michael haven't discussed the bathroom. You'll have to try and bring it up this evening, when you get back. Your mind scrabbles. Yesterday's shopping list, clutched in your hand, is crumpled and blurred.

Ian hesitates. Then he strides back to the till, pulling out his wallet.

On the shelves behind Mr Coyne's head are two packets of mothballs with a picture of a moth with open wings on the box. Summer evenings, windows flung open; a moth fluttering around the light bulb.

'Guidbye.' Ian nods.

'Goodbye.'

Stepping up to the counter, you pretend to consult the list to give yourself time to catch your breath. When the doorbell's tinkle tells you he has left the shop, you can hardly bear it.

Outside, minutes later, Ian's outline is just visible through drifts of fog as he makes his way along the towpath towards his boat. He must have called in somewhere else while you were trapped in the shop behind Mr Coyne's dirty blinds. You hurry to the towpath, but Ian's loping strides leave you further and further behind. He's almost disappeared.

'Ian.' His name, half under your breath, is swallowed by the fog. No one behind on the towpath, no one else around; you try again, 'Ian!'

He's at the bend in the river. Chest tight, you stop and yell through cupped hands: 'IAN!'

At last he hears. He pauses for a moment, looking back, and gives a small wave. It dawns on you that he can see you standing there on the towpath with your shopping basket, waving, but he can't read your mind. You hurry towards him, damp air filling your lungs, and he signs 'T' with his hands, as you used to if he was sanding in the house, or using some noisy piece of machinery.

By the time you get to the houseboat, you're out of breath. The boat sways beneath your feet.

'I'm sorry about . . . about Mr Coyne.'

Ian has his back to you, filling the kettle and there's Billy Eckstine's old song 'My Foolish Heart' on the wireless. He switches it off. He's wearing a navy blue Guernsey sweater that's unravelling at the cuff.

'He's such an old gossip.' You try to laugh, but feel a blush rising. Heat belches from a wood-burning stove in the corner and the boat tips towards the stove, towards Ian. The fog outside, the heat and the slope of the floor in here – your senses feel smothered. No, you mustn't faint again. Once is too often. You unbutton your coat, push up the sleeves.

'So—' He pauses and rests the kettle down on the wooden draining board, a tension about his shoulders and neck. His hair, as usual, is tousled curls. 'Are ye no wanting the bathroom tiled?'

'No. Well, yes.' It's impossible to speak. 'My throat – I was shouting. I need –' You swallow. 'I'm sorry – may I have a glass of water?'

He nods to a shelf behind you so you reach for a glass, then squeeze past him to the sink, every nerve ending aware of his body, the muscular bulk of him. Gripping the edge of the draining board, you pause before leaning across to turn on the tap, then the boat rocks a little and he's moved away, his breathing noisy in the tiny space.

Water gushes into the glass, a sparkling torrent.

What on earth are you doing here?

The glass is filled to the brim, water spilling over, streaming over your hand, your wrist. Tears well up. Briefly, watching him on the towpath, you'd thought you could talk to him about everything. Of course you can't. You can't even talk to Jean. Or Hoggie. You bite your lip, hard, to stop the tears, because it'll be the second time you'll have gone to pieces in front of him and there's a limit. Water is sluicing over the glass, swirling and gurgling down the plughole. The boat rocks and tips as he moves across and stands behind you.

'Come awa and sit down,' he says, his words a caress barely audible above the gurgle and rush of water. He knows then, must have heard. At least now you don't have to summon the words to tell him yourself.

You sit on the sagging settee while he rinses a couple of teacups under the tap and wipes them on a ripped hand towel. He has taken his wellington boots off and his feet are bare. Clean and white; naked. He has long, lithe toes with a sheen of blond hair. A stack of rolled canvases leans against the wall and a tattered telephone directory lies open, pages ripped from it and littering the floor – screwed-up balls of paper smeared with paint. Several jam jars filled with paintbrushes stand on the windowsill. Again you smell turpentine and linseed.

Ian opens an old Roses' chocolate tin and cuts a slice of something to put on to a saucer. 'A wee slice of my mother's Cut-and-Come-Again?' he asks, and licks the crumbs from his thumb. 'You're awfy peely-wally.'

The confusion must show on your face because he throws back his head and laughs, revealing those splintery hairs on his neck.

'Peaky. In need o feeding up.'

Michael has complained about the weight falling from you.

Ian lays a hand on yours, briefly, casually, comforting as if you're a child, as if it's the most natural thing in the world for him to touch you. And why isn't it? Why are you always so reined in?

One day in the summer, while he was still working in the dining room, Ian was eating flapjack in the kitchen when Michael came in through the open back door and you'd leapt up, guiltily clattering together another cup and saucer, breathless. Ian sat unperturbed, his legs splayed under the table, a toe poking through a hole in one of his socks. Michael would notice that.

'Looking after you, is she?' Michael said, hanging up his linen jacket.

'Guid baking.' Ian held up the half-eaten square of flapjack, glistening and syrupy. You'd been able to relax. Michael knew Ian – of course – because of the passing days alone with him, the shared conversations, you'd forgotten Michael knew his parents, had given Ian the decorating job because he needed the money.

Ian is turned away again now, cutting a second slice of cake, his back to you. 'Whit about the bairns?' he asks.

The children. You lift your hands to your face. Perhaps, after all, he hasn't heard.

You lower your hands again, observe them clasped together in your lap, your fingers twisting at your rings. 'Andy's missed you.'

You can't say her name just yet. You must steer the conversation, a skill you acquired while nursing. 'How's Jamie?' Your voice sounds level.

'I'm away to pay him a visit just now. I promised the park, though wi the fog we'll mebbe take tea instead. Wanny come?'

Take tea. Cosy, familiar, afternoon tea. Of course you must say no. Your sandwiches and thermos are on the passenger seat of the Morris, ready for the long drive ahead. Jean is picking the children up from school and giving them tea, as she does every Wednesday.

'Yes. Please.' You can't look him in the eye. 'I'd love to. Thank you.'

You walk beside Ian and Jamie, hands deep in your pockets. Wet leaves fall and stick to the pavement. Perhaps if you asked to push Jamie's wheelchair, the effort, the weight of it, would be something, your hands holding on to the rubber handles. Perhaps it would warm you just a little. Instead, you tighten your upper arms, elbows, against your body. Through the layers of cloth, your own muscles and limbs press against your breasts and the empty cage of your ribs.

The tearooms are steamy, filled with an aroma of toasted muffins and the clatter of china. The waitress, who's wearing a plain dark dress with a white apron, greets Ian with a shy smile and gives Jamie a kiss on the cheek.

'And how are we today, Jamie?' she says, crouching down to take hold of one of his hands in both of hers.

Without any fussing, a table is moved to one side to make room for the wheelchair. Ian angles Jamie into a corner because, as Ian explains, Jamie likes to watch everyone else. Ian pulls up a chair beside him. You sit opposite, with your back to the bustling tearoom and its ebb and flow of voices.

The waitress brings a teapot under a knitted cosy, tea-cups and saucers, plates, bone-handled side knives and silver cake forks. There's a jug of cream, a bowl of rasp-berry jam and a pile of warm scones. Ian helps Jamie, pours him tea, cuts up his food and feeds him, murmuring to him all the time. Something about their two heads bent together – Ian's head of cropped curls and Jamie's patchy wisps of hair – reminds you of Andy and Elaine, the way Andy liked to talk to her constantly, in a private undertone, lips brushing her ear.

Ian and Jamie wolf down the food. You manage a morsel of scone and jam, washing it down with the strong, aro-matic tea. On the wall above their heads are hunting scenes and watercolours of roses; some horse brasses. A fire crackles somewhere on the other side of the room, behind you.

Ian pulls a notebook from his jacket pocket to show Jamie, then you, some pencil sketches he's done of the river, the houseboats, the bridge at Henley. You nod and smile. Your brain is capable only of observing and labelling, thinking nothing.

Stepping out of the teashop into the swirl of fog, you sniff and rub your hands together.

'Cauld?' Ian says, looking up from Jamie.

You shake your head and force a smile, but he's already tugging a tartan scarf from under his sheepskin jacket and he comes close, lifting the scarf as if to wrap it round your neck. You jerk your head back, away. There's an awkward moment as you look, startled, into each other's eyes.

You reach out to take the scarf from him.

'Thank you.'

The wool is scratchy on the back of your neck and under your chin so you tuck your head down, rubbing, wanting the burn of soreness, burying your mouth in the remnants of his warmth and the smell of his boat, a mix of damp canvas and turps. You put out a hand to feel Jamie's blanket, to see how thick it is. There are two blankets, the heavy rug with a softer nylon one underneath.

'Mither will have put the woollen stockings on him, to keep his legs warm.' Ian rests a hand on Jamie's shoulder, rubs and squeezes. 'Ma brither's a wee Jessie, is he no?'

Jamie's mother has pulled stockings over his clumsy, fidgeting feet, up his hairy legs. She has guided his twisted hands into woolly gloves, tugged a hat firmly over his ears and wrapped him in two blankets. You banish an image of Elaine's sore chin, the baby's bib, her chubby hands in mittens.

THE FLUORESCENT TUBE IN the sun room buzzes and flickers. My watch says it's almost midnight. The room is filled with the scent of freesias. Was it today or yesterday morning Sarah brought them? I flex my fingers, rub my eyes. Vision's out of focus. I've been so absorbed in the painstaking handling of tension, the counting and lifting of strands into odd- and even-numbered spaces, following with my finger *Ashley*'s table of instructions on page 510, that it's only now, as I come to the end of working the sixty-one-strand pentalpha, that I realise my stomach is cramped with hunger.

When I remove it from the table, the sinnet's not as compact as it should be, but it's heavy and beautiful. No dead spots. The three dimensions enhance the planes and angles of the five-pointed star cross-section. It has the look of a shooting star. In the morning, the sinnet will need fairing with a pricker, working over each strand and tightening to adjust the tension.

I make toast. Cut a slab of butter from the fridge and lay it on the toast. Watch it melt, liquid and golden. As I take a bite, butter oozes and trickles down my chin, slick as sweat. I rub my chin, lick my thumb. Remember the back of her neck, my nose in the salty dip hidden beneath her tumble of hair. And the twin hollows high between her muscular spread thighs, each a curve fitting the curve of my thumbs, the sweep of my tongue. I wipe my chin and lick my thumb again. I pick up the plate of toast.

No answer when I knock on her door, just silence and darkness.

Back in the kitchen, the new roller and some squares of sandpaper in a brown paper bag and the unopened tins of paint on the counter remind me Susie may be down before long. Top of her 'TO DO' list is the kitchen. Sanding down the tongue-and-groove boarding will be a suitably mindless task; I'll just keep going until physical exhaustion sets in.

A taxi draws up outside and a woman gets out. I look at my watch. Late morning. I've been up all night then. Under-coating's almost done. The woman getting out of the taxi is wearing high heels and a leather jacket over a blue dress. The dress clings in all the right places, showing off boobs, but-tocks, the long lines of her thighs. Her mass of hair is bundled up into casual loops at the back of her head, which is turned away as she rummages in her handbag to pay the taxi driver. Spiral silver earrings swing. The curling strands clustered in the hollow at the back of her long neck finally tell me it's Sarah.

Today I am looking for an interruption, so I thump on the kitchen window and wave.

'Bring a jumper,' she shouts back. 'We're sitting outside. The sun is shining.'

She's stirring something in a white saucepan. Up close, there's the rich smell of chocolate. She's still wearing the heels and the leather jacket. The dress shows a good eyeful of cleavage too.

'Hot chocolate,' she announces. 'My secret recipe. You'll find you've tasted nothing like it, ever, in your whole life.' She

140

admires the flow of thick sauce twisting from the chocolate-coated wooden spoon. She's got some sort of eye make-up on today, her pupils big and dark in the pale irises.

'Unless . . .' she sidesteps swiftly, so close that our bodies are almost touching, then cocks her head and looks up at me through her eyelashes, 'unless you've been to Venice, city of lovers?'

'Never.' I lean back against the kitchen table so we're on a level. I get hold of her hips and pull her towards me. The material of her dress is thin. Firm flesh beneath. 'Looks like neat melted chocolate.'

'Tastes like heaven.' She whirls away.

I watch her ladle chocolate with the consistency of custard into two enormous mugs.

'Can't remember when I last had hot chocolate,' I tell her. But truth is I can. The chocolaty smell has me thinking of the hot chocolate grandfather used to make for me to take up to bed.

'Good. Follow me.'

We sit outside on a low bench made from what looks like a breakwater plank, silvered with age. It's sheltered by a higgledy-piggledy fence Sarah has made from different lengths of driftwood washed up on the beach – odd bits of planking from boats, fencing and beach huts. Some of it's silvery-grey, some flaking with paint or old varnish. With the white painted wall behind us, the sun is surprisingly warm for November.

'Cheers,' Sarah says, raising her mug. 'We won, so I'm celebrating. Well, celebrating again.' She leans her head against the wall.

'Won? What?'

'Tango.'

That explains her lithe muscularity, the sculpted thighs – she dances. The suppleness and strength she displayed in bed was a surprise, because she must be at least ten years older than me.

'My feet have blisters.'

'Congratulations.' I put a hand on her thigh.

'You dance?'

I shrug, moving my hand up and down her thigh, enjoying the slip of the blue material between my hand and her skin. 'No. No rhythm.'

She arches an eyebrow. 'Well, we know that's not true!' Her head drops back and she stares up at the sky. 'Anyone can tango. I do believe that. Tango's not about learning the correct dance steps. Not really. It's about listening – to the music, to the other person, their touch and the movements of their body.' She throws her hands in the air and rolls her eyes dramatically. 'God, don't get me started! You're not in one of my classes.'

'Classes?'

'It's all improvisation. You can do it. I'll prove it to you. Not today because my feet are too sore and I'm knackered. Now just look at that sky.'

The sky takes up more than 75 per cent of my field of vision from this angle, low down. It's a bowl of blue. I can hear the waves, out of sight beyond the high shingle bank, pound and rake the pebbles.

'Which reminds me,' Sarah continues, 'how's the rope stuff coming on? Done any more work on that big thing that looks like French knitting on a giant scale?'

I lean my head back beside hers. 'The sinnet? Finished it this morning. Today I'm painting and decorating, since I'm supposed to be earning my keep.'

'Your keep?'

'Well, my sister's more or less feeding me at the moment.'

'Your sister? Her place then, is it?'

'Not exactly.' I stretch out my legs. Twisting my neck, I roll my skull to and fro on the rendered wall and close my eyes. The sun's warm and red on my eyelids.

A pause.

Sarah's sucking up her hot chocolate noisily. She wipes her lips. 'That place has been empty a long, long time. Only the occasional mysterious visitor for a few days, then nothing but the odd-job man for months at a time.'

'Yeah.' I take my hand from her leg to pick up a stone and aim it at an old lobster pot collapsed on the pebbles. Perhaps Father was the mysterious visitor, though it seems unlikely. I chuck another stone at the lobster pot.

Sarah sighs.

'OK, mate, I get it. No Entry.'

I select another, smaller, stone. Weigh it up. Throw it.

Sarah unzips her boots. They thud on to the wooden decking. She stretches and wriggles her toes about, humming something familiar: *What shall we do with the drunken sailor?* She draws my attention like a magnet.

'What got you started on the rope?' she asks, after a few minutes.

I look at her in surprise. No one has asked me this, the right question, before. It's a shock.

'In general, or this time specifically?'

It's a sort of test for her.

Sarah's focused on picking nail varnish from her toenails. 'Oh I think in general, don't you?'

She's passed.

'My grandfather was a rope maker. He taught me about knots.' The hot chocolate brought him to mind and now he's here, in his rolled shirt sleeves and braces, making the *sss sss* noise of concentration between his teeth as he steps out into the daylight.

'A rope maker!' She stops picking her nails and screws up her forehead. 'I don't even know what rope is made from.'

'All sorts of things, these days, but it used to be mainly hemp.'

'Wow! Hemp? You mean like cannabis?'

'Yeah, hemp is *Cannabis sativa*; the strongest natural fibre.'

'Well, bloody hell!' Sarah goes back to picking nail varnish from her big toenail. 'Don't stop. I'm listening.' Her hands are lined and dry. She brushes them together, draws her bare feet up beneath her, and snuggles up. 'C'mon. Put your arm round me and tell me the story of rope; of you and your grandfather and rope.'

I put an arm around her shoulders, knocking her hair by mistake so that several looped sections fall down around her face. There are kinks and waves, tightening into corkscrews at the ends; blonde and grey hairs mixed in with the brown. I lift a strand. It smells of cigarette smoke and, somehow, sex. A pulse throbs at her neck, just below the ear.

She elbows me in the ribs. 'C'mon. Talk. Begin at the beginning.'

I unravel her hair bit by bit, winding the curls around my fingers, watching them unwind again and, as I sit in the warm November sun, it's easy to talk about Grandfather – about the cardboard boxes filled with lengths of different ropes that were kept in his hallway with its yellow light, his 'walking the world' stories.

'Why did he say that then, that he'd walked the world?'

'Because of the distance rope makers walked. Up and down the rope walk, every day. Someone calculated that, during a lifetime of rope-making, rope makers walked the equivalent of the circumference of the world.'

The way she listens, her total absorption, makes me want to keep on talking. I tell her about the first ball of string

Grandfather gave me. It came in a brown paper bag that smelled of the hardware store. I was about four. I had to stretch my hand wide around the ball of string to examine the overlapping whorls, the way they criss-crossed, deeper and deeper, into the empty core of the ball.

'Have you ever looked properly at a ball of string?'

She shakes her head. 'Never, but I will now.'

I try to describe it to Sarah, the excitement of going faster and faster round Grandfather's front room, putting string high up round the door handle, round the hook on the fireplace where the fire bellows hung, low down, round the bottom of the standard lamp, the feet of the piano stool. By the time I'd finished everything was joined by the lines of string criss-crossing the room.

Sarah's eyes are closed now, her breathing regular. Perhaps she's asleep. She opens one eye and says, 'I can see it, that room. Don't stop yet.'

But the sun is disappearing behind the purplish-grey clouds clumped on the horizon and the air's becoming cool. I've been talking a long time. I'm hungry.

'I'll cook you fried egg and bacon.' She reads my mind. 'If you tell me one more story.'

So, because she's asked and because she seems interested in the cannabis connection with rope, I describe the way they used to collect momeea, many years ago. About the hot season that came after the high snows and before the monsoon rain. Young boys ran naked through the cannabis stems and leaves until they fell exhausted among bruised plants. The natives would stroke the momeea from the limbs and torsos of the naked boys and knead it into balls between their palms.

'Momeea,' she says. 'What a wonderful word!'

I stand up, dizzy with words and hunger and lack of sleep. 'Momeea, churrus, sidhee, bangh, gunjah, hashish.' I stretch and roll the sounds. Sarah stands too, pretending to stir a huge cauldron. We chant the words together until a woman walks by with a golden retriever and swiftly turns her gaze from our antics.

We fall against each other in laughter.

Then, because I'm on a roll, I tell her about the doctor in Calcutta in Grandfather's time who experimented with majoon and tincture of hemp to treat convulsive disorders like tetanus and rabies.

'Cannabis to treat rabies? Sort of makes sense when you think they use it for multiple sclerosis.' She's looking up at the sky. 'Scary disease, rabies. The fear of water – where does that come from?'

I don't know the answer to this.

'The French call it "La Rage", don't they? They used to chain people up – grisly.' Her face lights up with a smile. 'OK. Let's do it.'

'What?'

'First tango lesson.'

'Now?' I'm drained from talking.

'Here is ideal. Take off your shoes. Close your eyes. We're going to walk, and you're going to keep your eyes closed. No cheating. The most basic tango pattern is *la Caminata*, the Walk.' She slips her arm around my waist. 'Feel the clues you get from my movements. I'm not going to say anything.'

The tide is high, halfway up the shingle banks, so I can relax: no wet sand. I close my eyes. We wander together over the shingle, me with eyes closed and faltering steps, body tensed to guess when to step up or down, when to move to left or right. She doesn't say anything to me except, 'Relax,' which she says quite often.

Gradually, a space opens up inside my head. My soles burn less and instead my body grows acutely aware of the varying sizes of pebbles beneath the arch of my foot, the slope of the shingle bank, the salt air on my lips, the sound of the waves – a constant presence – and the pressure of her hand, elbow, thigh against my body. Eventually level concrete is rough underfoot again. We come to a halt. I blink in the shadowless light.

'We need food,' Sarah says.

In the kitchen, she puts on music she calls 'techno tango'. As she cooks, holding her head high, back straight and breasts out, she tells me about Buenos Aires and immigrants who composed the original tango music. Every now and then she flips one long leg up and around the other, a quick flash of movement, fluid from the knee.

I sit at the table and watch her. 'Are there steps?' I say, thinking of the onetwothree, onetwothree of a waltz.

But Sarah shakes her head and gesticulates with one hand, chasing the eggs round the frying pan with a spatula in the other. 'Some of the steps are the same as other walking dances, like the quickstep, but tango dancers relate to their partners very differently. You touch throughout – and it should be an emotional connection, as well as physical. We talk about *el alma del tango* – the soul of tango.'

Her words, the concepts behind them, don't sink in. The kitchen is cosy and my face is glowing from being outside. I try to remember whether or not I slept last night. I stifle a yawn as she's scooting the bacon and tomatoes on to two plates. She stops mid-sentence.

'I am interested,' I say, hurriedly, 'just knackered.'

'Mmmm . . . You an insomniac or something?' She sits down opposite.

I shrug.

'Well, I'll bore you with tango another time. It's my passion, I guess. Eat.'

I'm too weary to query her and only when she's chucked me out because I'm fidgeting and she wants to sleep, do I wonder what place sculpture has in her life, if tango is her passion.

There's a half-empty bottle on the kitchen table. It's dark outside. The kitchen smells of wet paint. A woman I went out with briefly, years ago, was a professor, something to do with anatomy. I had a cleaning job at the university where she taught. She had big tits, looked good in a white coat and was into playing games, sex in uncomfortable places. Once she smuggled me into her laboratory, which smelt of gas and formaldehyde. She pretended I was a student. There was a soft hum from the fluorescent lights and the brush of starched fabric as the real students in their white coats bent over the wooden dissection bench. They were scraping tissue away from the undersurface of the cerebellum, near the stem of the brain, to reveal a knot of fibres, made of nerve cells. It was the size of a fingernail.

'That's the amygdala,' my girlfriend announced to the students, tapping the almond-shaped knot with the tip of her scalpel blade. 'It processes fear, houses memories of fear. And anger, we think.'

She described the appearance of inclusion bodies in the amygdala of patients with rabies, a discovery that first led to the connection of fear with anger.

'In rabies, the regulator for fear is turned up and up – but we don't know much about it, nor why fear seems to be indelible.' She detailed the neural wiring of the amygdala, explaining its complex connections to the senses. As she spoke I heard rain, smelt shoe polish, felt small round holes pressed against my fingertips: a bundle of nerves.

HE IS IN THE box room. He is taking Jelly's cot to pieces. They have been arguing in the kitchen. She has gone into the garden.

A scraping on the landing. He is moving the piece of wood that covers the hatch into the attic. He carries a side piece of Jelly's cot up the stepladder. The attic light bulb shines on cobwebs like witches' hair. When his legs come down out of the attic, I run and bite his leg as hard as I can. My mouth is stuffed full with material, choking. The ladder wobbles. His foot lashes out.

'For pity's sake, Andrew, stop behaving like an imbecile.'

He nearly falls down the ladder. He picks me up. I swing my legs and kick him. He smacks my face, hard, so that my teeth clunk. There is blood in my mouth. My cheek burns.

in the dark

I told Hugh and Stephen about Jelly when we were swapping marbles. Stephen said it was all for the best because Elaine was a Spasbo. I punched his nose. Stephen kept saying but she is she is Andy she is a spaz and I punched Stephen every time he said it again and again until Stephen's nose dripped blood all over his poxy yellow aertex shirt where Stephen's poxy initials were embroidered in poxy cross-stitch.

In the cupboard under the stairs I press the pads of my fingertips over the woodworm holes and wonder what else is in the dark, on the other side of the small dark circles.

Houdini wasn't born Harry Houdini. He was born Erich Weisz in 1847 in Budapest. Some people never grow out of playing let's pretend.

One day I let my alarm go on ringing and ringing. I put my head under the covers and breathed in my warm bed air.

'Andrew! This is not the way to behave.' His voice was low and hard.

'Please, Andy,' she begged. 'You need to get dressed for school.'

'Andrew. How many times do I have to tell you?'

'Not Andrew,' I told them. 'Houdini. I am Harry Houdini the Handcuff King.' If they don't call me Houdini I won't hear.

In the dark of the under-stair cupboard, I listen for The Voice. It will tell me what to do. It will give me commands. But Houdini's Voice doesn't come so I tell myself stories instead.

Here is a true story I tell myself in the dark of the cupboard under the stairs. It's 1906. Houdini is locked into a cell on Death Row. The cell door clangs. There are metal bars, cold and lumpy. They taste of blood. A dirty mattress has shapes like brown countries on a map and there's a toilet without a seat in the corner. The toilet is brown inside. There are dark corners all around the cell and brown tiles. Brown is the colour of old blood. The key turns in the lock and the jailer walks away, keys going jingle jangle at his hip.

In the sole of his left foot, Houdini has hidden something to pick the lock. He picks the locks on every single cell on Death Row and all the murderers escape. Pale thin men with striped clothes like pyjamas. Death Row is filled with echoes and shouts and cheering from the murderers.

This I will not tolerate. Pull yourself together.

YOU ARE IN A jostle of bodies, juggling a warm glass of white wine, cubes of pineapple with cheese on a cocktail stick that you're lifting to your mouth, and a tipsy Mr Robertson, whose nose is too close to your cheek as he asks you if he has ever told you how much you remind him of Ingrid Bergman, a dark-haired Ingrid Bergman, and you're trying to smile and say, 'Yes, yes, really, you *know* you have,' as you turn away towards the buffet table, holding your glass higher in an attempt to put some space between Mr Robertson's body and your breasts when, far across the crammed hall and above the crowd, you glimpse broad shoulders and the back of a head of coppery hair and it's so unexpected, hours into Mr Robertson's retirement party, among Michael's colleagues and wives, the Friends of the Hospital – Ian.

Your knuckles knock against Mr Robertson's watch as he raises his hand to your hair and wine is spilled, your blouse wet and clinging.

The kitchen is crowded with ladies laying out trays of green cups and saucers for tea and coffee, but you manage to make your way through to the sink. In the hall, the jazz band is just starting up – the opening bars of something by

Fats Waller. Michael will want to dance. Dancing means no need to make conversation.

There's a pile of unused tea towels by the sink, neatly folded blue and white. You use one to blot at your cleavage. As one of the ladies squeezes past with a tray, a palm rests in the hollow of your back, a light pressure. Good: Michael. You can dance and conceal the damp patch until it's dried a little.

'Oh, look what I've done!' You sigh, about to make some comment about Mr Robertson as someone else edges past between the sink and the kitchen table, and the man behind you – staggering in the press of bodies – leans against you to make room. Your buttocks brush against his groin as you turn, your shoulder squashed at an angle against his chest. Not Michael, but Ian. His face so close you can see, just at the base of his nostrils, the roots of the coppery hairs of his moustache, the way they pierce the skin. There's a glimpse of tongue and lower lip through his beard and alcohol on his breath mixing with a spicy, moist smell, an unfamiliar aftershave. You catch him staring down at your breasts – the clinging damp patch on your blouse – at your mouth, and you notice tiny flecks of green in the brown of his eyes when they meet yours. A jolt; the spark of attention: male, sexual. And an answering buzz between your legs. His eyes slide to your lips again, head dipping forward, and for a startled moment you think he's about to kiss you. He must have had too much to drink.

'Ian.' You lift both hands to his shoulders, one still clutching the crumpled tea towel, to hold him at arm's length. 'Have you come to ask me for a dance?'

'Excuse me.' Someone else squeezes awkwardly past the two of you.

Ian stumbles again, his beard at your ear. 'Jive?'

You laugh. 'Let's just get out of everybody's way.'

* * *

153

You must have been mistaken, because he doesn't seem drunk at all once he's on the dance floor and, to your surprise, he's a better dancer than Michael – better at leading. The two of you lunge and slide at first, and you're aware he's feeling his way, judging your ability. Michael is occupied with twizzling a petite blonde who smiles up at him admiringly, so you relax, forget about everything else, and focus on the way Ian tugs you hard towards him, a palm to palm hand-hold at shoulder height before he sends you spinning with an exhilarating increase in velocity, catapulting away and bouncing back.

'That was good.' Ian takes a carton of cigarettes from the back pocket of his trousers.

The two of you have joined a few other couples cooling down outside. His jacket is around your shoulders. Eyes on you as he lights up, he raises his eyebrows in query. In the past, at home, you've refused his offers of cigarettes, but the fleeting pull of intimacy in his gesture is irresistible. Your blood is still pulsing from the dancing as you slip the cigarette between your lips and lift your chin, keeping your eyes on the flare of the lighter he holds towards you. He's watching your mouth.

'Caught in the act!'

Jean plumps herself down on the bench beside Ian and, head on one side like a bird, introduces herself as your younger, single sister. She smiles at him coquettishly.

'I'll have one too while you're at it.'

Later, touching up your lipstick in the Ladies Room, you accused Jean of flirting.

'And why not?' she replied, eyeing you in the mirror. 'It's not as though I'm going steady at the moment and, as far as I can tell from his avid attention to various ladies here, neither is he.'

And you could see Ian enjoyed it, the way Jean monopolised the conversation, making him throw back his head and laugh, then coaxing him back into the hall to dance with her.

Michael rolls into bed beside you, his hand plunging between your legs.

'Feeling better tonight?' His breath is vinegary.

'Hmm.'

'We're all right, aren't we? Now? We've got through this?'

You concentrate on keeping your limbs relaxed, determined that your body will not reveal antagonism, but the hand staying there, his touch, persistent and careless as his words, forces you to shift on to your side to escape his thumb's rubbing insistence. He misreads the movement, slides his hand up under your nightie and begins stroking, over and over, the same spot on your hip.

'You seem more your old self. Dancing, having fun.'

You put a hand on his, to still it. He kisses your cheek, your neck, your ear, and pulls your nightie higher. There isn't really a choice. You will submit to his advances, go through the actions at least, because then he'll leave you alone. He'll go to sleep. Refusal will put him into a rage. There'll be an argument.

'. . . yourself again,' he's murmuring as he lifts his body over yours. 'My party girl.'

Afterwards, lying awake, your mind slips back to Ian's body pressed against yours in the crowded kitchen, that electric kick. Surely he felt it too. Or perhaps that's not the way it works, perhaps you merely gave yourself away. And, remembering you still have not talked to Michael about the bathroom, you imagine Ian back in the house, picture him – hands behind his head, shoes off, long legs stretched out beneath the kitchen table – and summon up other occasions, an alternative series of events unfolding.

TODAY IS BAD. Afternoon. Low tide. Sarah's not there. Dull skies crouch overhead and the horizon is missing, lost where milky grey sky merges with milky grey sea. Wind slices up through the floorboards, lifts and rattles loose weather-boarding, gusts at the window panes like some hefty beast prowling. I've had a drink but it hasn't helped. I can't shake off an image from last night's dream. Walls rising up, again and again, looming so high they must topple. Windows with bars. Always the same fucking walls, fucking bars on windows. Again and again. The retching fear.

I need to get out. Confront the wet sand. Its expanse.

Outside, wind punches into me. White-foamed waves are roiling. The sea's roar is all I can hear. Spray flies, my face soon damp with it. Flocks of birds migrating south, wheel across the dead sky. And four swans, necks stretched out. Salt on my lips, my hair tacky with it. The sea heaves. Once again the shingle banks have been pounded by the over-night storms into dramatic slopes and troughs, pebbles heaped high against the breakwaters. I stop at the edge. Rivulets of seawater drain from the pebbles and carve waterways into the sand. I step on to it with one foot and watch damp sand swell around the sole of my trainer.

Almost imperceptibly, my foot is sinking. My vision pulses in time with my racing blood. I have to turn away, step back on to the pebbles, heart smacking hard as a squash ball.

On the way back, I try again at Sarah's door. No answer. She hasn't been there for days as far as I can make out. Can't remember what she told me about when she'd be back. I walk west, out into the wind and rain, away from the wet sand and away from the shabby, ramshackle houses.

NO PARKING ON ANY ROADS. THIS IS A PRIVATE ESTATE.

I head for the salt marshes. Rain trails down my back. A curlew picks its way over mud covered with webbed prints. A few yellow petals flutter on the straggly clumps of gorse. Only three o'clock and so gloomy a light or two already glimmers across the reservoir from the caravan park on the other side. Scum congeals at the water's edge, where it can rise no further up the mud. Wind knives at my face and ears so I turn back towards the houses. Some new wire-and-wood fencing protects newly planted wisps of gorse that are struggling to grow. They don't stand a chance. Tough as it is, gorse grows distorted here, burned by the savage salt-laden wind.

I'm hungry again. I forget to eat.

I kick at a piece of masonry along the road.

I'll phone Susie.

The phone box smells of urine. There is graffiti on the concrete floor. I get halfway through dialling Susie's number, then put the phone down. I rest my forehead on the back wall of the phone box and read the cards advertising tarot readings, telephone sex, a 'Dreaming Workshop'.

Try again.

'Andrew! I didn't expect to hear from you so soon!' Susie's voice is bright. I picture her in the steamy kitchen of

The Vicarage. 'How're you doing?' A whistle blows, shrilly, over and over again in the background and there's a loud rhythmic clanging.

I run a hand over my face and beard.

'Andy?'

'Here.'

'Can't hear?' A door closes, muffling the background noise. 'Sorry, is that better? The boys have the music box out – got to keep them occupied somehow in this atrocious weather.'

'Susie . . .'

'You sound a bit rough. Have you got a cold? Are you keeping warm enough? Is the water sorted out yet?'

'I . . . No.' I pull the collar of the sheepskin jacket up. I don't know where it came from; it's way too large and scruffy to be my father's. 'I need to know—'

'OK. Fire away. How's the decorating going? I was thinking of coming down this weekend, wasn't I? I thought I'd bring—'

'About Elaine.'

'About?'

'Elaine.'

'What about Elaine?'

'About what happened.'

'I told you—'

'No! Not when she was born. Just listen for once, will you?'

There's a pause, then Susie says in a low voice, 'Have you been drinking? It's four o'clock!'

'Here. What happened – here, with Elaine. I want to—'

'I was only four or five. I don't really remember. Well, she was quite fat, wasn't she? I think. There are no photographs, or Dad never had any that I saw. You must remember her better, surely?'

'But down here, at The Siding. You and Mum went to get ice creams, remember? And you took so long, for ever, I—'

'Ice creams?'

'Yes.'

'I don't remember, specifically, anything about Elaine and ice creams.'

'No, you and Mum and ice creams. We never came down here again after it happened.'

'Well, Dad was never keen on the beach, was he? It was only Mum. I think he only kept The Siding in case, after Mum left, in case she went back there. Because she loved it.'

He bought it for her. It was hers.

'But, we never came down here again, did we?'

'Well, after Mum left we didn't, no. Jean thought Dad could make a packet renting it out, but he was adamant. He'd bought it for Mum. I've always thought it was a bit like a parent when a kid dies, you know, when they leave the bedroom exactly as it was, as a sort of shrine. The Siding was Dad's shrine—'

'I killed her.'

'Andy, you *must* have been drinking!' Susie's voice softens. 'Now you *know* that's not true. Parents leave because they fall out of love with each other, not because of the children, though children often blame themselves and—'

'Not *Mum*, Susie—'

'HANG ON, I'm coming.' She's yelling. I have to hold the receiver away from my ear. 'For goodness sake! Doorbell; sorry – got to dash. Let's have a really good chat when I come down.'

'Susie—'

The phone peeps. My money has run out.

On the way back to The Siding I knock again on Sarah's door; still no answer. No car. Not sure if there ever was one. I stand for a bit in the shelter of her driftwood fence.

The Siding: *a shrine*. Sarah said someone apart from the odd-job man came here, now and then. Would Father have come here, by himself? Susie might know.

I knock again: nothing. I stop by the Jelly Tree, unfasten a faded pink jelly shoe and put it in my pocket.

Inside, I put the jelly shoe on the table in the sun room. I open another bottle of Merlot and sit in the dark. On the steep bends of the mountain roads in Crete, where people have gone off the road, their souls flying from their bodies, the Greeks build shrines. Little houses with glass doors. Some elaborate, some simple. Sometimes they're built to look like Greek Orthodox churches. Relatives visit and pray and leave things that would have been important to the person who's died: a flower, a necklace, a shoe, a bottle of Coke, a page torn from a pad with a scribbled note.

The sourness of the wine slides down my throat and settles in my belly.

YOU HEAR HER KEY in the front door and only just have time to lift the needle from Jean's Elvis record as Mrs Hubbard bustles towards the kitchen, leaving a faint metallic smell of Silvo in the hallway. You slide the record into its cover, turning Elvis with his quiff and thrusting hips to face the wall.

Upstairs, you take an embroidered tray cloth from the linen cupboard. By the time you're back in the kitchen, Mrs Hubbard has vanished into the sitting room. The clang of the coal shovel tells you she's clearing last night's ash. You fill the silver sugar bowl with fresh sugar lumps, humming. It's Wednesday. Jean will pick the children up from school and give them tea. Today you won't be alone, hands on the wheel, your spine, your neck, rigid with the grip of need to see Elaine and to hold her in your arms.

Instead, you're meeting Ian and Jamie; going for an outing with them. It's not the first time. Hard to say how you've slipped into this. You had to phone Ian to let him know that Michael did not want the bathroom redecorated after all, and then you bumped into him more than once leaving Coyne's. You expressed an interest when he mentioned his preliminary drawings for the Christmas card commission; he invited you to drop by the houseboat to see them. Of course you were too nervous to take him up on that. Then, at the Fawkes Fair, Ian was there with Jamie and you had the children. He asked you again, standing close in the crowd queuing for the coconut shy, when *were* you going to come and see his drawings? He grinned at the cliché overtones. It was there, at the fair, possibly, he suggested another outing with Jamie and it had been easy, simple to arrange when Jean picks the children up from school on Wednesdays and the day is, more or less, your own.

You've told no one else what you do when you leave the house all day on these particular Wednesdays, but have rehearsed one or two stories. You have time now that each and every day no longer revolves around Elaine, time for 'good works': hospital visiting, taking groceries to Michael's more elderly and infirm patients, perhaps some sort of activity in the school – all appropriate occupations for a doctor's wife. You have the Morris you can drive and your skills as a nurse. You're going to make yourself useful and outings with Jamie will be a suitable activity.

'I can see it's doing you good,' Jean said last Wednesday, when she dropped the children back to the house, 'having time to yourself again. I told you it would.'

When you open the front door to leave, Mrs Hubbard is on her hands and knees, brushing red polish on to the front steps. She doesn't look up.

'I'm just off then, Mrs Hubbard. I've put out a tray in the kitchen for your elevenses.'

'Thank you,' Mrs Hubbard mutters, head bent to the brushing.

'I'll go by the back door, so as not to interrupt you.'

The winter sun is bright and the air in the car is hot and leathery. You'll park at Coyne's, go in for a newspaper, then take the footpath down to the river to meet Ian. You turn the key in the ignition and push in the choke, looking back at the house. By two o'clock, Mr Hubbard will have come in his car to collect his wife. You have never seen him, only the pale green Hillman Minx with its engine running. You imagine Mrs Hubbard's house: a dry Mr Hubbard waiting in an armchair, his newspaper folded, crisp and tidy on his lap, until his wife gets back. Or perhaps he's fat in a string vest, sweaty, his raw sausage fingers thrumming the table.

Mrs Hubbard's neat cap of hair gleams, smooth, edged with a roll of curls so tight and precise that the rollers could still be buried in there somewhere. When she gets home from a morning's cleaning, Mr Hubbard's meaty fingers caress the ordered curls until they tumble, wild and unruly, around his wife's thin face. She is transformed.

You laugh out loud at this image as you glance over your shoulder before reversing out of the drive. Something blossoms at your ribs. Today you're taking Jamie to Burnham Beeches, Ian will be folded into the passenger seat of the Morris beside you and there'll be glimpses of his profile in the flickering light beneath a tunnel of branches. Perhaps you'll pull up in a lay-by, unfold the wheelchair, spread out the picnic tarpaulin on a bank covered with copper beech leaves and drink coffee from the tartan thermos you've packed for the journey. Jamie will sit in his wheelchair. You'll throw leaves into the air for him and he'll watch them fall. Sun will filter through a canopy of leaves on to Ian's beard so that the purple glints shine through the red and brown and ginger. He'll throw back his head the way he does, and you'll see the hairs, thick as pine needles, sprouting from his neck, from under his ears, from the tender underside of his chin.

You reach the boat earlier than planned. Ian has bent down to pull on his Chelsea boots.

'What're we gonny do?'

'We talked about Burnham. It's so beautiful at this time of year.' You pace about the sloping kitchen of the houseboat, throwing the car keys up in the air with one hand and catching them deftly with the other. 'It might be tricky with his chair though. What do you think?'

'Ach, nae,' his voice is almost a whisper. 'Nae. I mean . . . ma heid is spinning.'

You stop throwing the keys. Ian's forehead rests on his knee, the zip on his boot remains undone. You stare at the curve of muscle in his upper back, the cinnamon-coloured hair lying on the rolled neck of his black sweater.

He stands very slowly, passing a hand over his beard. 'Ye ken.'

The car keys clatter to the floor. You pick them up and as you straighten, he's close behind you, hands on your hips, pulling you towards him. He rests his mouth in your hair. Blood crashes in your skull.

'Ian.' You put out a hand to the edge of the sink, its coolness. 'I can't.'

Immediately he drops his hands and moves away. 'Forgive me.' His face is tight. He's backed up against the cupboards on the opposite side of the kitchen, hands behind his back. 'Please. I shidny—' He looks at the floor.

'No.' Your fingers are white-knuckled, clutching the bunch of keys. You place them carefully on the draining board. 'No. It's not that.'

Water plops softly against the hull.

Your feet in the sensible lace-up brogues, freshly polished, are side by side on the dusty boards. His Chelsea boots are unzipped. In the space between your feet and his, there's a splatter of red paint on the floor. Left toe round to the heel of the right shoe. Without undoing the laces, easing your foot out, and then the same for the other foot, kicking the heavy shoes aside, you're stepping towards him, bare boards catching on your stockinged soles.

His breath is coming hard, laboured.

Another step.

Greasy turpentine and sweat: the oniony, locker-room smell of him, a young man in tight black jeans with creases behind the knee, around the bulge and thicker material of his flies.

He's motionless, watching you.

Your mouth is flooding with saliva as you focus on the ribbing round the bottom of his black polo neck, the smoother, finer knit over his chest where the blond hairs, shooting upwards, will push against your hands.

You step closer. The boat rocks.

Lifting your head to look at his face, craning back, and heat pools in your groin, fans between your legs, the inside of your thighs, flames your neck, your cheeks. Your breasts tingle, your body fluid as the incoming tide.

Close to, his pupils are huge. On his shoulder, the woman's hand, a wedding ring, engagement ring, is yours – and now – your held breath bursts out as a sob, your body tumbling – his beard in the curve of your neck softens your limbs, edges meld as you're pressed to the unfamiliar contours of his groin, his stomach, his firm muscularity. His shoulders are so much wider than Michael's. In your belly leap little licks, urgent as fear.

Now his hands graze the hollow of your back, stroking, sliding down, tugging at your blouse, freeing it and then his upper arm hardens under your palms as he pulls at the fabric of your slip, his breath heavy, his beard, tussocky, brushing your cheek.

'Let me feel your skin,' he whispers. 'Please let me feel your skin.'

I HAVE A NEW, cloudy blue marble in my pocket. It's a Saturday and I want to knock for Hugh and Stephen.

Mum has put lipstick on. There's a cardboard box in the car packed with bottles of whisky and ginger ale, chocolates and some tins of soup. In her shopping basket under the tea towel there's a spiced lamb roll and flapjack which she was baking yesterday when I got in from school. She's wearing a little red hat and a red silky scarf. She stands in the kitchen doorway waving, her gloves and the car keys in her hand.

'Mmmm, you smell nice,' Father says. 'Be off with you now.' He kisses her on the lips.

She puts her hand up to her hair. 'If you're sure you're not too tired, Michael?'

Father has just come in from morning surgery. He's hung his jacket on the back of the kitchen chair and is unfastening his cufflinks. He begins rolling up his sleeves. 'I think we'll manage, between us, don't you?' He winks at me.

Father never winks at me.

Mum's going to visit one of her nursing friends. She's got a new flat and Mum's staying the night because it's a long way away.

I wanted to go and stay with Grampy, or go and visit the new flat too, but Mum laughed and kissed the top of my head and said it's a boring long drive and anyway it will be all nurse talk.

'Leave them to it. Nurses and their chatter.' Father pulls a face, blowing from his mouth so his hair flies up. 'You want to avoid that at all costs!'

'And the new flat has no garden, nowhere to kick a ball about,' Mum adds. 'Daddy's got lots of projects for the both of you up his sleeve, you just wait!'

She makes it sound like a treat, staying at home with him and not even being allowed to call for Stephen and Hugh. Susie made a big fuss about staying the night with Auntie Jean. 'Want Daddy! Want Daddy!' She stamped her feet up and down, up and down like she was running on the spot. I don't know why they didn't just let her stay here.

Father and I spend the afternoon hammering and sawing to make a run for Susie's rabbits from wood and chicken wire. When we finish the rabbit run we make a bonfire with bits of wood and empty cereal boxes and sugar cartons and newspapers. The sparks fly up orange and red.

Father says, 'Time for tea, do you think?'

I watch Father's back while he's busy on the other side of the kitchen. I lick my finger and rub it along the blue Formica of the kitchen table. Then I put my finger in my mouth and suck it. But I need to lick the blue to feel it properly.

Father puts slices of Spam on to two plates. 'Sit up straight, Andrew. Stop swinging your legs about.'

I don't know how Father knows this is what I am doing, because he has his back to me. I swing one leg a bit.

Nothing.

Both legs; the chair makes a little squeak.

'Andrew, what have I just said?'

Father comes across to the stove and picks up the pan with the mashed potato, goes back to the counter again and dollops potato on to a plate which he puts in front of me. On the plate are lumps of beetroot in a puddle of dark red. The bottom of the pile of mashed potato is dark red. I poke a slice of Spam with my fork and push it to the side of the plate, away from the red. I cut off a piece of Spam and put it in my mouth but there is some red taste. It stings. I swallow the lump of Spam whole. I am very hungry so I fork mouthfuls of mash from the top of the heap before it all goes red.

'Don't use your fork like a shovel,' Father says. 'Your mother . . .'

My mouth is filled with potato that doesn't taste of potato. I spit it out. The smell of the dark-red vinegary liquid is in my head and my mouth and makes my throat squeeze. I run to the sink and cough and spit. I'm hot.

'Andrew, for heaven's sake. You—'

'I HATE the red stuff! I HATE beetroot!' Words and bits of potato jump out. 'And Mummy says I DON'T have to eat it if I don't want to.'

I am already at the kitchen door when Father shouts, 'Go to your bed. Now!'

My heart is a football in my chest. The house is wrong when she's not here. I lie on the bed, then slip off and roll underneath into the dust and dark. I shut my eyes tight and think of Grampy's front gate, clicking it shut and running up the garden path, in through the back door, feeling my way in the dark hallway past the snake skin from India and the wooden bear that's taller than me. The bear is sharpening its claws on a tree trunk and there are wooden branches for coats to hang on. There is the smell of buses on wet days. Between the bear's legs there's a metal bucket for umbrellas, but there are no umbrellas in there. There are two bottles of linseed oil and Grampy's sail-maker's palm and needles. Next to the bear are Grampy's cardboard boxes with different bits of rope. I put my hand in to touch them.

Under the bed I say the names of the different types of ropes, one after the other. In the top box that says FAIRY LIQUID:

house-line
cod-line
nettle-stuff
and samson lines of hemp.

Underneath:

hawser rope
shroud laid rope
cable laid rope.

I am still awake.

I creep downstairs and past the sitting-room door. Father is reading his *BMJ* under the circle of light from the standard lamp. I let myself out of the back door, leaving it open because of the noise the metal strip makes.

Outside it is very dark and I don't stop running till I get to the bridge. There's the slimy mud smell of the water sliding underneath. The river is black and shiny. There are plipping sounds.

The metal handrail on the bridge smells like blood. I take a deep breath of cold air and I am Houdini standing on the bridge. I wait for The Voice to give me commands. The black water is ice. There is a round hole for me to dive into. The policemen put the long chain round me first, then the handcuffs and leg irons. From the banks, the crowds watch.

'Handcuff me and put leg irons on! I am Houdini the Handcuff King!' My words are puffs of white on the air.

At the freak shows or in the police stations I always escape. I am in the newspaper. I make lots of money by magic.

The ducks flap their wings and make a noise. I don't have any bread. The swans glide by like they are kings and queens, their wings snow white in the dark. I could fly into the night sky on a swan's back, white feathers soft and warm around me.

When I get to the other side of the bridge I run as fast as I can down the narrow footpaths between the high walls and fences to Grampy's back gate.

'What have we here?' says Grampy, coming out of his front room with the newspaper in his hand and spectacles on his forehead. 'Pyjamas? You'd better come in and get warmed up, my Treasure.'

Knots keep treasures safe.

HEAD ON MY ARMS at the table in the sun room under the fluorescent tube's hum, I'm startled by Sarah's loud rap.

I reach for her as soon as the front door is open but she ducks to evade my arms and storms into the kitchen, pacing up and down, relighting a skinny spliff. Her hair is up off her back, wrapped in a strip of multicoloured material. She's wearing her clay-splattered overalls. Smudges of clay coat her forearms. I sneak a look at my watch: 2.30 am. Has she been working at this time? Where was she earlier?

Every time I touch her she twitches my hand off, or twists out of reach. She refuses a drink of any sort, refuses food. I ask her what's up and she mutters, *Nothing*, glaring at the black window. I sit at the kitchen table, where I've been working on Hangman's Knots.

With a sigh she flounces from the kitchen and flings herself on to the old sofa, untying her baseball boots. I trail after her. She complains about the stark light from the naked bulb over our heads so I switch it off. I tell her about some netting and two old lobster pots I found today, but don't mention the nooses or the jelly shoe. Maybe she'd like a look tomorrow, if she's around. She doesn't appear to be listening so I don't say much. 'Where've you been these last few days?' I add.

'For fuck's sake, Andrew! I can't be at your beck and call. A couple of drunken shags do not equal a long-term commitment. Go and find someone your own age.' Sarah grabs a baseball boot and pulls it on again. She struggles with the laces. With every tug she gives them, the broken old sofa springs lurch.

I can't imagine why she's in such a foul temper. I only asked her what she was doing tomorrow.

'I just can't be doing with it. Why can men never accept that a woman might just want sex without any strings, like they always do? They want to have their cake and eat it. It always boils down to ownership, possession, putting a label on a woman saying MINE and then going off to fuck someone else in secret because it's more fun.'

I can't follow her argument but her energy is infectious; I'm slightly fuzzy from an afternoon's drinking and would really like to get her into bed right now, while her blood is up. She's trying to plait the great mass of her hair, a rubber band between her teeth, but her hands are shaking.

'Sarah—'

As she leans forward to search under the sofa for her other baseball boot, the tops of her buttocks swell over the waistband of her jeans. I plunge my hand down there, deep to the fatter flesh where her skin is cool. She leaps like a scalded cat and the baseball boot flies through the air, catching me on the chin.

I grab her wrists, holding her arms above her head as she struggles. Wanting to avoid a kick in the balls, I get behind her, strapping her arms down with mine. She grunts, stamping her feet and trying to jab her elbows into my guts. I bury my nose in the damp wisps of hair at the back of her neck, groin zapping and buzzing, my erection pressed against her.

Suddenly she freezes, panting. Through her T-shirt, her nipples are up. I take my chance, scoop her in my arms and fling her over my shoulder in a fireman's lift to carry her to my bedroom. Then I remember the child-sized bunk bed. It'll have to be the sofa. She's inert as a sack of coal as I ease her down, but as soon as her back is on the cushions she's lithe and slippery, trying to get away. I pin her wrists easily with one hand. With the other I grapple with my flies, watching her face. Her eyes are unreadable, until she catches sight of my erection. She smiles, a broad slow smile with white even teeth. Mimes a bite, her teeth clashing. I can feel her lips smile beneath my kiss.

Later, lying on the sofa, she smokes a fag and tells me that tomorrow – or rather, later today – she will load the Diving Woman into a van and take her to the warehouse where a mould will be made. 'I hate it,' she says, jabbing her cigarette stub into a saucer, 'I hate this stage – the whole fucking process from now on, the way she'll become something else. Brass; a metal thing I've never touched. She'll be a water feature in somebody's garden. It's like a death. Every time: a death.'

I spring up from the sofa and pull on my jeans. She watches as I buckle my belt. I'm almost out of the room when she calls, 'Andrew?' her voice soft.

'Going for a run-off. Coffee?'

When I turn from the toilet bowl, she's in the doorway. The wild mass of her untied hair smells fusty, of warm skin after sex, and its silver and brown corkscrews more or less shield the front of her body, head to hip. Like mermaid's hair. She puts a hand on my arm. 'Andrew, did—?'

' 'Scuse me.' I walk past her.

'I'll do without the coffee, thanks,' she says minutes later, walking into the kitchen. She's fully dressed, wearing one of my jumpers over her overalls. 'I need to get some sleep.'

What chance do I have of sleeping?

She comes over to the stove and leans on me, slipping a hand into the back pocket of my jeans. She has shadows under her eyes. It's the first time I've seen her looking tired; exhausted. She's usually so feisty. 'Tell you what,' she says, 'how about we make a dancing date? Not tomorrow, the next day?' She eyes my feet. 'Got any shoes with slippery soles?'

'No. Will this be—?'

'Don't worry. I'll have something that'll fit in one of my boxes of teaching gear. You up for it?'

I could cover my tracks a little here. I put an arm around her and kiss the top of her head. 'Sorry.'

'For—?'

'Some things I'm no good at talking about.'

'Want to try?'

'You're tired.'

'Yes. We could get into bed and talk. Cuddle up. That would be nice, you know?'

If I get her into bed, I can probably persuade her into more sex.

'It'll do me good to stop thinking about the Diving Woman,' she adds, wearily.

We head back to her place. The night is clear. Stars scattered like glitter remind me of Crete.

She makes hot chocolate from a jar. Takes off her clothes and climbs into bed. No elaborate routine washing or slathering creams and lotions on her face. Her big white bed takes up the entire floor space of a Pullman compartment. It's so much more comfortable than anywhere at The Siding. Lying on my back under the thick duvet with her body curled up next to me, I'm surprised to have no desire for anything else, just to lie there.

'It was something I said, wasn't it? About the Diving Woman?'

So, she's not giving up. I don't say anything.

'Andrew?' She runs her spread fingers through the hairs on my chest, rests her palm where the hair grows thickest, the centre line between my nipples, floats her fingers on the bounce of hair and presses down lightly, then lifts her hand away – the space between her hand and my skin like something missing – her touch returning to move lightly up over the hairs on my belly, slowing again as she reaches the curls of chest hair. With her strokes, something coiled within me loosens. My body grows loose and heavy.

'I'm listening.'

'It's such a long time ago.'

'Think of it as a story about someone else, that helps with murky things from the past, I find. You know that thing people do for agony aunts: "*Dear Virginia Ironside, I've got this friend who's got pregnant by her brother and has already had two abortions . . .*"? Try that.'

A part of me is irritated at the way she makes it sound light and inconsequential, but I'm comfortable and not sleepy yet so I experiment with a beginning. 'Many years ago there was a small boy who loved this beach—', and my memory of that terrible day becomes the story of Elaine.

I reach the part where the man digging for lugworms starts to run, and I can't go on. I roll on to my stomach, fists clenched, holding my breath. I have to get out. I get as far as the edge of the bed, head down, unable to think where my clothes are, my knee and thigh jiggling uncontrollably up and down, up and down, but there's a grunting choking sound that must be me because my chest and throat are strangled. A cry comes out. A yelp.

Sarah's there, taking my head into her arms. I'm struggling away from her because I can't breathe and will explode and have to get out.

But she's still there, holding my head and stroking my hair and saying, over and over again, her voice soothing, 'It was an accident, Andrew, an accident. It wasn't your fault.' And finally I'm exhausted. There's nothing left.

We lie down together. She strokes my hair.

When I wake in the morning her hand still rests on the back of my head.

YOU CLUTCH THE GLOVES, cream suede with scalloped cuffs, to your handbag. The handbag, also cream suede, makes you wish for something more stalwart. Today, in the muted green of the waiting room, the raspberry red of your suit is frivolous and garish – a reminder of another self. Yesterday Jean pounced on this outfit, whipping the suit from your wardrobe with a rustle of laundry plastic, exclaiming with delight that it's the image of one Oleg Cassini made for Jacqueline Kennedy.

It's only been a few days. You feel exposed.

You bought the suit to wear for your weekend together – although once you arrived, the two of you hardly stepped out of bed, just stayed there, cocooned together in The Siding as wind and sea railed outside. Undressing each other that first afternoon – the lunch you'd so carefully packed abandoned on the kitchen table – he gazed at your body with delight. You could read it in his eyes, his smile. He couldn't believe how beautiful you are, he kept saying. He kept repeating *how beautiful* as he contemplated your body, smiling and reaching out for you again and again. Later that afternoon, bubbling with a laughter urging you to fly, you bounced from the bed, jumped into slacks, pulled a sweater of Ian's over your head and danced out, barefoot, into the wind, bounding across the pebbles and on to the sand, swooping and shouting, mouth wide to breathe in the air, to lick the salt. The wide sky was layers of smudged purple and grey, frothy with wind-flurried white. Ian followed, chasing, vaulting over breakwaters, as the two of you raced across ripples of sand to the sea's edge.

'It's not suitable,' you told Jean yesterday. You took the suit on its hanger and put it back into the wardrobe.

In your head, you have to keep things separate. Wearing this outfit while being Andy's mother and Michael's wife, frays the edges.

'Why ever not? Come on, it'll make you feel better.'

'I don't believe what I wear will make me feel any better at all.'

'Look, it doesn't help anyone when you're walking round looking like a wet weekend. You're taking Andrew to see this psychologist because he'll make suggestions that will improve things. He'll have seen it all umpteen times before. So, stop agitating. Be hopeful.'

Jean didn't add, as you knew she was tempted to, *or you'll end up as bad as you were after Susie, after Elaine.* Today Jean is not here to boss you into a more positive frame of mind. Silence wads your throat and lungs. *Breathe, breathe.*

You will have to tell Ian. It's making you ill, the deceit. You will be strong and you will stop it. He'll find somebody else in no time at all.

The thought makes a sob catch in your throat. Michael, nose in a newspaper, pats your thigh. A wave of nausea washes over you and, pushing the red jacket sleeves up from your wrists to cool them, you wonder where, through which of these closed doors, the Ladies will be. You've not been sick but this nausea has been a nuisance for a couple of days, a bug perhaps, that the children have brought home from school. Thank goodness you got through the family interview. Three wooden chairs lined up, in an uncarpeted room, and the psychologist's desk. The psychologist's hair, receding from his forehead, was white and so too was the neat beard hiding his mouth. He wore a three-piece suit, a bow tie and horn-rimmed spectacles.

Michael did most of the talking, and you listened to his mellifluous voice, almost hypnotised by the calm recounting of the details of your lives. Andy swung his legs and snapped the catch on his toy gun. Then you and Michael were ushered out, leaving Andy in front of the desk, cowboy hat pulled down over his eyes, legs still swinging and one fawn sock down at his ankle.

He's still in there with the psychologist, your little boy. The little boy you adored so much that once he was born you hadn't wanted another child, didn't really want or need any other human being. Michael's desire for you after Andy's birth was an intrusion. No wonder Michael quickly grew so jealous. It is your fault.

But, four years later – too long a gap, Michael kept on and on – came Susie. In the nursing home, you'd wondered if it was the wrong baby they'd given you, because you felt nothing except a bone weariness. A few days after Susie's birth, you turned your face to the wall when they wheeled her in for her feed. Back home, the repetition of nothing on nothing, day after day, inside your head, became a barren wilderness. And the days folded in on themselves, all those endless blank surfaces. Then, to fall pregnant, just three months after Susie's birth, with Elaine – the tears prickle up behind your nose again.

'Come on, Andy! Don't be chicken.'

Hugh's voice echoes up through the darkness of the hole. I sit on the ground and put my legs in first, the way the others did. The sides of the coal chute are gritty cold.

'Come on!' Stephen calls up. He's fat, but he didn't get stuck. I shift my bottom forward a bit and then I'm sliding down. I can taste sooty dust and I've landed on a knobbly heap of coal and coal sacks.

'It'll make a jolly good den, won't it?' Hugh runs up and down the slope of coal, de-rrum de-rumming the tune to the *Lone Ranger* and pretending he's galloping on a horse. 'Yee hah!' he shouts. 'Yee hah!'

Everything is shadowy. Stephen stands with his back flat against the wall, biting his lip. He has a smear of black on his forehead and it gives me an idea. I lift my hands to my face and rub my cheeks.

I put a finger to my lips and whisper, 'Camouflage,' I wait, to make sure they're both listening, 'will be essential while we explore.'

The three of us mess our hands about in the coal dust and rub our faces. Hugh and Stephen look like the Black and White Minstrels Mum watches on television. Their teeth show up white in the dimness.

The house sits above us like an attic – dusty floorboards and sheets over things. It's not properly empty. The ghosts of the people who once lived here are going to come out of the walls as soon as we've gone. On the outside the house looks different from all the other houses in our road. The windows have no curtains and the paint is coming off the front door in flakes. It made me want to come and look inside.

'It's a mental institution, this place.' I nod my head at the others. 'We're going to explore the wards and find all the padded cells. There may be mad men. Lunatics!'

The others go quiet and nod their heads back at me, fingers to lips.

'Maniacs!' Hugh nods back.

I've told them all about the lunatic asylums where maniacs in straitjackets are tied up and left to wriggle like maggots in padded cells.

Hugh goes first up the twisty stairs leading out of the cellar. Stephen goes last behind me because he's slow and puffy. The door at the top is ajar and dusty. Sunlight comes through the gap.

You undo the clasp on your handbag and finger the familiar jumble: the compact in its velvet pouch (from Paris, the honeymoon, a gift from Michael); lipstick, handkerchief, door key, Eau de Cologne. You dab cologne on to your handkerchief and press it to your forehead, the sides of your nose, your forehead again. It's the waiting, the silence, the high-ceilinged room with its waxy dark floorboards. Green foam, an oasis, shows through the sparse colour of a floral arrangement: an unnatural place for flowers.

Unnatural.

'Why would you, of all people, be like this?' Jean had said, after Susie's birth.

A telephone rings from behind a closed door and is answered straight away, then, at last, a woman with red lips sashays into the room with a clipboard: a questionnaire to fill in. Her stockings and petticoat make rustling sounds beneath her narrow skirt as she walks.

'Just some family medical history for our records,' she says, as she shakes your hand and Michael's. She rustles around to sit beside Michael. Her sweater is tight over her breasts. Fluffy angora – too girlish for her age. Smoothing her skirt along her thighs, she turns towards him. Oh ruddy well let him answer the questions then. You dab your forehead. The Ladies: where is it? You must powder your nose before seeing the psychologist.

The angora woman has raised her eyebrows in query, red lipstick lips curved in a smile; she's asked something you haven't heard. She repeats the question – the children's birth dates – Michael never remembers. He takes over to supply the details of childhood illnesses: chicken pox; mumps; measles.

The woman writes in the column beside Elaine's name: MENTALLY DEFICIENT.

My book on Houdini says he thought the freak world was normal and straights were freaks. Houdini performed at freak shows. One day, Bess and Houdini arrived at Huber's dime museum in New York to do a performance with the other freaks. There was Unthan the legless wonder, Emma Shaller the ossified girl, and Big Alice the fat lady. Houdini and Bess waited in the entrance hall. While they waited another exhibit was unloaded: an electric chair.

It was the electric chair from a prison in Auburn, used to electrocute a murderer.

Houdini cannot forget the electric chair arriving at the freak show at the same time as he arrived with Bess.

There is a reason for everything. He knows.

He thinks about the chair a lot.

In 1910, when Huber's dime museum was sold, he bought the electric chair and took it home to put in his Manhattan brownstone. Bess hated the chair and, when

Houdini was away, she got someone to help her carry it down to the basement.

But Houdini liked to sit in it every evening so he missed it straight away and brought it upstairs again.

In this empty house there is a big chair with arms and a dust sheet over it.

You are ushered in to the psychologist's room. The three chairs are empty.

'Andrew's next door.' The psychologist gestures towards a panelled door in the opposite wall. 'We have lots of games and toys there to keep him happy.'

He moves to the desk and notes something down. His fountain pen is black and gold. For some reason you think of that first meeting with Michael in the hospital corridor and it makes you feel hopeful. *Hope*, that's what Jean always says, *stay hopeful*.

He replaces the cap of his pen. There are raised veins on the back of his hands. You must tell him about everything; all of it. You put your handbag on the floor at your feet. It will be a relief.

'Now, let's put all this aside for a moment,' he waves a hand across the wad of notes on his desk. 'We'll begin with a few details about your pregnancies. Can you tell me what age you were when you first conceived?'

Those somnambulant weeks before Andrew's birth: the baby's weight pressing down between your legs; the hard stretching of your skin with the bulge of a heel or an elbow; expectation a heavy ripeness as you stood in thick fog on Westminster Bridge with Michael, queuing to file past King George's coffin.

'I was twenty-seven – no – I'm sorry – twenty six.' You correct yourself. It's not Andrew's conception that you remember, but his birth: Michael cradling Andy, moving his nose over the downy head, breathing in the baby smell of scalp. Michael, accustomed to other women's babies, handled his own newborn with practised skill.

Your eyes fill. What have you done? What have you allowed to happen?

'Take your time.' His gentleness makes your throat constrict. 'There is plenty of time.'

He waits, unruffled. His stillness is calming.

'I'm so sorry.' Clear your throat. 'When Andrew was born . . .'

The fragile boughs of the silver birch at the window signal an indefinable loss. You see Michael, standing in the light of the bedroom window, caressing a miniature foot, his lips to the wrinkled sole.

'Perhaps you would like one of these?' The doctor comes around his desk, proffering a box of tissues. He tugs up his trouser legs as he sits on a chair beside you.

'I think that things were – Michael couldn't – he didn't like—' Weeping distorts your voice and makes it difficult to continue. 'I think I might have loved my son too much.' You press a tissue to your mouth. Tears stream down your cheeks.

After a while, he puts a hand on your shoulder.

You shake your head, eyes filling again. 'It's my fault.'

He lifts his hand from your shoulder. 'There's no reason to apportion any blame. Perhaps we should get you a cup of tea. Let's fetch Janice, shall we?'

The fluffy woman arrives in a talcum waft of Coty's, murmuring solicitously as she guides you to the door. She goes back for the box of Kleenex. Michael stands and enters the room with the psychologist. The door is closed.

Janice brings a tray with tea in a teapot and four lemon puffs on a plate. The ritual of pouring – milk jug, strainer, sugar cubes and tongs, the teaspoon stirring – steadies you, but one bite of Lemon Puff and the nausea washes through you again. The teaspoon clatters down in the saucer and you ask Janice where you can go to powder your nose.

I whack the chain on the floorboards.

'Found it down by the river, near the boatyard,' I tell them, passing it through my fists, squeezing my fingers around its hardness. I whack it on the floorboards again.

'You stole it?' says Stephen, his mouth all loose. He pushes his glasses up his nose.

'I've got a padlock.' Hugh ignores him. 'It's on my bike.'

Hugh and me look at each other. We've already got some handcuffs here, hidden in the pile of coal in the coal cellar. My new Timex says a quarter to four. It's Pancake Day today. Today would be a good day to do it. Stephen probably eats loads of pancakes.

'How long would it take to go and get it?'

'Let's all go,' says Hugh. 'I'll get Mum to give us some lemonade and biscuits and while you two distract her, I'll sneak into the garage and get it. Pretend I'm spending a penny or something.' Hugh snorts and the two of us double up with laughing. 'Spending a penny' is what Stephen says to our mums when he wants to go to the loo at our houses.

'Why do we need a padlock?' Stephen asks. He doesn't want to run all the way there and back again to our den because he runs like a duck.

'Stay here then, if you want.'

Stephen looks at his feet. He's wearing black plimsolls like the ones we wear for P.E. at school only his are too small and his fat feet bulge out over the elastic bit. He won't wait here by himself. Hugh's been here on his own, I know. I crawled through the broken bit of fence one afternoon after school and peered in the French doors and Hugh was lying on the floorboards in a patch of sunshine reading the *Beano*. Blimey, he didn't half jump when I rapped on the window.

After half an hour or so, the door opens again and the psychologist shakes Michael's hand in the doorway, and you stand, stuffing your balled-up handkerchief into a pocket, waiting to be invited in. But the appointment time is over. The psychologist will send a written report; another appointment in six months' time.

'I didn't take off my cowboy hat,' Andy says, jutting out his chin in the way that Michael does. 'He asked me to.'

You crouch down to wrap your arms around him and bury your face in his neck. Your eyelids are swollen and stiff. Andy wriggles away.

'Did he make you do pictures too, Mummy?'

Perhaps you could have managed some drawings. A picture of Andy licking the soles of Elaine's feet and making her laugh, that funny little yelp she used to give. A picture of Andy curled on your father's lap. Andy locked in the cupboard under the stairs. Pictures would have been much easier.

You take hold of Andy's hand. He twists in your grip but you keep holding as the three of you pass through the corridors lined with closed doors and the sounds of muffled voices, down the stairs and out on to the glittering pavement. There's a cold wind. Andy finally slips from your grasp and shoots at the pigeons, his fingers held like a gun.

Ptchew! Ptchew! He shouts and leaps along the pavement.

Michael keeps looking at his watch. He's calculating whether or not he'll be back in time for evening surgery. The tyres and wheel hubs of the cars parked along the kerb are dusty and worn. You pull your car-coat closer.

Me and Mum were making butterscotch Angel Delight, pouring it into four little glass dishes, for tea. Stephen's mum came round. Susie was unwrapping the Cadbury's flake, ready to sprinkle it on top. Stephen's mum had angry red lips and wobbly cheeks like Stephen's, only hers were all powdery. When I saw who it was at the door, I ran and hid in the laurel hedge at the bottom of the garden. I stayed there until it was nearly dark. Stephen's mum told my mum what we'd done. She threw my Angel Delight away and shouted at me. Susie ate all the Cadbury's flake. There was none left for me.

I had to write a letter to say sorry and take it round with Mum. Stephen sat on the sofa at his house. He was wearing his too-small plimsolls and looking at them. While I said sorry, he put one foot and then the other up on the edge of the coffee table, over and over, one foot then the other.

Stephen's such a tell tale tit.

The car glides along. Andy is curled up on the back seat under the old hospital blanket, sound asleep. Michael's silent, looking straight ahead as he drives. He's wearing his gold cufflinks. Semi-detached houses line the road. Lights come on in bow-fronted windows and give glimpses of lives: a book-case in an alcove, a standard lamp throwing a circle of light over the white antimacassar on the back of an armchair. A couple stand at their bow-fronted bedroom window. The curtains are half drawn. He's behind her, kissing her neck as she wriggles to one side, trying to reach for the curtains, laughing and smiling. *Ian.* Blood leaps to the surface of your cheeks, your body's automatic reaction. There is no point. It's tearing you apart. You have to try to hold everything together.

It's half past five. On an ordinary day you'd be in your blue-and-white kitchen, peeling potatoes, cooking mince for the children's tea. Yesterday you made apple snow with Bramleys from the garden for Jean to give Susie for pudding today. You turn from the bow-fronted houses and stare ahead at the tarmac.

'Well, that was very productive.' Michael's voice makes you jump. 'His opinion is that Andrew's trying to deal with the fear of separation; from you. Attention-seeking, as I've thought all along. He used something he refers to as the "squiggle game", and came up with some very interesting—'

Michael and the psychologist shaking hands in the door-way; Michael's gold cufflinks and his St Andrews tie.

'What is this squiggle game?' You twist to face him. 'Andrew told me he had to finish some drawings.'

Michael glances at you. 'Well, clearly that's a child's perspective and therefore somewhat limited. I believe he draws a line or two, and then interprets the drawings that the child goes on to produce from those starting points.'

'And this is the basis for a diagnosis that could affect Andy's whole life, the way we live *our* lives?' Blood pounds at your breast bone. 'A few scribbles on a piece of paper!' You loosen the scarf at your neck. 'It sounds about as accurate as reading tea leaves!' You clap a hand over your mouth.

Listen to Michael.

Take slow breaths.

The scarf slithers on to your lap, its silky raspberry colour cools your hands.

'Are you feeling nauseous?' Michael's eyes assess you.

'No!' Too abrupt. 'No, no, I'm fine. Really.'

breathe

'so – what did he say about Andrew's drawings?'

'Well, apparently Andrew translated seven out of the ten drawings into something associated with rope or string, and—'

'Surely *any* little squiggle of pencil on paper could look like string!'

Michael thuds the heel of his hand on the steering wheel. 'Would you like to hear what he said, or not?'

You look out of the window at the houses again. Most now have drawn curtains. 'Sorry. Yes. Please. Sorry. Sorry.'

'Well, out of ten drawings, Andrew's included a lasso, two whips, two crops, a yo-yo and a knot, indicating an unhealthy preoccupation with rope.'

'And how does he get from that, to the idea that Andrew is worried about losing me?' But as you say it, you can see how. String. Joining. Umbilical cord. 'No – I see how he might.'

You rest your head in your hands. 'Michael, he was wearing his cowboy hat. He had his toy gun with him. Is a lasso so surprising? Did you tell him what my father's occupation was? Why do *you* think he's so interested in rope?'

Michael shifts his hands up the wheel, placing them in the ten-to-two position that he taught you to use. He says nothing. You lean back and close your eyes, seeing Andy in his cowboy hat, his toy gun in the holster at his hip. A lasso whirls through the air, falling around a horse's neck. Rope tightens on the bulge of muscle. The animal strains, eyes rolling as it bucks and paws the ground. A whip cracks and raises dust. You've watched the cowboy and Indian films that Andy loves so much. You lift your chin up from your coat collar. 'He didn't even bother to speak with me.'

'Don't overreact. He has to take into account your medical history. You were too distressed for him to pursue the interview. Incoherent, was the word I believe he used. Besides, I was able to give him all the necessary details.'

In profile, the familiar shift of his jaw bone warns you. Heat flares behind your eyes, making them water. This time it's anger. You want to force him to look at you and recount his conversation with the psychologist. Because it will have been a conversation, not questions and answers. You want to ask Michael about the 'facts' he gave. He'll have changed things. Andy's love of stories, his vivid imagination, will have become a tendency to tell lies. A fascination with texture and colour and smell will have become the indicators of some sort of mental abnormality. You've failed Andy today, yet again. *Your medical history to take into account.* Your throat squeezes tight and the tears come once more. Your nose is running.

'Mummy?' Andy's head bobs near your shoulder, his hand gripping the back of your seat. 'Mummy? Where are we?'

Michael glances in the rear-view mirror. 'We just got a bit lost here, Andrew. Got our bearings now.' He passes you a neatly folded handkerchief with the laundry mark at the corner. 'Let's just concentrate on getting home in one piece, shall we?'

SARAH'S WEARING THE BLUE dress – 'Turquoise, Andrew,' she tells me, when I say it's sexy, 'turquoise, not blue' – and high-heeled shoes. Her calves are bare and tanned. I wonder how that can be, in November. There's energy in her movements, the flex of her well-developed calf muscles, the taut line of muscle in her thighs that shows through the draping fabric of her dress as she walks to and fro across the kitchen.

She brings three more wine glasses to the table. I stand up. I didn't expect this, the looming threat of a social occasion with strangers.

'Before you say anything at all,' she says, looking me in the eye, 'they're childhood friends of mine. They're more family than my family so if you think you can't handle it you can leave now.'

So she has her priorities.

I swill a mouthful of Shiraz. 'Am I that predictable?'

'Oh, I know your sort of old.'

My 'sort' doesn't sound favourable. As I gather myself to leave, the doorbell rings. They don't wait for Sarah to get to the door. A grizzled guy with a thin grey ponytail and a bushy beard carries a guitar into the kitchen. He reaches for my hand immediately. 'Tom,' he says. His hand is huge and calloused. 'You must be Andrew.'

I nod and smile. It doesn't seem necessary to say anything in response because behind him follows a Mary Hopkins lookalike, slender with blonde hair flopping down. They both fling their arms around Sarah at the same time. Sarah has tears in her eyes. Some back-rubbing and kissing and murmuring about 'Such good news' goes on, so I finish the glass of wine and pour myself another. I can feel myself retracting, snail-like, but can't leave now, much as I want to.

Mary Hopkins slips her shoes off, comes over and bends down to kiss me on both cheeks. Her face is round, scrubbed-clean. 'I'm Denise. Can I sit here, next to you? Or will Sarah fight me for this seat, do you think?' Her voice is so soft that I have to lean towards her to catch the words.

'Yeah, I bloody will. Piss off and sit over there next to your own bloke.'

Everyone else laughs. This might be OK. The three of them have enough to say between them without me being required to even open my mouth. Sarah leans her thigh on mine and the conversation leaps and bounds. We share tapas which Denise has prepared and brought. Often they interrupt or talk over each other, quarrel over the accuracy of details that they want me to know, like how long they have all known each other.

Sarah and Tom met building sandcastles on this beach when they were still in terry nappies. Denise was a late arrival to the sandcastle gang, but no one can remember the exact dates of anything, so they argue and discuss whether or not to search for childhood photos. Their childhood summers sound uncannily similar to mine: crowds of children gathering on the sand at low tide, parents sitting in deckchairs, distant on the pebbles, everyone digging and patting as fast as possible to build a castle big enough for six or ten or maybe more children to stand on as the tide comes in.

'I gather you're one of us too,' says Tom. 'Childhood holidays here, now living the dream full time? A common story round here.'

'I'm only here for the time being.'

'Perhaps we all built sandcastles together,' says Denise looking across the table at me thoughtfully. 'I had twin brothers. Everyone remembers them. They wore matching multicoloured striped jumpers knitted by my mother.'

Knees and feet, are what I remember, the imprints of fingers on the sand; salty white skin, sand-coated calves; girls' hair in rat's tails, stiff with salt. But, thinking about it, I maybe remember two boys in striped jumpers, blond, older than me. Or maybe they're in one of the old photographs, pictures of a row of children, in jumpers and sagging knitted swimming costumes, standing on a sandcastle as the tide came in.

'It's a bit like college reunion after twenty years,' Sarah says, 'something incestuous about it somehow.'

I watch her laugh. I didn't know that she'd had childhood summers down here. I put a hand on her knee and she covers it with hers.

Tom and Denise are happy to talk about themselves, their lives together, and I listen. Tom was in the music business until five years ago when his father died and left him the Pullman carriage house. He gave up gigs and hotel rooms and took up fishing. It's his boat I see out there, just offshore, most nights. He's passionate about the Pullmans and promises to show me a photograph of their carriage being transported here by Ted Broadbridge's drogue timber wagon and a team of six horses.

Since their children have grown up and left home, Denise has got into various New Age alternative therapies –

aromatherapy, something called 'shamanic dreaming' – and sees clients in a room in their Pullman, 'Buffers'.

'What's yours called?' Denise asks. Her question startles me. My guard has dropped.

'The Siding.'

'That one! Been mostly empty for years and years, hasn't it? Such a shame. Did your parents own it originally? I'd love a look inside.'

Denise, I suspect, is one of those intense women, like a counsellor I was sent to once, with a tendency to probe into every microscopic and painful detail of other people's lives. I know exactly what Denise would say about my dreams, because I've been told before. My subconscious mind is telling me something. Tonight Tom and Sarah have dominated the conversation; a one-to-one with Denise would be beyond sufferance.

'Music?' Sarah deflects Denise's question by turning up the music full volume. 'What do you think, everyone?'

I smile at her, but she doesn't seem to notice my gratitude. Now that I listen to the music, I think it sounds old-fashioned, almost music hall. Lots of accordion.

Tom and Denise, it turns out, are two of Sarah's tango 'pupils'. They have brought a bag full of tango gear and they take it into the studio to prepare themselves.

'Now,' Sarah says, standing behind me and running her fingers through my hair. 'Can we tie this back? Do you have anything?'

I hand her a length of string from the front pocket of my jeans. The brush strokes are firm as she smooths my hair back into a ponytail. Only my mother has ever brushed my hair before. I lean my head back against her groin, but she moves away saying, 'Now, shoes.' From the hallway she fetches a pair of smart black shoes with a slightly stacked heel.

'Haven't worn stacks since the seventies,' I joke, as she crouches down to put them on me. She's fed me, brushed my hair, now she's putting on my shoes. I look down on her bent head, the fluid curve of her swan-like neck and the intricate weaving of her hair into its neat pleat. I run a forefinger slowly down the side of her neck, seeing her head flung back, her breathing hoarse in her throat. She gets up from her knees.

In the studio, Sarah has made floor-space. The other two are already gliding around, concentrating on each other. Sarah stands in the centre of the cleared space and beckons me over to stand close to her. She's looking to the left, into the middle distance. I look in the same direction.

'It's important,' she articulates slowly, 'that you under-stand that the improvisational nature of tango requests the complete attention of both of us, each to the other.'

She's speaking differently, with a sort of serious politeness.

Complete attention. Her eyes are green-blue glass, sea glass. I won't ask her to say it again.

'OK.' She straightens her spine.

I do the same.

The posture has lifted her breasts, making them prominent, tilting towards my chest and I find I'm mimicking her stature, lifting my rib cage. She puts a hand on her belly to indicate I should hold my stomach muscles taut. I look down at the top of her head, waiting for eye contact.

'Now, I'm going to lead, and it's my body movements you need to be listening to.' Her eyes are focused at some point over my shoulder, her face serene. 'I'll not be giving clues with my eyes. On a crowded dance floor, as the male dancer, I would be looking for spaces to move into.' She takes my right hand in her left, and then opens her hand. 'Palms flat: a light pressure.'

Her right hand is light at the small of my back. 'To begin with, I would suggest you close your eyes so that your other senses will be more acute.'

'Other senses?'

'Mainly touch. Close your eyes. We'll just stand and listen to the music.'

I close my eyes. I smell her hair, think of sex, my head between her thighs, the arch of her body, and my erection is growing. Then she's backed away, creating a space between us that I move to fill, a few hesitant paces forwards, as she steps back. I'm terrified of treading on her toes, so I open my eyes briefly and see our feet, the dusty floor. I stumble. She stops.

'Wait,' she says in my ear.

I close my eyes again. I find I can judge the size of her steps through the dip of her back beneath my palm. She's turning us in another direction, a slight pressure of one hip towards me and we're moving sideways, slow paces, a twist of her hips and it's a swift turn I don't quite keep up with. Another turn and her upper body moves beneath my fingertips, a slight pull of her raised hand tells me I must step backwards.

'Don't think,' she whispers, 'let your body listen to my body.'

The track ends and she stops, but it's a pause in motion, she's going to dance on to the next track. She's waiting, soaking up the new pulse.

We stop dancing before I want to, my mind and body so absorbed by the dance that I haven't been aware of anything else.

'It's like a trance,' I say, without thinking, and check her expression in case this is a crass thing to say.

'Better, because it's a shared experience.'

I'm keen to start dancing again; no more talk.

'It's a wonderfully de-stressing activity, wouldn't you say?' She moves away from me to the sink in the corner of the studio and fills a blue wine glass with water. 'I'm trying to advertise tango as something that anyone can do, maybe if life is getting too much, if their jobs are stressful. For example, I visit offices in London, where I teach, and encourage businessmen to come along. I go into hospitals and speak to the doctors. I send letters to headmistresses and headmasters.'

'You sound like a missionary.'

'It is a sort of mission, I suppose.'

'I could dance all night with you. Let's do some more.'

'We should take a breather. Come up to a class with me sometime. Let's make some coffee now.'

Everyone declines coffee in favour of the Jack Daniels that Tom has brought. Sarah lights little candles in glass cups and switches off the electric lights. Denise falls asleep, her head on Tom's lap as he talks on. He's a born story-teller, demanding nothing but an audience of listeners, and I wonder where he gets that confidence from, the knowledge that people will want to listen to him.

By the time they leave we're all wilting. Tom has extracted a promise from me that I'll look at an old seaman's chest of his. He wants some beckets made for it. Denise, predictably, wants a doormat like the one I made Sarah last week.

Sarah and I fall into her bed and I'm asleep instantly.

LAST NIGHT, IT WAS so cold you were worried it would snow. Then what? Even though today is the day you're going to tell Ian it's over, all you could think was, *then what?* Michael eventually got up and went to sleep in the spare room, complaining you were keeping him awake.

You stop at the postbox on the corner of Sutton Road and there he is, his Lambretta parked just up the road. Just the sight of his face, the way he stands looking into the middle distance because he hasn't seen you yet, brings a leap of joy. He nods a greeting as he squeezes into the passenger seat, wrapping his sheepskin jacket more closely and sinking his beard into his scarf. No Jamie today; another reason to feel guilty.

He won't kiss you until you're at least as far as Maidenhead – because it's not safe, because you might be seen.

This is part of what you can't cope with, the pretence. When you're not with him you are stripped, brutally, turned inside out like a sleeve – you become both the empty sleeve, soft lining exposed, and the arm left cold.

'We'd manage,' Ian has said, over and over again. He wants you and the children with him in the houseboat.

He phoned the house last week, breaking an unspoken rule, and Michael answered. Ian made some excuse about a friend, or someone wanting a painting job done, with a similar telephone number, and Michael came off the phone chuckling, but it gave you a scare.

Then he'd written to you – another risk – because he was desperate to tell you about a small house he'd seen that you could renovate together, perhaps if you went back to nursing, and he worked in the evenings. The letter was filled with drawings, of the house, of ideas for the house, of you standing in the doorway, together.

'But then, when would we have time to renovate the house?' you'd asked him later. 'We'd either be working or looking after the children.'

It's just make-believe. Michael would never allow it, would never tolerate the loss of face. Michael would make life impossible.

You shake your head, trying to clear your thoughts.

Ian winds down the window and rests his chin on his hand, elbow propped on the car window, looking out. There is frost on the grass.

'Ian, could you—?'

'Sorry,' he winds up the glass again. 'I'm sorry . . .' He twists round to face you.

'What is it? What's the matter?' You fiddle with the heater control. The fan is rattling but there's no heat. 'Has something happened?'

'Ay.' He pulls off his scarf. 'A job.'

The traffic lights are green but the car sputters and almost stalls. It doesn't like the cold. A few flakes of snow are falling like clumps of feathers.

'But that's wonderful! A job? A decorating job? Another commission?'

'Teaching.'

'Ian—' You're wondering at his bleak tone, then it hits you – where around here would he teach art? Your voice comes out as a croak: 'Where?'

He leans close, a hand on your thigh, and he's talking, fast and soft, about being together, about the rarity of love, about not living a life that's a lie. You can tell he's rehearsed this speech – the reasonable phrases, the believable possibilities. Perhaps if the two of you took on Jamie as well as your three children, his parents might help financially.

His optimism is young, naive. It would be a scandal. You would be the scarlet woman, labelled unfit to care for your children. You keep your eyes on the road, saying nothing.

'I'll be needing tae let them know.'

'Where?'

A lady steps out on to the zebra crossing but it's too late to stop the car. She waves her walking stick and scowls her disapproval from the kerb.

'Pull over.'

You glance in the rear mirror and swerve into a bus lay-by. The engine stalls. You pull the choke further out and try to start it up again, wanting to keep the heater going, for what it's worth. The starter motor coughs and splutters.

Try again. Don't look at his face.

Try a third time. The starter motor is fainter.

This day is not right.

'It's flooded, the engine.' He puts a hand on your arm, takes your hand in both of his. 'Paris.'

You've been struck, the breath knocked from you.

'Come with me.'

You shake your head, wordless.

Part Four

'THING IS, ANDY,' Susie tugs her flapping coat across her body, shouting over the roar of the tumbling shingle and the slap of the canvas above us, 'we should probably think about a prospective buyer.' She lifts her hands to her ears and, again, the wind wrenches her coat open. She looks like a starvation victim – jumper stretched over distended belly, legs spindly in leggings that bag round the knee. I look away.

'The tatty old canvas . . . I'm just not sure.' She winces and pulls her collar up. 'This *wind*! Please can we go inside now?'

I've brought Susie straight round to the seaward side of the house to show her the work I've done on the veranda, hoping she'll be OK with it. Maybe even pleased. We're on the new decking area. A shipload of two-by-four was washed up during the last storm. Planks scattered break-water after breakwater for miles along on the beach. Sarah and I hefted more than fifty up the beach and piled them in a satisfying stack between our two houses. Good, broad planks for decking. Susie just looks miserable huddled in her coat. She hasn't even glanced at the star-shaped sinnet that sways, thick and heavy, in the wind. I've hung the sinnet around three sides of the decking area, suspended from three-foot-high steel needles at intervals along the rope's length.

'What about that?' I point.

'The rope?' Head tilted, eyes narrowed, she considers. 'Looks nice. You made it, I suppose?'

'You can tell?'

'Well, it looks sort of weird, with that pointy-edge.'

Thanks, Susie. 'It's star-shaped.'

She cocks her head again, squinting. 'Is it?'

'In cross-section, it's star-shaped.'

'Well –' She seems about to add something, but she then sighs as if she's bored with the whole thing. 'Bit like a seaside pub, with all this.' She gestures towards my collection of battered lobster cages, the heaps of nets. 'People will be wandering in off the beach and ordering a pint!' She laughs, lifting a red-knuckled hand to her mouth. It's not a happy laugh.

'None of that's permanent.'

I shove the door open with my foot, then remember, too late, I'd intended to steer her away from the sun room. It's full of rope work and stuff I don't want her seeing. But, hands shoved deep into her pockets, shoulders hunched, she hurries through the creaking sun room, stepping between the piles of jigsaws, books with no covers and squashed tubes of paint from the old trunk. She's so busy watching where she treads she doesn't notice much else.

'What a mess! Looks like the boys' room on a rainy day.'

The kids aren't setting foot in here. I've put a bolt high up on the internal door of the sun room. I'll tell Susie the bolt is to stop them escaping on to the beach. Richard was supposed be left in charge today, but there was some last-minute 'commitment'. Henry's at a friend's, but the twins are here, asleep in the car.

'Kitchen looks good.' She sniffs the air. 'Fresh paint!'

She goes to check on the twins, leaving the front door ajar. It shudders back on its hinges, wind frisking through the house. When she returns, she's out of breath, her nose red against the pallor of her skin. The twins are still asleep, thank God. I light the Calor gas heater.

'Drink? To warm up?'

She wipes her nose with a lumpy piece of tissue from her coat pocket. 'No. I'm fine. Give me a quick guided tour while they're out of action.'

We start off along the corridor of one of the Pullmans. Although it's narrow – only about the width of my shoulders – I've repainted all the wood, white, as agreed, and with the row of south-facing windows the corridor's bright with light from the open sky beyond.

'I love these windows,' she says, tracing SMOKING with her forefinger. 'Are they Victorian? That's when the carriages were made, isn't it?'

She turns into the last compartment opening off the corridor. I've used white gloss on the wooden walls and curved ceilings in here too, and repaired the rope luggage shelves above the bunk beds. The rectangular frames that used to hold the advertisements I've painted light blue, at Sarah's suggestion. Looped along the sides of the beds is a three-strand rope made from the corn-flower curtains, ripped linen sheets and some ancient, thin beach towels. Susie will probably mention pubs again.

I scuff my foot on a flap of old linoleum. 'Floor still needs doing.'

'And maybe something simple at the windows?' she says.

She touches everything and sighs. Now she's running a hand over the gleaming gloss.

'It all looks so much better, doesn't it?' Her hand is on the blue-and-white rope. 'Where did you get this?'

But before I can answer, she's pushed past me and opened the door to the next compartment, the one Elaine shared with our mother.

'Goodness!' She steps in.

I've reused rope from fishnets, new ones, fanning knotted rope above the bedheads. Tom gave me the nets in exchange for the doormat I'm making for Denise. He not only supplied the necessary rope and twine for the beckets for his old chart chest, but insisted on paying me for my time making them. We consulted *Ashley*'s. He flicked through the book, reading out phrases which, for some reason, he found uproariously hilarious. Finally, he chose beckets with Six Strand Round Sinnet bails and Manrope Knots which suited the carved cleats very well.

I'm telling Susie most of this, but she has her back to me, fingering the fan of net above the low iron-framed bed that was once our mother's. She's not listening.

'Our old spirograph, do you remember it, Andy? That's what it reminds me of, this shape.'

I can see how the parabola of interlocking lines might remind her of spirograph patterns.

'It's very pretty; so feminine. Expensive?'

'No . . .—'

Susie winces again, passing a hand over her eyes. She flops. Her knees give way. Before I get to her, she's steadied herself, a hand on the iron bedhead. Back straight to counterbalance the weight of her belly, she lowers herself down on to the bed using one arm as a prop. Head hanging, she draws deep, shaky breaths.

'Susie . . .'

'I'm OK. Little woozy. Probably blood sugar.'

'Tea? Some toast?'

Her drooping head, a ragged line of scalp parting thin hair, turns from side to side. She takes more deep breaths, a hand stroking the paisley eiderdown, sliding a finger in and out of rips in the silky material.

I begin to tell her, again, where the netting came from. Her shoulders rise and fall. I can't see her face. Finally, when she looks up, her face is blotched with tears.

'I haven't heard a thing, Andrew.'

'About the—?'

She sniffs and drags out the lump of tissue. I gather she's not referring to the netting or the beckets.

'Sorry.' She blows her nose and dusty bits of tissue float on the air.

Her body tilts towards mine as the mattress sinks under my weight. I put an arm around her shoulders. I'm shocked how loose and haphazard her bones feel beneath my palm. No flesh or muscle to give strength or hold them together.

'It's a long drive. Perhaps you—'

'The twins! I'd forgotten.' She levers herself up to vertical, then rocks as if she's losing her balance. I leap to catch her. Briefly, she collapses on to me before sighing and pushing herself upright again. She wavers unsteadily back down the corridor and out to the Volvo.

I carry the box of food supplies and a plastic crate of stuff for the boys in from the car. Susie shuts herself in the kitchen, a barricade of old deckchairs around the gas heater, and tries to keep the twins contained in the one warm room. The twins flick the light switches on and off, on and off. Open drawers and slam them shut. Take saucepans and lids and chopping boards out of cupboards and bang them around. Condensation runs down the window. I pace about a bit, wondering how we can possibly spend the whole day like this, then hit on the idea of going out to fetch fish and chips for lunch. After some dithering over what the kids are allowed to eat, Susie writes a list which she presses into my hand. 'No salt. No vinegar. Don't forget!'

It's a relief to escape the noise and stifling air. I dawdle, going the long way round to the fish and chip shop via the harbour mouth. The mudflats are glazed with watery light but far to the west a dark bank of cumulus bellies, mountainous on the horizon. Rain will come before the day is out.

Fish and chips under my coat to keep warm and dry, I shoulder open the front door. Voices.

'No, I'm sure it hasn't been,' Sarah is saying as I enter the kitchen, her hand on Susie's, her head tilted. The two women are sitting side by side at the kitchen table, turned towards each other confidingly. The table top is littered with coloured card, glitter and felt-tip pens. Wind gusts in through the front door and folded pieces of card with cotton wool stuck to them blow on to the floor. Susie is peeling glue off her fingers. A pile lies on the table like shed skin. She doesn't look up as she says, 'Shut the door.' Another gust lifts the newspaper covering the table. Looks like Susie's crying again.

Sarah gets up to kiss me, a flake of glitter on her nose catching the light.

'We've introduced ourselves and had a good long heart-to-heart,' she says, pouring Susie another cup of tea from the pot. 'And we've managed to keep the boys amused at the same time. See?' Sarah holds up what appears to be a loo roll covered with cotton wool.

'A snowman,' she says, laughing at my confusion. 'To be filled with sweets.' She claps a hand over her mouth in mock horror. 'I shouldn't have told you that; it's a surprise!'

Today Sarah's hair is lifted up and back the way I like it, exposing the swoop of her neck, the line of her jaw.

'Do you want fish and chips? Or are you hurrying back to work?'

'Not a difficult choice, is it?' She arches an eyebrow and angles her head. She looks at me, the tip of her tongue touching her upper lip. Time slows, syrupy between us. A pulse throbs just below her jaw line.

'Use a fork, not your fingers!'

Sarah and I pick up our cutlery.

When the boys finish eating, Susie clears their plates and gives them the loo roll snowmen which they point like guns at each other, making firing noises. Before long one of them stomps around the table and lifts up his arms. Susie hauls him on to her lap, where he picks up a dessert spoon to examine his reflection.

'Sarah's been talking to me about your—' Susie shifts awkwardly to pour herself a glass of water, a hand on the boy's head as she lifts the glass jug over it '—*sculptures*.' The word is loaded with a sneer.

My hackles rise. 'Yes, well, she knows more about it than I do. It's how she earns a living.' I don't want to discuss this with Susie. 'It's the same old thing.'

'Mmm. That's what I told her.' Susie grimaces and presses a hand to her side.

'Sue, believe me. People are interested. I know it.' Sarah's hand squeezes my thigh under the table. 'I've emailed photos to one or two people and had a great response. Some of his knot and rope work is extraordinarily beautiful, you know. That amazing sinnet! Wouldn't mind betting this gallery in Glasgow are on the verge of sending him an invite.'

'Glasgow?' Susie's doughy face is slack.

'The shipbuilding history is a good connection.'

Susie's expression remains uncomprehending. The boy

on her lap puts the spoon into his mouth and takes it out again, teeth clashing on the metal.

'Well, all I can say is, it was always an awful nuisance, his thing with rope.' She darts a glare at me.

Oh, here we go. Susie has never met one of my women before. My instinct to steer well clear has obviously been spot on.

'He tied a washing line around my neck once, you know. Got him into all sorts of trouble.'

'I can imagine,' Sarah says smoothly. She picks my hand up from the table and studies it. Sarah makes a habit of examining my hands, exclaiming over their size, the thickness of my fingers. She'll circle my palm with her thumb, lick the hair below my knuckles. My cock stirs.

'The things boys get up to,' she says, smiling broadly at Susie, showing those even white teeth.

I stand up to pull off my sweater and fiddle with the heater.

'Yes, well. And then, after—' Susie stops, seems to change her mind about what she was going to say. 'He was always up in his room messing about with string and rope when Dad thought he should be out playing rugby.' She shifts to the edge of her seat and slides the little boy – I don't know which twin it is – back to the floor, then faces Sarah as she flicks her hair over her shoulder. 'It's not statues, is it? It's not pottery. Not – what's the word? – *ceramic*. So how is it sculpture? I don't understand.'

This'll get Sarah started. Sure enough, her eyes flash as she takes a breath ready to launch into discussion, but the kid has a thumb in his mouth and distracts Susie by tugging at the front of her dress with one hand.

'No, darling.' Susie strokes his hair. 'Do you want a little nap?' She struggles to her feet. 'Please excuse us for a minute. I'll just pop him in one of the bedrooms.'

'Can you manage?' Sarah rises quickly. 'Will he let me?' She holds her arms wide. He takes out his thumb, frowns at her, then burrows his head in Susie's shoulder.

'Don't worry. I'm strong as an ox.' Susie wades out of the kitchen, the kid tangling his fist in her hair. The other twin slides down from the table to totter after her.

'Phew.' Sarah fetches another tumbler and helps herself to the open bottle of red standing by the breadbin. She puts both hands on my shoulders and propels me back to the table. 'You *are* a quiet one! Sue's told me the whole story.'

'Story?'

Sarah's words are slightly slurred. Perhaps she had a drink before she arrived. She drank tea with the fish and chips, but she seems slightly pissed. I'm not the only one who keeps erratic hours. A positive thought. She'll never want me to move in.

'About your parents.' Sarah pushes her chair back at an angle, kicks off her shoes and lifts her feet on to my lap. 'Your *mother*.' She swirls the red wine around her tumbler.

Outside, the feathery tamarisk branches blow like hair in the wind. Right now, I'd like to go into the sun room and close the door. Leave the women and kids to get on with it.

Sarah plays with the tip of her plait, fanning out the hair between her thumb and fingers, inspecting the ends. She sweeps her cheek with the little brush of hair, staring into space, preoccupied.

'Has she.' I make it a statement rather than a question. I'm not going to be manipulated into a conversation I don't want.

Sarah looks up. 'Has who what?'

'Susie. Told you.'

'Oh. Yes. She says you're not at all keen to trace your mother.' Sarah rolls her head around, bending her neck this way and that, rotating her shoulders as if warming up for a dance session.

'I'm not.'

Sarah lifts her feet from my lap, swivelling off her chair to stand behind me and slide her fingers deep into my hair. She massages my scalp. It's like a drug. My shoulders sink, my eyelids grow heavy. The sensation gradually blankets my thoughts. Sarah's breath tickles my ear.

To keep the edges of myself clear, I bite my lower lip. 'He drove her out, our father. Now he's dead.' Staccato words. 'That's the story. Perhaps now she'll get in touch – but that's up to her. Unless she's locked up.'

'Locked up?'

I raise my eyebrows at her.

'You mean . . .? But she wouldn't be in an asylum,' her fingers pause momentarily, 'or whatever, after all this time, would she? Though you *do* hear . . .' The circles of pressure on my scalp begin again. 'Anyway, Sue gave the impression—'

'Susie needs money.'

'Money? She didn't—'

'Our father left everything to our mother. If she's dead, doesn't make a claim, it will all come to us two.'

Sarah says nothing for a while. She continues massaging my head. I close my eyes. My mind floats and bobs.

'It's quite romantic that he never remarried, isn't it?'

'*Romantic?*' My eyes fly open.

'Well, he had a lonely life. She is sorry for him, Andrew.'

Sarah doesn't know what she's talking about. No idea.

'Now his life is over. She's carrying a new one. It's a balance. She's a mother; she wants to confront her own mother. Makes sense to me. Karma, if you like. If Susie wanted the money, why would she make any attempt to find her? No. I reckon anger is what drives our Sue and, what's more—'

'Bloody hell!' I sit up straight. *Karma?*

'What?'

'You sound like some kind of counsellor.'

'Not surprising.'

I'm wide awake now, ducking my head away from her hands.

'One of my many accomplishments.' She perches a hand on her hip. 'I've worked in Marks and Spencer's underwear department too. Very nice uniform,' she says, pouting provocatively over a shoulder at me, boobs up.

'Sarah—' My chair scrapes the floor. Sarah is missing the point. No one, so far, has mentioned Elaine.

'Shh! Sue must have dropped off.' Sarah looks at her watch and picks up a long woollen scarf from the back of her chair. 'I'd better shoot. Tell her goodbye. Only came round for a coffee.' She winds the scarf round her neck several times. 'Forgot you said she was coming down.' She's not meeting my eyes.

I put a hand on her arm and feel the gritty powder of dried clay on her skin. 'Can I show you something? Before you go?' I want to see if she understands what I have done with the jelly shoe.

I lead her through to the sun room.

'What's all the secrecy?' she says, as I reach up to unbolt the door. I say nothing, all the time watching her face, noting her lifted eyebrows, the wry smile, the saucy glance up into my eyes. We stand in front of the upturned cardboard box on the table. I put my palms to its sides. Wait.

I lift the box. She looks down.

Sees the wooden box and frame, the jelly shoe with its toe immersed in freshly set concrete. Her face sags. Her head drops. A hand covers her mouth, fingertips pressing white into her cheek. Her pupils are huge.

I want her to stand like that, holding that intake of breath, to go on staring, like a woman grieving at a grave, because, today, yesterday, ever since I poured dark wet concrete around the pink plastic tip of the jelly shoe, I haven't been able to lift the cardboard box to look at it myself.

Finally, she takes the cardboard box from my hands and replaces it. Neither of us says anything. She picks up each of my empty hands and kisses my fingertips. We walk out of the sun room and Sarah closes the internal door, sliding the bolt across.

In the kitchen she put the back of her hand against my cheek. 'I'm sorry, Andrew.'

Now perhaps she understands why I have no wish to see my mother.

Her plait swings as she reaches for the door, then she pauses. 'Oh, I'm up in London for a few days. Be in touch when I get back.'

She holds on to the ends of her scarf and steps out into the wind.

I begin to clear the table and wash the plates. The nooses are made, waiting to be hung from the rafter in the sun room. I'll attach the jelly shoe to one. I haven't yet decided what to hang from the others but they will be against the ceiling almost, and the rope ends will hang down to suggest the ropes of a bell tower. But the jelly shoe in its bed of concrete – this still needs some work – will rest on the ground, the rope end high and out of reach. Like an unreachable note. The Devil's Music. Because one of the final things I did, while Elaine was still here, was practise my whistling.

'You awake, Andy?'

The sitting room is shadows. Outside, a full moon lights up a mackerel sky. It must be late afternoon. The wind has dropped, but the sea swell is heavy. Bad weather drawing closer. I lift my feet from the chair and stretch my arms above my head. 'Am now, aren't I?'

Susie doesn't laugh. 'I didn't mean to fall asleep.' She lowers herself gingerly on to the sofa. 'I do it all over the place. Put the children to bed and wake up, fully dressed, on one of their beds or on the floor in the middle of the night.' She sighs. 'I'll have more energy once I'm not carrying this extra weight around.' She rests a hand on her belly.

'Will you get someone in to help?'

'*Someone?*' she echoes sarcastically. 'Like who?'

'Well . . .'

We both stare out at the moon.

'Andy . . . don't be cross with me, will you, but because I hadn't heard a thing and it was getting me down, waiting and not doing anything constructive so, when I found it, her address in America – I was having a clear-out, getting ready for Christmas – I sent a Christmas card.'

She's not making sense.

'Sent a Christmas card?'

'Yes. Most likely it will never reach her, she's bound to have moved, we haven't been in touch for years and years, but . . . it'll probably be a dead end.'

'Susie, hang on a minute, *who* have you sent a Christmas card?'

'Hoggie.'

'Hoggie?'

'Yes. Believe it or not I had to write "Dear Hoggie" because I've no idea of her first name.'

'Harriet Amelia.'

'What?'

'Harriet Amelia Hogg!' I always loved her name. And it strikes me, although her hair was red, it was like Sarah's – long and wild – and she sometimes let me take out the combs and Kirby grips that kept it in place, and play with it. 'Harriet Amelia Hogg. Remember?'

'You're not cross? I should really have consulted you first.'

'Yes.' I run a hand over the stubble on my jaw. 'Susie, even if—'

'I know, I know. Even if we find out where she is, she may not want—'

'That's not what I was going to say.'

But I don't know what I was going to say.

We sit in silence once more. The twins clatter and burble in the kitchen. The moon races through the sky. The logical part of my brain works out it's the cloud skimming the sky, not the moon. The visual confusion of speed and stasis is disorienting.

Sudden silence from the kitchen.

'MUMMY!' A shriek.

Susie jerks and hauls herself to the edge of the seat, using the arm of the sofa to lever herself up. She pauses. 'I meant to say, *she's* nice. Sarah.'

'Yes. She said to say goodbye.'

'I'm so glad she'll think about Christmas. She was brilliant with the boys. She got kids?' Susie is on her way to the kitchen. Both boys are wailing now.

'Christmas?'

'What?' Susie shouts from the corridor.

In the kitchen the twins have dolloped glue and glitter on to newspaper, cotton wool stuck to their fingers and jumpers. The yoghurt pot containing the glue has fallen on to the floor; both twins are still seated at the table, their faces screwed-up and red from yelling.

'Only a glue emergency,' says Susie, feet apart and breathing heavily as she watches the white puddle of glue spread on the lino.

'I'll do it.' With the end of a cardboard tube I scrape the glue back into the pot.

'Bread and jam for tea before we go home?' Susie asks nobody in particular. She takes eight slices of white bread from the bag and lines them up on the bread board, spreading a thin layer of the butter substitute she's brought down with her.

'When're you coming up? Shall I come down and get you? Hungry, boys?' She's struggling with the lid on the jam jar. She passes it over. The outside of the jar is sticky. I twist off the lid and stand, holding it and the jar. She notices my expression. 'What?!'

'Christmas?'

'Yes, you know – big happy family time of year that's about three weeks away. Or had you forgotten?' She snatches the jam jar and begins spreading the buttered slices. 'You had, hadn't you?'

'I don't usually—'

'I know you don't usually.' She presses two pieces of bread together with her palm and hacks them into quarters. 'You don't *usually* do family funerals; you don't *usually* do family weddings!'

Here we go again.

She starts on another two slices, waves the knife at me. 'But this year you're here, not in some goddam foreign country miles away, and—' she wipes her nose on the back of her hand '—and our father has just died.' She fishes up her sleeves for the lump of tissue.

'AND,' she continues, voice shrill, 'I'm just about to give birth to your nephew or niece, so it would be nice, just for ONCE, if you deigned to spend Christmas with your FAMILY!'

She flings open a cupboard door to find side plates. A sense of helplessness washes over me. The Vicarage: all of us cooped up there for days on end.

Susie puts two quarters of jam sandwich on to each of two plates. 'Eat up, boys,' she says brightly, putting the plates on the table and kissing each child on the head before walking towards me. 'What were you planning?' She's lowered her voice, is almost hissing at me. 'To stay down here and spend the whole time pissed out of your brain?'

'Susie, I just haven't thought—'

'No. You wouldn't.' The skin is tight around her mouth. 'That phone call last week, *were* you drunk?'

'I've left home, Susie. I'm a grown-up.'

'Yes, but . . .' Her voice is suddenly flat. 'You sounded – weird.' Her shoulders droop. 'I was worried.' She's chewing the inside of her mouth. It would be so nice to see her smile for a change.

'OK, OK.' I hold up my hands, palms towards her, apologetic. 'It was the rain. You know how it gets to me. Here it's so noisy – with the wind – there's no escape.'

Susie shudders, nodding.

'I'd a bit to drink at lunchtime then, after I phoned, I slept it off.'

'Another thing that drove everyone crazy.'

'What?'

'You not sleeping. Wandering about in the middle of the night.' She rubs her forehead with the heel of her hand. 'Oh, let's not argue. Why don't you come back with me now?'

'Christmas is three weeks away!'

'Don't sound so aghast.'

I think rapidly. 'Susie, you want to get sorted here first, don't you?'

'I suppose.'

'Sit down. Let me make you some tea.' I pick up a quarter of jam sandwich from the breadboard and offer it to her. She shakes her head so I pop it, whole, into my own mouth, pick up another quarter and do the same, checking the boys aren't watching. I lick jam from my fingers. And, obscurely, she's smiling, her heart-shaped face lighting up. I smile back. 'Tea, then?'

I've got my back to her, filling the kettle when she says: 'You'll come, won't you? It'll be so nice to have you for Christmas.'

'Earl Grey or PG Tips?' She's brought both down. I don't drink tea. Perhaps she imagines I'll invite guests.

Then she's fussing over the children, wiping jam from their fingers and mouths, putting them on the lavatory and chattering about the trials of the early stages of potty training. Every now and then she pauses, a hand to her side, to catch her breath. I return glue and glitter and cotton wool to the plastic crate and carry it out to the car.

At last, I wave them off, promising to phone in a week or so. A light rain is falling. A taxi pulls away from Sarah's house. Sarah – eyes dark and dramatic with make-up, hair piled up – blows a kiss from the passenger seat.

Christmas.

In avoiding the question of Christmas, I hadn't found out exactly what Sarah had said. *Glad she'll think about Christmas.* Why would she want to? It will be unbearable.

I get the sheepskin and walk out towards the harbour mouth. The full moon casts shadows, mudflats liquid grey in its light.

In fairy tales, parents send children out to the forest to die, or be killed. There are wicked, murdering stepmothers. In real-life murder cases, the first suspects are close family. Strange that I've ended up in Crete where they draw their families together, three generations often living closely with each other.

I don't know where these thoughts are leading me.

Families: Sarah never mentions children. I've never thought to ask. She never mentions parents either, only friends – although perhaps it's only that she refers to people by name rather than by a label of ownership. I gather from something Tom said that her parents were hippies. A 'wild child', she spent her childhood in one commune after another. Perhaps that sort of extended, patchwork family works better. A circle is so difficult to escape.

JUDY CLUTCHES THE WHITE bundle. Punch shrieks and whacks a stick on the side of the stage.

Something terrible happens to the baby. Perhaps Punch strangles it – you can't remember. Already a headache throbs.

'Take care of Baby while I go and cook the dumplings,' squawks Judy. She shoves the bundle into Punch's arms and bobs off stage. Punch places the scrap of white on to the ground and rolls it from side to side.

'Hush-a-by, baby, on the tree-top,' he croons, batting the bundle between his flat wooden hands. His hooked nose and the slant of his painted eyes give his face the menace of a mask but Susie, cross-legged on the floor with the other children, mouth slightly agape, appears entranced. You crouch down behind her and run a hand over her blonde head.

Several more children join the watchers on the floor. Their mothers step back a little into the folds of the curtains at the windows of the darkened social hall, turning to each other, their heads close in conversation. One of the women has the Marilyn Monroe look: peroxide blonde, arched brows and pouting, red lips. When she tilts her head back, laughing, breasts prominent in a tight-fitting top, you recognise her as the woman Michael danced with at Mr Robertson's retirement do in the autumn.

I open the front door with my new key.

'You stupid, stupid woman!' From the kitchen comes Father's worst voice. The quiet, hard voice.

Susie, clutching her satchel, tucks her head into her school scarf and runs with fast little steps through the hall and up the stairs. I follow, but in slow motion. I'm not scared. I step past his bag by the radiator. Past the tallboy; past the coat-rack. The kitchen doorway is just after the coat-rack. With each step, blood swishes in my ears. One STEP, another STEP: *What's the* (STEP) *time*, (STEP) *Mr* (STEP) *Wolf?* The stairs – patterned carpet, stair rods – are just past the kitchen door. Then in-between my big steps and the blood swishing in my ears, there is a little voice, a tiny voice – like a blow of air, like someone whispering behind their hand, lips tickling my ear. I stop. And there it is again. The Voice!

When you heard about Marilyn Monroe, you'd stood in the kitchen and wept. It was on the wireless one morning last August. Her death: the police discovering her body; the talk of sleeping pills; suicide.

Susie and Andy were in the garden, the two of them fighting over the swing.

Today your eyelids are swollen, eyelashes falling out. You mustn't cry here.

No contact, as agreed. You have heard nothing. Some nights you wake at the brink of orgasm, his beard between your thighs. During the day, it's his voice haunting you, or his smell. Sweat and skin, the male smell of him caught in the roots of the thick hair on his chest.

I shiver. There it is again.

'*Now!*' The Voice says.

I breathe very deep into my lungs, and I am HOUDINI THE HANDCUFF KING!

I can bend over backwards and pick up pins with my eyelashes.

I'm in the hallway, almost at the kitchen door.

'*Now!*' The Voice says, '*Now!*'

I drop my satchel and leap past the kitchen door. I pull open the door of the cupboard under the stairs and climb inside, shutting the door behind me.

Straight away, Father opens it again. My eyes are screwed up tight, my arms round my knees.

'A word with you, young man. Out!'

I screw my eyes tighter, press my fingers to my eyelids. The Voice is fading.

'Do you hear me? Out!'

Rolling over, hands flat over my ears to get rid of HIS voice, I curl into a ball.

Father grunts. His hand grips my arm, my ankle, pulling at me. 'Do as you're told, Andrew!'

'Look out! Look out! He's behind you!' the children chorus. One little boy jumps up and down. 'Be-*hind* you! Be-*hind* you!' The words thud out as his feet hit the floor.

'What's Andy up to today?'

You jump at Michael's voice in your ear and straighten too quickly from bending to Susie, pushing the balled-up handkerchief up your sleeve. Blood rushes in your ears; the Punch and Judy furore ebbs and flows in waves of sound. Punch flings the white bundle out of the window and one or two of the children giggle uncertainly. You put a hand on Michael's arm.

'Oh, hello.' You kiss his cheek. You mustn't think about Marilyn Monroe, mustn't think about Ian and cry here at a hospital social function. People will be watching. 'I didn't think we'd see you today. Andy's with Hugh and Stephen.'

Michael still has his white coat on, so it'll only be a dart around the hall to show his face before he goes back to the operating theatre. He's given Susie a sugar mouse from the Christmas tree. She holds it loosely, still wrapped, staring up at Judy, who is back on the tiny stage, screeching and beating Punch with the cudgel.

Michael puts a hand on your shoulder to turn you back towards him. 'You don't think he might be spending a little too much time running wild with those boys? Mrs Cunningham told me she saw the three of them on the bridge throwing stones at the ducks on Tuesday.'

A knot of tension throbs at the base of your skull. You can't get it right.

But, you don't want Andy under your feet all the time. For the past few days of the school holidays it's been a relief to have him out of the way, down by the river with Hugh and Stephen, not ricocheting around the house baiting Susie. It's exhausting keeping an eye on him all the time.

Michael's watching your face. You rub your forehead. 'Most of what they get up to is harmless, Michael.'

Hugh's parents are musicians: Leonard plays in an orchestra; Mary sings. They have stage names: Leo and Maria. Maria wears flounced skirts with net petticoats. She plucks her eyebrows. These are all reasons for Michael to be wary of Hugh's 'suitability' as a friend for Andrew.

I tuck my head right down, my nose resting on the skin of my knees. It smells like blotting paper. Father grunts again, using two hands to pick me up. I'm in a ball on the carpet.

'Stand up!' His voice is very, very quiet.

I'm rubber-ball hard. I rock to and fro, hands over my ears.

'I'm waiting.'

'*Now you're ready*,' The Voice says clearly, '*to begin your dance with death.*'

Houdini stands in a cage. He's wearing swimming trunks. His ankles are in manacles, his wrists bound behind his back.

A policeman on the stage whacks Punch with a truncheon.

You lift your chin and look Michael in the eye. 'It's the holidays. Andy's got to be able to let off a bit of steam, wouldn't you say? He doesn't want to be cooped up in the house with Susie and me all day.'

Michael glances at his watch and is distracted by the time. 'We'll discuss it later,' he says. 'I'd better go.' He reaches down to give Susie's back a little rub. She lifts a hand as if to wave goodbye but doesn't turn her head from the puppets. Her hand falls back to her lap.

Michael weaves through the audience, pausing in the shadows at the back of the hall to speak to the Marilyn Monroe woman. Then he continues, stopping now and then to greet someone – a hand on a man's shoulder, a smile and a dip of his dark head towards a group of ladies.

He rarely suggests you bring the children into the hospital for a visit these days; it's as if he tries to put them out of his mind. He never talks of Elaine.

Gales of laughter ripple out as a clown swings a string of sausages around the stage. Punch smacks at them with his fingerless hands; Susie smiles and claps.

Michael has a way of holding himself, his slender body charged with an energy and purpose that invigorates those around him. When he greets people, he touches them – a handshake, a pat on the back – or tilts his body towards them in a way that suggests concern, interest. It's part of his charm, this attentiveness. It's why the nurses blush and giggle, matron bustles and checks her watch before his ward rounds. You were once the same, drawn to his magnetism. Now you're in bed before him, lying on the edge of the bed, as much space between your body and his as you can get, feigning sleep.

'Andrew! Do you hear me?' Father's voice is hard, hissing.

'I'm listening,' I whisper to The Voice.

'Muttering now?' Spit lands on my arm.

I open my eyes, inside the ball of my arms and legs. The

skin on the inside of my wrist looks like a petal from one of Grampy's roses.

The ease of Michael's movements through the hall some-how lends the impression that he's host of this entire event, his own private Christmas party. And it's not just the women that look at him. He's in charge. His white coat sails out as he disappears out through the lighted doorway.

A voice cuts into your thoughts: '– until you are dead. Dead. Dead.'

'Michael! Please. Let him be.' Mummy's voice.

His hands hold the top of my arms *and at three-fifteen Houdini goes into his cabinet, wrists handcuffed in cuffs that have taken a Birmingham blacksmith five years to make* and Father points at my chest with a finger *and twelve minutes later Houdini reappears but with his wrists still fastened and his knees hurt so he asks for a cushion to kneel on* and Father shakes me and *at ten past four Houdini is floppy and sweating and* she's crying out again and *Hou-dini asks if he can be unlocked to take off his coat but the crowd jeer* and Father's mouth is hot and words come out *and Houdini uses a penknife to cut himself out of his coat then* I taste my snot salty *and ten minutes later Houdini is free* but Father's spit is on my face *when the crowd carry him shoulder high around the Hippodrome* and the wall is hard on my back and Father's breathing on my face and everything is fuzzy and

'I am Houdini the Handcuff King,' I say, staring over Father's shoulder at the gold-and-white wallpaper. 'People still don't know how I did what I did.'

'Michael! He's going to pass out.'

'Pull yourself together!'

darkness

until I see sense

Press my fingers over the woodworm holes.

On the little stage there are the gallows and the hangman: Jack Ketch. Punch peers out from behind bars. You finger the pearls at your neck. You should have said something to Michael when Andy tied that noose around Susie's neck. There was a look in Andy's eye you couldn't fathom. That was months ago. Now it's far too late. And the notebook – perhaps you should have told Michael about that. The incident in the empty house Michael heard about from Stephen's mother – how long might the poor boy have stayed there, tied up?

What is best you no longer can tell. You seem incapable of making any decisions. What had you been thinking of, keeping these things secret? You look down at the top of Susie's head, the white-blonde plaits tied with tartan ribbons, and bend to unwrap the discarded sugar mouse, even though you know Susie won't eat it.

The woman by the curtains has moved to the light of the doorway. She pats her Marilyn Monroe hair and plucks at the white cardigan around her shoulders. Glossy as a photograph, she's like the women in *Good Housekeeping*'s *The Happy Home*. She flits out through the doorway, following Michael.

'That's the way to do it,' Punch squawks.

On the puppet stage Jack Ketch hangs, swinging limply, noose around his neck. Punch lurches around the gallows, back hunched, the bell on his jester's hat jangling.

You should tell him, tonight.

'That's the way to do it,' Punch repeats. 'That's the way to do it. Now I'm free again for frolic and fun. Free for frolic and fun.'

I'M WIDE AWAKE IN Grampy's spare room. His snore comes through the wall.

The bed is high, like in a fairy tale, with lots of mattresses piled up. I've been here a month now and only wet the bed once. The night Father made a bed up in the bath so that the mattress would not be ruined, the Voice said: '*Now!*' and I ran through the snow to Grampy's.

Houdini wore a black silk blindfold to help him sleep.

Under the cool of the pillow is Mum's blue-and-turquoise scarf. I tie it around my head like Houdini's blindfold.

After the first night at Grampy's, Mum brought shepherd's pie and sat in the kitchen while me and Grampy ate. She'd brought homemade lemonade and Traffic Light biscuits too. She stamped the snow off her boots in the doorway and held her arms open for me and Susie.

'I can't think what has got into him,' she said to Grampy later, shaking her head and pleating the seersucker tablecloth with her fingers. She had her coat on even though it was hot in the kitchen. Her face was red. 'I can't think. He is so angry. It's all my fault.'

Grampy put a hand on hers and said, 'He'll be fine. We're good company for each other.'

Mum said, 'No, you—' then just shook her head and looked at the tablecloth again.

One day after school I went home to fetch my toboggan. It was Wednesday 7th February because I wrote it in my exercise book. Our teacher said ten inches of snow fell overnight. Even though it was not spring, Mum was spring cleaning. The doors of the kitchen cupboards were wide open and the packets and jars and bottles were all over the table and work surfaces. She held two jars up to the light. Her hair was messy and flat at the back. She had a jar of cinnamon in one hand and a jar of Robinson's Golden Shred in the other. She whirled round and held the two jars right next to my face. There were sticky fingerprints on the marmalade jar.

'What do you think? The colour? Which? The marmalade . . .' Her eyes moved fast from one jar to the other and then she looked at me, blinked and snatched the jars away, holding them behind her back. 'Of course it doesn't matter, it doesn't matter. Silly me!' and laughed. 'Silly me!' She kissed the cinnamon jar as she put it back on the table with all the other jars and kissed me, squashing my face with both hands, her breath smelling of Sundays and sherry.

'Now then, what have we here?' Auntie Jean was on the back doorstep with Susie. They both had snow in their hair. 'Let's find out what's on the television, you two.' She shooed me and Susie into the hall.

'Sit down now, duck,' she said to Mum and took the jar of marmalade out of her hand. 'No good for anyone this now, duck, is it?' It was her baby-cooing voice, the one she uses with Grampy. And 'duck' is Grampy's word. Mum's empty hands hung down by her sides; she was smiling but then she started to cry and shake her head as well. Auntie Jean pressed Mum's head against her chest.

'Why don't you put your wellies on and take your sister to see Gramps for a bit? Make sure you have your hats and gloves. Your Mum's a bit under the weather. All this snow! I'm going to run her a hot bath and get her into bed with a hot-water bottle.'

Auntie Jean used to run Mum a bath and put her to bed after Elaine was born.

When I say No that is what it means. The Voice is angry like Father's.

Auntie Jean came to Grampy's with clean pyjamas and took Susie to her house for the night. Mum was poorly. The day after that, Auntie Jean came round with Susie after school and said Mum was going away for a big rest. It would be fun because Susie was going to stay in Auntie Jean's spare room and I was going to stay with Grampy and perhaps we would all go skating on the Thames.

Susie started to cry. 'Who will feed my rabbits?'

I picked the scab on my knee.

Auntie Jean comes every day after school with Susie and Honey and we have tea together. Then Auntie Jean clears the table, tells me to learn my spellings and tables and takes my shirt and pants and socks away for washing.

Grampy's house is warm.

'Let's get a good fug up,' he'll say, and turns up the little metal heater he calls his Aladdin's lamp. He has this as well as the coal fire, because of the snow. 'What's next on our schedule, my Treasure?'

Grampy has two armchairs that used to face the fire but now they face a bit sideways towards the television Father bought him for Christmas. We watch *Thunderbirds* and *Crackerjack* and even *Juke Box Jury*. Grampy says he'll watch anything, but he must draw the line at *The Flower Pot Men*.

Sometimes we get out the sewing twine and cord and sail needles. Grampy teaches me some Two-Strand Lanyard Knots.

A rope maker, he tells me, knows that yarns are spun, strands are formed, ropes are laid and cables are closed. These are the correct terms, but some people mix them up by mistake.

To see if a hemp rope is damaged, he tells me, force open the strands and examine the heart here and there all the way along the rope's length. The heart should be a little lighter in colour than corn or vanilla fudge. If it is rust coloured, or greyish, it is utterly worthless.

Utterly worthless.

Just before bedtime Grampy lights his pipe and has a smoke. Some evenings he goes out into the garden and makes a path to the front gate through the snow. His daily constitutional, he calls it.

Then we make Hot Chocolate and I can take mine up to bed, while he stays downstairs and watches a bit more telly. His favourites are *Sunday Night at the London Palladium* and *Coronation Street* because it's about up north and he says it reminds him of home.

'Helps me to get out,' he says, laughing through his false teeth because that's what Auntie Jean is always telling him. 'You ought to get out more, Dad.'

I'M SWEATING, MY THROAT squeezed. Gale force winds and the sea's restless prowl. Four o'clock in the morning and my body is on red alert, heart ricocheting. Pointless, as well as undesirable, to try to sleep. I take toast and coffee into the sun room to rework the Hangman's Knots: thirteen turns to each noose, I've decided, not nine. Changed my mind. Not a random choice. I wonder if anyone will ever even notice. Or ask why.

The sky lightens.

I think of going out for a walk, but the sea is a grey scribble in the distance. Not a good idea.

Instead, in an attempt to get my head somewhere else, I fish about in the bottom of the old trunk. There's a dog-eared pad of drawing paper, some embroidery thread, poster paints, plaster of Paris, a pencil stub. With my penknife I slice the blunt tip of the pencil into edges and planes.

With the sharpened pencil I doodle experimentally on the cover of the pad, adding my squiggles to faded paint smudges. The edges of the pad are wavy with damp, but the paper is thick and good quality. On the first page I draw a lasso, then another.

I wore my cowboy outfit when they took me to the clinic: waistcoat, chaps, bandanna, holster. The Lone Ranger galloped and hollered through my head. *Yee Ha!* And hooves beat, thundering beneath the wooden chair legs. The smooth seat was a glossy conker brown. I hauled the chair around, sat astride it and laid my silver gun on the table. The doctor wanted me to take off my Stetson. I didn't.

The doctor called it the squiggle game, doodles with a pencil on paper. He started them off: lines that lay like string on the paper.

I added my own:

The doctor set a lot of store by them, removing his round, horn-rimmed glasses to peer closely.

They were arguing, as usual, in the car on the way home. The hospital blanket prickled my face. To shut them out, I'd pulled it over my head.

I run pencil over paper, one page after another falling to the floor. One more – I brush the page with the side of the hand holding the pencil. A Reef Knot; left over right and under, right over left. The dimensions do not translate accurately to the page. I sketch lightly, trying to correct the pencil lines as I go, but the flat page defeats me. The act of tying a knot, as Grandfather once told me, is an adventure in unlimited space. I was nine. The first Russian astronaut had just orbited the earth.

I rip out the page, screw it up and let it drop. I select several of the jewel-coloured twists of embroidery thread, a pair of scissors and begin to cut and tie, cut and tie, using Reef Knots to join the different coloured lengths. The knots are very small and flat, the sheen of the thread enhanced by interlocking dips and curves. Most people think, because they know how to tie a Reef Knot, they know when to use one. Not true. According to Ashley, when employed as a bend the Reef Knot is responsible for more deaths and injuries than have been caused by the failure of all other knots combined.

After a while I stoop to the scattered pages and shuffle them. The pencil lines are different widths, thin where the pencil was sharp, thick and smudged where it was blunt – the suggestion of time passing. It gives me an idea. I select half a dozen scribbles and order them, according to thickness of pencil lines, sharp to blunt.

By the time Sarah knocks on the window of the sun room, making eating gestures through the glass, I'm surprised to see the clouds are red-bellied: sunset. The pencil scribbles are pinned on to the blistered tongue-and-groove boarding of the sun-room wall and I've almost finished making copies of them, using brown string and cotton rope in various lengths and widths. The cotton rope is coated with a mixture of paper pulp and powder paint, to add colour and bulk. For the final drawing in the series, a dense scribble I drew with my eyes closed, I've used the coloured embroidery thread, choosing turquoise and purple and royal blue from the assortment in the trunk, knotting lengths together with Reef Knots, to make one unbroken line.

I tug the door open to let Sarah in, aware of an ache in my fingers and arms now that I've stopped. And, in my T-shirt,

I'm cold. I pull on my jumper and collapse on the old kitchen chair, running my fingers through my hair. I'm weak with hunger and too much caffeine – my perpetual state.

'Wow!' says Sarah, stepping in for a closer look. She studies the drawings and rope work, her back to me, hands in the pockets of her overalls. The way she stands now, motionless but quivering with energy, reminds me of the Diving Woman. Sarah's body has the same mesmerising pause of muscle and movement. Under her baggy white dungarees, she's wearing a low-backed vest top and from her lower neck down to between her shoulder blades, the knobs of her vertebrae are visible. Fine hairs lie on her skin. The tip of her long plait grazes at the swell of her buttocks.

'I love the way this one stands out from the others.' She peers at the silky embroidery threads, then steps back to study the piles of snippings on the floor. 'Is it finished?'

I nod, light-headed. 'More or less.'

Sarah clutches her stomach when it rumbles. 'Got any food?'

I cut mould from a block of cheddar in the fridge, while Sarah rummages through the box of supplies Susie left. 'It's like a Christmas hamper,' she exclaims holding up jars of Marmite and olives. 'Look! Even cocktail sticks!'

The remnants of the sliced bread are stale, so we toast it with cheese and Marmite and take our plates into the sun room, where she sits apart from me, cross-legged on the floor, shaking her head at the offer of wine. She wolfs down three slices of toast, licks the grease from her fingers and unplaits her hair, fluffing it over her shoulders. Today her hair smells of apples. She slips a tobacco tin and Rizlas from the pocket of her overalls and sprinkles a pinch of tobacco on to the paper. She runs her tongue along to seal the edge, and glances up at me, lifting an eyebrow, but she smokes in silence, gazing out at the darkening sky. I can't work out what's going on in her head. Haven't enough energy to try too much. I move closer, lifting a spiral curl and wrapping it around my forefinger. The slip and cling of her hair arouses me, my cock shifting, but she leans away to spear an olive with a cocktail stick and the strand of hair slides from my grasp.

I brush the dust from my jeans and walk to the window. Outside, the sea is back, breaking waves gleaming white in the darkness. It's early evening. The fluorescent tube sparks overhead. I could suggest some tango, but I've no music. Her face looks empty, turned in on herself.

'How's it going then?' I say, finally, picking up our plates from the floor.

She seems to come to, get her bearings. She takes a long final drag on her roll-up. Her latest commission, I already know, is from a friend of the couple who bought the Diving Woman. They, too, want a water feature, something similar.

'My production line, you mean?' She stubs her cigarette on the plate I'm holding. 'It's crap.' Her face is sharp and white. One slip and she's biting.

'Crap?'

'Yes. The nursery at Bosham House phoned me today.'

'About?'

'The same old thing: water features. They want some – big, bloody expensive ones, of course.'

'Isn't that good?'

'Oh, yeah, I'm behind with the rent.'

'Then . . .?'

'Then why am I in such a foul mood?' She pops the olive into her mouth.

'Well, you're a bit quiet, but . . .'

'You don't have these dilemmas.' She neatly retrieves the stone between thumb and forefinger and drops it on to the plate. 'And you don't know how lucky you are. It's another world out here. You live in your sister's house, no worries about a roof over your head. She even brings you food supplies.'

This is about money, then. 'Well, it's not . . . I don't—'

'No, you don't.' She's pacing up and down, waving her Rizla packet about. 'You have an idea and you get on with it. No one tells you what to do and how to do it. Or, worse, gets you to make copies.'

'But the point is it's not my *work*, is it, the rope stuff? It's just a – a hobby. It has nothing to do with other people.'

'My God! The ultimate self-centredness of the True Artist.' She gestures inverted commas around 'True Artist' and grimaces, before scooping up her hair in both hands and rapidly plaiting it again.

'Not at all.' She must intend to provoke. 'I'm not an artist.'

'And I am? I might as well be making concrete gnomes, except that my water features are for rich people who imagine they have taste!'

I should have told her – I realise five minutes after she's left and I'm alone adding our plates to the pile already balanced on the draining board – tourists constantly boss me around when I'm waiting tables in tavernas. But it doesn't matter. It makes life easy. That's the difference. Waiting at tables doesn't interfere with my head. I don't have to converse with anyone about anything at all except the food and drink. And, when I don't feel like talking to the tourists, I simply pretend to have no German, no English. I smile winningly at the most attractive female in the group, the one I might want to get into bed at a later stage, and shrug. Usually, they quite quickly stop trying to talk to me. Vasilis vanishes into the kitchen and opens the lid of the chest freezer to hide his laughter. I'm meek, subservient, head tilted, attentive, but elsewhere. In Crete, it's easy to be alone when I need to be. There are the lonely mountain tracks and narrow dirt paths worn by goats. The simple white mountain-top churches.

And it's not Susie's house. Surely I have told Sarah this already.

Too unsettled to stay in and get on, I decide to walk to the phone box at the far edge of the village to make the promised call to Susie. The phone box smells of curry today; there's a takeaway carton upside down in the corner. Wind whistles through a cracked pane. *Behind with the rent*. Perhaps that's her problem. I'd assumed she had a private income of some sort. I turn up the collar of the sheepskin jacket.

'Oh, I'm so glad it's you! I was worrying about how to get hold of you.' The chink of crockery and Susie's voice is breathy, coming and going. I picture her in the chaotic kitchen, phone tucked between shoulder and ear, unloading the dishwasher. 'I thought I'd have to drive down to tell you. Hang on.'

The clinking stops.

'Tell me?' I can't hear her voice any more, only a sound like wind blowing across the telephone receiver at her end. 'Susie?'

Her voice is back, hushed and urgent. '—been in touch – asking me what I want her to do.'

It must be leaves in the trees I can hear. She must have stepped outside the back door. 'Who?'

'Hoggie . . . over the years . . . says she must tell her about Dad . . . but . . . my address . . . should I . . . told Richard yet.' Her voice comes and goes.

'What? Slow down.'

'She's written to me. Hoggie – Harriet, I mean. I knew, the moment it landed on the doormat. I had to sit down. Mum's in Spain.'

I rest my forehead on the smeary glass and poke at the yellow-stained takeaway carton with my toe. Her voice is fading, tinny.

'They've visited each other quite recently, Hoggie and Mum. She will definitely want to see us, Hoggie says. But it's up to us. Can you believe it? I thought I should ask you. I've started to write back but there's so much – Andy, I can't believe it, can you? I don't know what to think.'

Outside, a Jack Russell sniffs at the door of the phone box, cocks its leg, urinates, then scampers up the road after a hooded figure in a cagoule.

'I'm so excited I can hardly keep still. Andy? That's why I was thinking – Christmas—'

Her words pound, crashing through my head. I'm drowning. Substance and breath knocked from me. My throat constricts. I slip downwards, fumbling with the receiver, trying to bury it, with Susie's voice, beneath the sheepskin jacket, clamping the receiver against my ribcage, shoving it, until I'm hunched on the concrete floor of the telephone box with the hard lump of plastic rammed high into my armpit. Still Susie's voice squawks and fuzzes. My head tumbles with her incomplete phrases. Words in smithereens.

My mother stood on the sand at the edge of the pebbles, her mouth open in a wide O.

I withdraw the receiver from my armpit and hold it out in front of me. Let it go. Plummeting, black, shiny: the receiver twists and spins as the wire takes the weight, curls elongating and shrinking again. Finally, it dangles. Chirpings escape from little circles in the earpiece. Neat woodworm holes pressed against my fingertips in the blackness. My hands cover my ears. Silence roars in, my head awash with underwater turmoil. I tuck head and elbows down between my knees, hold on to my breath.

*　　*　　*

241

My eyes open. I'm gasping, my lungs tight and airless. Don't know where the hell I am. Concrete, curry: the telephone box. It's dark. I stagger to my feet, cramp in both legs, my whole body seized up. Was it dark before? God knows. I'm stiff with cold so I've been in here a while.

Outside: rain on my face; a juddery breath of salty air. I stamp my feet to get sensation back. Moonlight on the wet track. Time's jumped; it's night time. I must have passed out.

The impulse to run is strong. But my rucksack; *Ashley*'s; Grandfather's sailor's palm: I have to go back for them.

At The Siding, I stop at the gate. Susie's Volvo is there, engine running, headlights on. This doesn't add up. Her voice on the phone . . . must have been out of my head for hours for her to already be here, now. The front door's open, banging back against the wall. I go nearer. Susie's in the car, slumped over the wheel.

As I heave open the car door, she lifts her head. She's crying. She moves robotically, holding open her arms and then, mind still reeling as if I'm pissed, my head's on the softness of her breasts.

'Thought I was too late, Andy, too late.' She keeps saying it over and over, her breath hiccupping. 'I thought you'd gone again.'

Eventually we sort ourselves out and get into the house. I'm parched, downing glass after glass of water, splashing my face, my head under the tap, trying to decide whether I need alcohol or just a long sleep.

'Andy?' Her voice is thick. She blinks across the kitchen at me, looking dazed. A phlegmy cough has her shoulders heaving. 'Andy, there's something . . . where?' and then something happens to her face, a momentary spasm, like terror, and her eyes roll back in her head. I glimpse the whites just before she falls off the chair and is thrashing on the floor.

A snatched thought, *Is this labour?* but the twitching and kicking of her legs and arms is so violent, her mouth foaming, that it's obvious she's having some sort of fit. Fuck.

Useless objects illuminate themselves with a startling clarity: the different shades of a lifting patch of brown linoleum; the mottled blue-grey metal of the leg of the old stove; her bunch of keys fanned on the Formica table top. My thought processes move excruciatingly slowly while my body races to the door and I shout out into the empty evening for help. Nobody. I glance at the Volvo. Could I drive it? Not a clue. Quicker, safer, is Sarah's phone. On the wall in her kitchen.

Of course, she's not there.

Pick lock.

Dial 999.

I rant.

A calm voice tells me to move all furniture out of my sister's way in case she hits herself, to check her airways once the fit has passed.

'She's pregnant,' I remember, just as I'm about to slam the phone down and run back to Susie.

'Pregnant, did you say?' The voice is sharper. 'You're sure?'

'Huge.'

Susie lies on her back, shuddering. Her face is waxy. There's vomit in her hair and the skin on her forehead is broken and bleeding a little. She must have hit herself on the chair leg. I touch her cheek and tell her I'm there. She goes limp and lies still. I don't want to touch her any more.

Quick footsteps behind me: Sarah. Her smile disappears. Her perfume wafts as she crouches down.

'Andrew, for God's sake – an ambulance!'

I nod.

'Help me, quickly.'

We turn Susie on to her side as if she's sleeping. Part of me wants to fetch a blanket, put it over her face and leave her be.

Sarah bends her head close, brushing Susie's hair back, making soothing noises as she fishes with her fingers in Susie's slack mouth.

Blue lights.

Sirens.

A stretcher and men in bulky uniforms storming in. Their movements jerking across my vision in the blue flashing light as Sarah's fingers emerge covered in vomit.

I'm heaving. Get to the sink, retching, just in time.

Sarah's striding across the grass alongside the stretcher.

She climbs into the ambulance.

The doors slam.

A woman in uniform, helmet in one hand and a walkie-talkie at her shoulder, is behind me. She pulls out a mobile phone as the ambulance moves off, sirens wailing. 'I'll phone for a taxi to get you to the hospital,' she says. Without waiting for an answer she speaks rapidly, side-ways, into her walkie-talkie.

The taxi drops me at glass entrance doors and swings off into the night. I'm not setting foot in any hospital. It'll take about thirty minutes to get back to The Siding on foot. I start jogging.

I hesitate before closing the front door to leave. Take a deep breath. Taste the salt. I'll miss The Siding, its boxy rooms and curved ceilings, the rows of windows looking south to sea, the creak of the sun room's corrugated plastic roof. I can smell fresh paint but beneath it, still that rotting apple smell. It's comforting to think I'll probably carry that smell with me on the sheepskin jacket.

Chances are I won't be back.

I push the front door key into the coal dust just inside the coal bunker where, until a few weeks ago, it has lain for years.

I'm on the south coast of England. I could head north; miles of land to cross. I've never been to Yorkshire, never seen where my grandfather made rope, where he walked the world. I'll walk. I step off the front step into the dark.

THE SNOW CAME BEFORE Christmas and it's stayed for weeks and weeks and weeks. At Grampy's, we're cosy and I sleep all through the nights. One morning, snow drips from the gutters and I'm eating my porridge when Grampy blows his nose and says, 'Let's go to Marlow in the boat. Go and get your warm things on.'

It's a school day. Upstairs, I take my school uniform off and fold it on the chair ready for tomorrow.

The sky and the branches of the trees are reflected in the water. The boat moves between the two sets of trees and the two skies. It's dreamy, like being nowhere.

Last week it hailed in the night and I had a nightmare so I got into Grampy's bed. Grampy told me the story of where rain comes from and where it goes to, and that all water has a memory, always trying to get back to where it came from. Like rivers always flowing back to the sea.

Willows hang low at the edges of the river. Grampy points to a grebe's nest, a mother grebe feeding its baby with a fish. 'Your mother's home tomorrow, you'll be pleased to hear.' He mops his forehead with his hand-kerchief.

My chin's on the back of my hand on the boat's edge. I press my chin down and move it, backwards and forwards over the bones. It feels like all I am is a skeleton.

Grampy puts his hanky back in his trouser pocket. 'Will we make her a cake? I've got a chocolate mix somewhere. When we get home?'

Grampy often makes suet puddings, or cakes from mixes. He says he misses cakes since Granny Clementine died, but Mum and Auntie Jean scoff and say that their mother never once used a cake mix in her life. I see a cake with candles and Smarties on top and Mum getting out the special cake forks because it's a celebration cake.

I pick at a quick. 'Have we got any candles?'

Grampy shakes his head. 'But we can pop into Coynes on the way home. Now, duck, will we go as far as Temple Lock?'

There are swans on the bank by Bisham Abbey, white feathers all over the muddy grass.

'Look at that big cob.' Grampy points, wiping his nose with his hanky as some grey-brown swans swim past. 'Wonder which pen is his mate. They mate for life, you know.'

Grampy sleeps alone in the double bed under the eaves, always on the side nearest the door because Granny Clem was frightened of burglars.

'A strong homing instinct is the reason, so they say. But they also say a swan mourns when its mate dies.'

Grampy goes once a week to take flowers to Granny Clementine's grave. He doesn't put them in a vase, just lays them on the rectangle of soil that's over her coffin. He talks to her. He always says she's gone to a better place. Like she might come back one day when, really, she's dead.

I put my fingers into the icy water. The swans are clicking softly.

'I don't want to go to the Swan Upping ever, ever again.'

At the Swan Upping the men arrive in their skiffs with red-and-blue sails and pictures of swans stitched on to them. They wear hats with white feathers which means they are cowards.

'Why not?' Grampy has cut the engine, so the boat goes a bit sideways. Straight green weed is floating below the surface, like hair combed out by the river.

'I hate it, the swans being ringed. They should all belong to the Queen.' The water slips like shiny material over my fingers, like Mum's scarf.

'Ah, they do check the birds for injuries as well, you know. Fishing hooks, cuts made by fishing lines and so on.'

'Ban fishing.'

'It's a tradition, Andrew, from the days when swans were served up at banquets. Can you imagine that?'

'No.'

Grampy blows his nose. The cold air is making his eyes watery. I keep quiet for a bit.

A swan glides past. Once, when a swan tried to escape the Swan Uppers, it waddled up the bank on crooked black legs.

'I was sick.'

The swan moved on its bent black legs like an old person. I couldn't bear the thought of it being caught.

'You had the heatstroke.'

'Heatstroke?'

'Scorcher of a July, that year. And you were in bed by teatime. Quite poorly.'

'I don't remember.'

'Yes. High temperature. Your mother was worried. Made a big fuss of you.'

Grampy coughs and his breath puffs out on the air as he

pulls on the starter lead and the engine revs into life. 'I'm surprised you don't remember.'

I walk into the kitchen holding the cake with its four candles already lit. Auntie Jean is at the sink peeling potatoes and Father leans on the work surface telling a joke about Matron losing her glasses. Mum is sitting on a kitchen chair with Susie on her lap. Under Mum's eyes is all dark like coal dust but she's wearing lipstick and a dress. Grampy is breathing loudly, like he's just run a race.

Everyone claps and says things about the cake all at once.

'Come here and give me a cuddle,' Mum says, lifting Susie to one side of her lap and opening her other arm wide. I put the cake carefully on the table and stand next to Mummy, leaning into her softness. She puts her arm around me and squeezes. I lean a bit more, but the softness and the silky material of her dress make me feel like I'm going to cry. She has powder on her cheeks like Stephen's mum and her face smells different. Susie's shoe buckle catches my arm. I move away.

The cake has lots of chocolate icing that isn't quite set and some of the Smarties have slid off, but Auntie Jean puts it on the tea trolley with the cups and saucers and plates and napkins in their rings and she wheels the trolley into the sitting room. We all sit round the fire and my face gets hot. Auntie Jean cuts up the cake and gives everyone a slice on a plate, with a cake fork and a napkin.

'Dad, have you been out and about? You look done in,' she says when she gets to him. Grampy's eyes look at me across the room.

'Just going down with a bit of cold.' His voice is all thick.

Auntie Jean bends close and puts her hand on his forehead. 'Feels to me like you're running a temperature.'

Grampy puts a hand on her wrist and shakes his head.

'I'll be right as rain after a cup of tea.' He puts his plate with the slice of cake on to a side table.

When me and Susie come in from feeding her rabbits and pouring hot water on the ice in their water bowls, Auntie Jean is helping Grampy up from his chair. 'Let's get you home. Hot-water bottle and whisky is what you need.'

'Let me find the Vick.' Mum jumps up.

Grampy bends over his stick, his breathing noisy again. Auntie Jean holds his arm.

Grampy has left his slice of cake on the wobbly table so I pick up the plate and run out to Auntie Jean's car with it. Grampy is in the passenger seat, leaning his head back. He lifts his head up and takes the plate on his lap.

'That'll do nicely for later.'

Father is out on call at bedtime. Mum reads to me and Susie together in Susie's room. She reads *The Lion, The Witch and The Wardrobe*, which I have read before but that doesn't matter.

While Mum stays to kiss Susie, I go to my room to wait for her to come and say goodnight. My feet are cold. The sheets are freezing too. I want a hot-water bottle and hot chocolate like at Grampy's, but we're not allowed drinks upstairs at home.

Mum kneels by my bed in the dark. There is a narrow beam of light from the landing coming in through the open door. She rests her face near mine on the pillow.

'I'm not really tired.'

'You're not?'

'No. I go to bed later than this usually.' I think of the two armchairs and the television and Grampy's Aladdin's Lamp.

Mum strokes my hair. She smells of face powder. She yawns.

'Didn't you have enough rest?'

'Pardon?' Her hand stills.

'It's nearly Easter and you went away just after Christmas.'

'Yes. I'm sorry it was such a long time, darling.' She leans over and kisses my forehead. 'It—'

'It went really fast. You might need some more rest, that's all.' My insides are screwed up.

'More rest?'

'I could go back and keep Grampy company.'

Mum straightens up. 'I—'

'He needs someone to look after him.'

'You can go and stay whenever you like, Andy, you know that.'

'Live, not stay.' My nails are digging into the palms of my hands, which are by my sides under the covers.

Mum kisses me on the forehead again. 'I'm glad you had a nice time. How about a cuddle, Fatty Arbuckle?'

Fatty Arbuckle is the name she called me a long time ago when I was little, because I was skinny. I've nearly forgotten it.

I turn my head away on the pillow. Mum puts her hand on my chin and turns it back. With the landing light behind her head, I can't see her face. 'Andy, I know it's been hard. Don't be angry.'

'I'm not.' I pinch the flesh on both my thighs. 'I just like being at Grampy's.'

'Well, I need a cuddle even if you don't.' She leans towards me again and tries to slip her arms around me. I keep my body rigid.

'Night night,' she whispers against my ear.

I close my eyes. She sighs and gets up. I hear her leave the room, pulling the door to with a click.

THE PINK SPIN CURLERS, in their open box by the wireless, are like the tiny bones of a foetus. You look away from them, down to the egg nestled in the hollow of your palm.

The key turns in the front door and Jean hums in the hallway as she hangs up her coat and hat. She bursts into the kitchen, drags out a chair and flicks open her compact.

'Thank God that's the snow gone at last. How're you feeling today?' She holds the little mirror high.

'Oh—' You cover the curve of the egg's lightness with your other hand '—a bit dazed I suppose, if I'm honest; a little – overwhelmed.'

'Mmm.' Jean snaps her handbag shut. 'Right then, we'll do the eggs first and afterwards you can sit back and relax while I do your hair.' She nods towards the eggs lined up on the blue Formica. 'How many?'

The eggs balance on the table top, a tiny part of each shell resting there.

'No idea.'

Sun has angled into the kitchen, slanting on to the wallpaper: blue lines, red lines, horizontal and vertical; a pattern of pots of ivy on a shelf, repeated over and over again.

The roller towel on the back door needs washing.

The coal scuttle is empty.

'Dad was quite poorly this morning.' Jean squeezes past to reach the wireless. 'I'll nip in again later. His chest . . .'

She bends her head, twiddling dials. Crackles, hisses: halves of words slide away.

Jean has a new permanent, a gleaming cap of waves with curls like sausages behind her ears and at the nape of her neck. She's thrilled with it and brought the curlers yesterday to show you. She wants to give you a Toni Home Perm today.

She finds the Light Programme and joins in: *'Just to sprinkle stardust and to whisper—'* her singing sharp-edged as the key on a corned-beef tin.

Above Jean's head, through the window, you can see the tops of the row of elms at the bottom of the garden, swaying. In Morningside House you'd sat in the austere room with its narrow bed and watched an empty sky. You'd floated in the bubble of a different life, drifting, gazing down out on the world: in orbit. You thought about Yuri Gagarin, the first man ever to leave the earth, and wondered if he had felt the same peace in vast distances.

You didn't miss the children.

Jean picks up an egg and holds it between thumb and forefinger up to the sunlight. 'I thought you'd have made a start without me.'

'No.'

Jean circles the base of her egg with the ball of her thumb, then tweaks a needle from the pincushion on the table. Tongue between her lips, she jabs the point of the needle through the shell, then pauses, grimaces as she pushes the needle, firmly, further into the egg.

'I always think of a little fluffy chick just as I'm stabbing the needle through the shell.' Her fingers turn the needle round and round, side to side, stirring, to mix the yolk and the white. 'Don't you? Are you going to have a go, or wait for that one to hatch?'

The brown egg is warm against your palm. There are specks on the shell, pieces of grit, eggshell coloured. Your stomach lurches. You should not have eaten breakfast.

'*I was all right for a while, I could—*'

You leap up, the corner of the table catching your thigh '*—smile for a while—*' and Jean's hands, fingers spread, hover protectively over the eggs as they roll.

'*But I saw you last—*'

Reaching out: 'The wireless – please.'

'Steady!'

'*—held my hand so tight, When you stopped—*'

Your fingers find the dials. A blare of music, then it's off. Your throat squeezes around a breath that forces itself out as a sob.

'It's—' but you can't speak.

'Roy Orbison.' Jean nods. 'Yes!' Then she starts up again. '*Cry-y-y- ying . . . ov-er—*'

You smack the flat of your hand, hard, on the worktop. 'For God's sake, Jean!'

Jean dips her head and pats a curl. 'I thought you liked that song.'

'No.'

Jean considers her egg and jabs the needle into the other end.

'I don't.' You sink back into the chair. 'No.'

'Well, as it happens, it's one of my favourites.' She sighs. 'You're very jumpy, I must say.' Egg to her lips, she bends over the Pyrex bowl and blows, puffing out her cheeks; a gelatinous mix of yolk and raw egg white trails out through the other needle hole. She dabs at her mouth with a folded handkerchief. 'Are you still on anything?'

'No.' Your palm is hot from slapping the table, stinging. You roll the egg to and fro on the Formica, only brittle shell between the heat of your hand and the hardness of the table top. 'I wasn't "on" anything very much. And they don't let us out of the loony bin while we're still loonies, you know.'

Before Jean arrived, you'd crushed the eggs. The ones that you'd just blown: one by one, beneath the flat of your hand: crushed. You scooped up the fragments and buried them in the compost colander under muddy potato peelings; wiped your fingers on the roller towel.

There is no way to explain.

'I just can't . . . Some kinds of music are too sad.'

'I see.' Jean places her empty eggshell in the wicker basket. 'Feeling fragile? Perhaps something more cheerful: *My Fair Lady*?' She starts to sing again, warbling. '*I could have danced all night! I could have danced all night! And still have begged for more. I could have spread my wings. And done a thousand things . . .*'

Placing the tip of your little finger between your teeth, you bite down and keep on biting until the flare of pain dies back. Then you rest your palm on the brown egg.

Jean wiggles her fingers over the eggs, as if choosing her favourite chocolate from a selection box. 'You weren't ever a loony exactly.' Her voice is softer, almost a croon. 'Just a bit tricksy.' She flutters her fingers.

The egg turns below your palm.

Jean fishes in her handbag for her cigarettes and lighter. Inhaling, she nods towards the eggs. 'Shall we save some for the children to blow later?'

'No.'

She puts her hand on yours, to still the forward and backward movement.

'Relax. It's nearly Easter. It's spring. Soon be warm enough to go to The Siding. Sea air will do you good.'

She takes another suck on her Senior Service, blows the smoke out fast, tight-lipped, angling it upwards. 'You have a loving family.' She gestures into the air with the cigarette. 'This is an optimistic time of year.'

Her eyes are pale blue, the black pupils shrinking. She knows.

A heartbeat.

She can't know, but she might have guessed. How well does Jean know you?

You shift your gaze to the poster paints on the kitchen table, the slender paint brushes and three tiny yellow balls of fluff, each stuck on to a pair of plastic claws. There's a reel of shiny ribbon on the table, un-spooling. The twigs, from which the decorated eggs will hang, lie knobbly and dark on newspaper, a damp patch spreading beneath them. Your stomach churns again.

'I don't think I can do this any more,' you whisper, burying your head in your hands. The skin smells of potato peelings.

'Right you are.' Her voice is brisk. Jean's taken a fortnight's holiday to ease you back into 'real' life, because Michael thinks that to be too much on your own would be unwise. They're both watchful, anxious not to allow you near whatever brink it was you toppled over before. You're never alone.

The chair creaks as Jean leans forward to rest a hand on her arm. 'Tell you what, old thing, I'll make you a cup of Nescafé and then we'll go to the copse and pick some primroses before the kids get back, shall we? They're perfect now, the primroses. We could dig up a few for the garden. Dad might like some too.'

You smell cigarette smoke and a faint whiff of perm solution in Jean's hair and see the primroses shut in the boot of the Morris; bags filled with the breath of soil and roots and crinkly green leaves, petals pressed against misty plastic: creased; fragile and dying.

You drop your hands into your lap, holding them there. 'I'd just like to walk by the river. On my own.'

Jean hesitates, cigarette between two straight fingers, elbow poised on the palm of a hand. Her eyes slide over you, up and down.

'Just half an hour to myself, down by the river. If you could take Susie to Brownies, I'll be back before Andy's home.' Fingering the pearls at your neck, you smile brightly.

You go along the river to Cock Marsh, trying to amble. Three swans glide by: a lamentation. The cows turn their heads, chewing. There are dangling catkins, rolled leaf buds like fairy cigars on the beeches and, among the trees, glossy bluebell leaves. In the distance, water rushes over the weir.

There's a houseboat tied up by the lock so you walk towards it, although it's not his. This one is empty for the winter. You rub at the rust on the padlock securing the door and listen, as you did that first day outside the dining room, hearing his heavy shoes on gritty boards, his sigh, your voice echoing in the uncarpeted room that smelt of damp glue and soot. He strides towards you again, huge, the top part of his overalls hanging from his waist, thick coppery hair surging at the neck of his shirt. The sudden dipping movement as he bends to his shoes, the bulk of him so close, his head near your feet, shoulder muscles shifting.

You take a breath, let go of the padlock and make yourself face towards home, walk in that direction. Watching your feet, you almost bump into Mrs Reeves stepping through her garden gate with secateurs in one hand and an empty trug over her arm.

'My dear, how nice to see you out and about! Feeling better?' In the March sunshine, the face powder on her jowls is dusty. 'How about a cup of tea, it's almost that time?' She peers at her wristwatch as you shake your head. Before you have time to voice a reply, Mrs Reeves has put down her trug. 'And how is that adorable daughter of yours?'

Mrs Reeves is one of Michael's wealthiest patients. She's been extremely generous to the children. Toy trains, dolls, even a Wendy House. You must prepare yourself to listen. Mrs Reeves shakes her head over the misdemeanours of somebody's daughter. You have been ill for months; village life has passed by. You should catch up with things. You look up; wisps and smudges of white on the blue: clouds. The easterly wind bites.

'And, my dear, shocking news about the Sinclair's eldest, Ian; such a *dashing* young man. Have you heard? Eh?'

The prick of goose bumps on your neck and cheeks: his name.

Mrs Reeves has cocked her head to catch the reply. 'No? Surely, Michael . . .? Eh. Yes? Not long after he went out to Paris. Well, it's a terrible tragedy, terrible tragedy.' Mrs Reeves smacks her lips together, rummages in her pocket for a handkerchief and gives her nose a hard blow.

Your stomach has fisted. You must hold yourself very still. 'Mrs Reeves, no, I *haven't* heard.'

The springy curl of his beard at your neck, his smell of turps and sweat; *my darling*, he sighs at your ear – but when you glance over your shoulder there is just grass in the breeze; cows ripping at it.

Mrs Reeves wipes her nose thoroughly, shoving the handkerchief up each nostril. 'Well, yes, my dear. That contraption he rode around on, his "scooter". And the roads in Paris – well, I don't know if you're familiar—?'

In your ears, the boom of blood. You shake your head, tasting metal.

'His mother would be very grateful if you were to call in, eh? I'm sure it would be a great comfort for her, my dear.'

'Tell me—' you enunciate each word with care '—what happened.' It sounds like an order. You put your hand to the flint wall. 'I mean, pardon me, Mrs Reeves. Please. I haven't heard—'

'Well, it was right in the centre of Paris. You knew he went over to teach art out there? Delightful city, but my dear, the traffic! And he was knocked off the—'

Fierce as labour, the pain has you hunched, pressing a hand against the rough tweed of your skirt. 'He's *dead*?'

'Oh no! No, he did come out of the coma, finally – *such* an ordeal for his poor mother. She was quite exhausted by it all. But now, of course, they want a second opinion, because they're saying he'll never walk again and as for his painting—'

Your legs are numb but you're stepping for the last time into the tiny space that rocks as he ducks through the doorway behind you and there's liquid movement, bright with the sun pouring in through windows on three sides and ripples of light on the ceiling, reflections from the water, the air dancing with dust motes on streaming rays of light, canvases stacked against a wall, the floor splashed with crimson paint, his beard thick with its reddish glints, the white line across the back of his neck where his hair's been cut. He's asking about the children and wiping his hands on an old cloth, his fingers with the blond hairs above and below the joint; he lifts a hand to your cheek. He's asking again, cajoling. *Paris*: a glimpse of yourself, washing at a basin under the slope of an attic room – a low bed, canvases – but the children . . . Your ears thrum with the sudden fog of absence. You turn and tear along the towpath towards the weir, stumbling on the hummocky grass, choking, hand to your mouth.

'IT'S ME, MUM.' I kick the front door closed and let my satchel thud to the floor. A pile of post is spread across the doormat. I'd better pick it up.

'Mum?'

The house is cold. Today Mrs Spencer pointed her cane to the globe and told us more snow was coming from Siberia. If you live in Siberia you have a fur coat and hat and log cabin on the Siberian plateau. Most probably, the bear that holds the coats in Grampy's house is a Siberian bear.

She must be in bed again.

Utterly worthless. It's our favourite saying, me and Hugh.

I tread on the heel of first one shoe then the other, flattening them, wriggling my feet out. Then I tread on the toes of my socks until they're wrinkly on the hall carpet. I scramble up the stairs on all fours making as much noise as possible.

The door to their bedroom is closed. There's an icy draught across the lino. I put an ear to the wood and my hand on the doorknob and then something happens. Something weird in my head makes me stop. Like trying to remember a dream.

No bag in the hall; Father must be out. I knock on the door. Nothing. I open it. Freezing wind from Siberia rushes in through the open windows and the net curtains rise up in the air. The bed is tucked in and neat.

I shut the windows and sit on the big bed, hands on the candlewick tufts. Bouncing gently, I watch my reflection in the mirror on the wardrobe bounce too. Today is . . .

This week I am Register Monitor so I missed writing the date in my exercise book because I was collecting all the registers from all the classrooms to take to the headmaster's office.

Yesterday was *Captain Scarlet* and *Mysterons* on telly, so today is . . .

I'm too hungry to think.

The wardrobe is stupendous, like a monster alien landed on the flowery carpet. It has four doors that are dark and shiny as beetle wings. Along the very top wood is carved in swoops and curves like stag beetle antlers. The panels on all four doors have swoops and curves too.

I'm not allowed in here by myself.

I stop bouncing and move to the end of the bed, away from the wardrobe, but it's still there, its four big dark doors reflected in Mummy's dressing-table mirrors.

Once we played Sardines and I shut myself in the wardrobe. I hid underneath Mum's fur coat. It was covered with a plastic bag that rustled. The fur was silky and smelt of mothballs. There was a leather smell too. I pushed both hands into a wobbly pair of high-heeled shoes. Green shoes, to go with the dark-green ballgown she wears to hospital dinner dances, when she wears the furry scarf thing with its rows of tails.

I bounce, slide off the edge of the bed, roll across the floor and jump up like in *The Magnificent Seven*. I pull open two of the wardrobe doors: white shirts, sleeves sharp; dark jackets and trousers. Horrible hospital smell. One brass pole on the inside of the door has ties in lots of colours. Two brass poles along the bottom of the wardrobe have a line of shoes in pairs.

The black telephone by the bed begins to ring. I am not allowed in here. The ringing stops. It leaves a space in the air. I slam the wardrobe door – a puff of mothball smell – and run out of the room, throwing a leg over the banisters, sliding down.

The telephone rings again.

I stand at the bottom of the stairs.

I'll go to Grampy's, get fish and chips for tea like we did last week. Money in the bus-money box on the tallboy: lots of shillings and sixpences. Tipping coins into my hands, I fill all my pockets, shorts and blazer.

The newspaper package of fish and chips is hot and a bit wet. I won't unwrap it. I'll save them until I get to Grampy's.

I switch on the light. The kitchen table is cluttered with stuff.

'Only me, Grampy!'

The tea-plate with yesterday's slice of chocolate cake, not even a bite gone. Next to the teapot under its cosy, another plate. Toast and marmalade. Water in a Pyrex bowl covered with a tea towel. A Vick smell. Half a cup of tea, gone yucky.

'Gramps?' I call down the dark hallway.

Raw liver-and-kidney from a half-opened tin of cat food mixes with the Vick. It makes me cough into my hand. I run to the front room: empty. The bedroom: empty. Greenhouse? I knock over the metal watering can.

The damp newspaper package of fish and chips is still squashed under my blazer. Pushing the toast plate to one side, I put it on the kitchen table. The smell – another cough, splattering spit into my hand.

Sindy the cat shoots through the flap in the back door, meows round the licked-clean bowl. I finish opening the tin, scrape out jellied spoonfuls that Sindy gulps as they wobble into the bowl.

The grandfather clock in the hallway chimes half past five. The cat flap swings again. Sindy's gone.

Now.

My head's a muddle. My gut hurts from hunger. I should set the table. Clear it first.

I stack plates and cups on the draining board, leaving the special chocolate cake on its flowery plate for Grampy's pudding. The table's sticky. A cloth, grey and crispy-dry, hangs on the tap. I rinse it under hot water, squeeze, rinse again. I get out two plates and the knives and forks. I look at the kitchen table and the newspaper package. My tummy bubbles.

Perhaps it's Grampy's day for visiting Granny Clementine.

I can't wait any longer.

The chips are good, fat and floury in the middle. I scrape slimy black fish-skin into the bin, put a bowl over Grampy's plate of fish and chips, a clean tea towel from the drawer over the chocolate cake.

Big trouble I'll be in – they must have told me where they were all going to be. They must have told me where I was supposed to go. Only I wasn't listening. I keep trying to fill the gap in my head. Telly, I think, but the two empty chairs in the front room and grey ash in the grate are all wrong.

Back home, the telephone is ringing.

Where is she? She said she'd be in when I got home – and Auntie Jean. Yes, today they were decorating eggs. We were going to do some after school, when Susie got home from Brownies. At breakfast, she showed me the jelly stuff that she'd blown from the eggs into a mug.

The inside of my nose hurts with the cold. I'll light the fire – it's laid up ready. But then I'm upstairs again, looking at my face in the wardrobe mirror. All that the mirror is really, is glass with silvery paper behind, that's all. Utterly worthless. It's not what it looks like.

This time, Mum's side of the wardrobe.

Hands on the metal handles, I open both doors at once and the first thing is mothball air. The second is a shiny pole, with wooden coat hangers clacking like Susie's castanets. No coloured sundresses, no furry sleeves of coats, no tweed skirts. Two shiny poles along the bottom. No gardening shoes, no high-heeled ball shoes, no beach shoes; no nothing.

Inside, the wood is not shiny like the outside. Normally it doesn't matter. Wardrobes are usually full of stuff. A wardrobe is only empty when it's in the shop, brand new. Or when someone dies.

I climb into the box-space to make it not empty any more.

I wrap my arms around my knees so I'm all crumpled up. My chest is filling with something like hard pebbles. I think about closing the doors to keep the mothball smell in here too and then staying here in the dark until

until

but

I get to the window. Open it; hang out, mouth wide open, coughing up the dry, cold air.

The telephone rings. I run downstairs.

On the kitchen table are two painted eggs, paints and some yellow chicks. On the stove are hard potatoes in a saucepan of water. Muddy potato peelings in the sink colander. The refrigerator hums.

I wait on the bottom stair by the kitchen doorway, biting my knuckles.

The telephone rings again.

In the toilet under the stairs I cough and spit over the lavatory pan, insides kicking, but nothing comes up. I wipe my mouth on a bit of crispy Izal paper. All of a sudden I feel so tired I have to rest my head on the cool white. I crawl back to the bottom stair. Chin on my knees. My lungs lift and fall, my heart bangs.

The telephone rings. Lots of times.

After a little time it gets like being on the river in Grampy's boat, floating between two sets of trees and two skies. My head's all empty, gliding like a swan. The house round me is cold and dark as icy water.

A key in the lock.

Father stoops in the doorway with his bag, trilby and mackintosh with damp splatters across the shoulders, hair over his forehead. My eyes can see in the dark. Father lifts a hand to his hat; I leap. An animal screech. Father's hands fly to his face.

'Good God!' He gasps as I land on his chest. He staggers back against the still-open door, his head cracking on the edge. Scrabbling up from the floor, I can smell his armpit sweat. Father's hands, one on each shoulder, hold me at arm's length.

'It's you. Good God, Andy. What are you doing, sitting here in the dark?'

'Where is she? Where's Mum? Where've you sent her?' I leap up and down.

'Andy, Andy.' Father's voice is calm, his arms holding my body against his.

SHE'S DEAD. The words are in my head, written in capitals. Father has killed her. He has made her kill herself. *She's dead.* The Voice.

'Andy, what has got into you? Of course she's not dead.'

265

Father grips me, but I am thrown over the bridge into the icy river dark.

The ice was seven inches thick.

Father sinks to the floor, holding me with him against his mac and its smell of shut doors in corridors. I open my eyes and see over his shoulder, through the open front door. More Siberian snow is falling. Big white flakes. One or two green leaves poke up. The path is white.

Easter, not Christmas, but it's snowing, white.

I'm sinking into snow-white feathers.

'Andy! Wake up.' Father's voice is a long way away, a long way down. I hear him from the sky. 'Andy, can you hear me?'

A gentle shake; my head rolls.

'Let's get you warm.'

He heaves himself up from the floor, carrying me, pushes the front door shut with a foot. 'Where on earth is your mother?'

On the settee, a velvet cushion behind my head.

'—get you warmed up. You're frozen—'

A circular hole cut into the ice.

A match flares. Newspaper balls ripple with red. Father's face flickers with orange.

'Why on earth didn't anyone answer the telephone?' Father's on his knees beside the settee, the fire throwing orange into the room behind him. A blanket is laid over me, my body rubbed; words, voices.

The easiest way to draw a crowd.

My legs are treacle.

'Jean found him on the kitchen floor and took him straight to hospital, this afternoon.' Father's words.

I struggle up. My mouth won't work.

'He'll be fine. He's having assistance with his breathing now. Why is the house so cold? In darkness? Where on earth is your mother?'

The crack of kindling; the sooty chimney smell; the rub of rough blanket on bare skin, my legs; Father talking in questions: it all goes small and far away from me.

The telephone rings and Father goes out to the dark hallway to answer it. From the settee, I watch his head dip down, close to the receiver. It must be a secret. His voice is so quiet, I can't make out the words.
And now I will begin my dance with death.

Auntie Jean and Susie stamp snow off their feet at the doorway; Susie wails and sniffs, her nose pink.
Auntie Jean says things like:
'She is a grown woman, Michael'
and
'You'll need me to stay the night, then.'
She makes Hot Chocolate just like Grampy, tucks Susie and me into bed together, blankets and eiderdowns pulled high, two hot-water bottles. She'll sleep in Susie's bed, she tells us, but her voice and Father's voice come up through the floor all night.
My insides are squishy like the streaks of black in sinking sand.

THE DAYS HAVE GONE PAST.

Houdini's most famous exploit is the Bridge jump. Houdini wrote about it in the *Strand Magazine*, 1919. Today the top of the rope ladder easily takes me high enough to touch the first big branch that hangs over the roof of the Wendy house, but then it's a struggle to pull myself up and swing my legs over so that they're either side of the branch. I shuffle along, legs scraping on rough bark, towards the trunk, where I yank the coil of rope around my waist up higher and start climbing. Above me, branches move against the sky.

The ice was seven inches thick. A big crowd watched while I was manacled with two sets of the best and latest police handcuffs, shut and padlocked in a trunk and pushed off the bridge into the frozen river. Bess hid in the hotel room. She thought I would definitely die this time.

Cracks in the bark and a green smell. One or two of last year's acorns in cups. The loops of rope tied to my belt keep getting caught and come undone. I have to keep stopping.

From up here the lawn is a neat oblong splodged with

orange and purple where Mum planted crocuses under the apple trees.

She's hiding in a hotel room like Bess.

A hole was cut into the ice. Underneath the ice, I freed myself from the manacles, escaped from the trunk. But I couldn't find the hole. The current had carried me away downstream.

The policemen looked for her by the river. Father was cross.

'She has taken all her clothes,' he told them. 'That's not the action of a suicidal woman.'

But if he has murdered her, Hugh said, he might hide her clothes on purpose to trick the police. That's what Hugh's parents think.

Auntie Jean and Hoggie and all her other nursing friends must think that too, because they went up and down the towpath, calling, beating snowy hedges with rolled umbrellas.

They went out in boats.

'If it makes you feel better to waste your time,' Father said.

Houdini was an illusionist. He made people think one thing when really he was busy doing something else.

I escaped from Mrs Hubbard and ran to Mum's favourite houseboat in case she was there. By the weir, I lay in the ivy, its metal smell on my hands. A dead leaf in my hair when I got into bed. No one tells me to wash. Most nights Father takes the torch and goes out into the dark. When I ask him where he's going, he says out for a breather.

I press myself against the tree trunk and poke my tongue into cracks and scrapes in the bark.

*   *   *

269

I am able to hold my breath underwater for three minutes. So I have three minutes to find the hole cut into the ice. If I do not reappear in three minutes, something is wrong and my assistant must jump in and look for me.

After three minutes, my assistant was too frightened to jump into the icy river. Instead, he threw the rope down the hole and into the water.

They looked through photographs and chose one. Father put notices in the newspapers, Auntie Jean put missing notices on lamp-posts and inside the parish council noticeboard, Hoggie put missing posters up on hospital noticeboards and at the cinema. They chose the photograph taken on the beach at The Siding, me and Mum by the breakwater. Mum smiling, saying 'Cheers!'

Then five minutes was up, and everyone thought the great Harry Houdini was dead underneath the ice.

Newspaper boys called, 'Houdini drowned! Houdini Drowned!'

Bess cried.

But there was a little bit of air trapped between the ice and the water. I swam in the dark, my mouth up near the ice so it stuck to my lips when I tried to take a breath. Pitch dark. The water made plipping noises. At last I found the end of the rope my assistant had thrown in.

Seven minutes after they'd thrown me in, I climbed out through the hole. The crowd cheered and threw their hats in the air.

My teeth chattered and my body took hours to warm up, days to stop shivering. But I survived.

*   *   *

Seven minutes – is that right? The ice was seven inches thick, I remember that. But how many minutes did Houdini stay underwater?

It's very important to get the facts right.

Father said to Jean, 'There's no knowing what went on in her head.'

Although it's Houdini's most famous trick, some people say it never happened. They say the man that did Houdini's publicity made it up. There are lots of different versions of the same story. I don't know how to find out which one is true.

One version says he jumped off the Belle Isle Bridge into Detroit River on 27 November 1906. Other people say the Detroit River never freezes because it flows too fast. Some say Houdini was in Europe on that date. Houdini himself says he performed the trick in Pittsburgh. But Houdini played Let's Pretend.

I can see the manacles, feel them all heavy on my wrists; the trunk like a coffin shutting my body in. Alone. The tip and fall from the bridge, the slopping creep of freezing, watery dark – I can feel these things too, but I don't know exactly, what really, actually, in real life, happened. There are too many different stories about Houdini's most famous trick.

Houdini used seizings to secure together two ropes so that neither would give or slip when under strain. Seizings kept him safe.

I'm up high now. The sky moves beyond the uppermost twigs.

'She will be back soon.' Father tells us over and over. 'She'll be back.'

'She's tired.' Auntie Jean pulls off her woolly hat, scratches her head with both hands. 'She's just gone on a little holiday.'

*   *   *

I open my eyes to the blue sky but close them again. I add my voice to the voices in my head:

'You will be back soon. You are somewhere with a blue sky.'

Father shouts at Auntie Jean, 'Why on earth did you let her out of your sight? How could you let her out on her own?'

Auntie Jean jabs her cigarette in the ashtray.

'She's a grown woman, Michael.'

'She's a grown woman, Michael.'

'She's a grown woman, Michael.'

'Mummy, Mummy, Mummy,' Susie calls at night.

I pull the pillow over my head.

The whole sky moves as if it's falling. Auntie Jean's voice is shouting from the garden. She's small and pointing. Then her hand covers her mouth. My foot slips. Hands graze, grabbing branches, but my chin hits a branch, then my stomach, and my body bounces and flops and breath is punched out of me until at last I hold tight to a big branch with all my arms and legs. The rope has gone.

'Andy! Andy!' Auntie Jean's voice comes up to me. 'Hold on. I'm coming.'

I breathe the green roughness of the branch. Auntie Jean is all blurry. She hitches up her tweedy skirt and climbs the ladder.

Her hand's on my foot and she's saying in her sing-song voice, 'Well now, Houdini. Let's see if we can get ourselves out of this pickle, shall we?' She pats my foot. 'What we're going to do is this: I'm going to look for a good place and take one of your feet and put it in the good place, all right? We'll do that, one foot and then the other one, and we'll get out of here in no time at all.'

Her voice is bright and cheerful like I'm a baby. For once I don't mind.

When I'm on the rope ladder, my arms and legs start working properly again. Auntie Jean jumps off the ladder and flings herself on the ground, her skirt still all pulled up and her arms and legs out like a starfish.

She's laughing and saying, 'Oh dear God, Oh dear God. What will you get up to next? Come and lie down here with me.' She pats the grass. We lie and look at the sky and the clouds through the bare branches.

'Doesn't the sky look better from down here? When you're safely on earth?' She picks some grass and throws it at me. 'You need to keep your feet on terra firma, Andy, that's what I advise.'

We're all having scones that Mrs Hubbard has baked. There's jam and cream and butter. Father comes in from the hospital.

'We're celebrating some expert tree climbing,' Auntie Jean says. 'Come and have some tea and scones with us, Michael.'

The doorbell rings. I look at Auntie Jean.

'I'll tell them you're not in, shall I?' she says. I don't know how she knows I don't want to see Hugh and Stephen today.

'It's not necessary to start telling lies,' says Father, and he gets up to answer the door.

We hear a voice and it's Mrs Reeves, not Hugh and Stephen. Her talcum powder smell dusts into the kitchen.

The police have said that, as far as they know, Mrs Reeves is the last person to have seen her. This means she is a Very Important Person in their investigation.

Everyone in the kitchen is quiet. We jump when Father puts his head round the door. 'Jean,' he says, beckoning.

Mrs Hubbard clatters plates into the sink. 'Upstairs, you two,' she says. 'Shoo!'

Later the doorbell rings again. I'm at the top of the stairs just in time to see a policeman take off his hat in the hallway and follow Father across the hall to the sitting room. Father closes the door.

Next day Father has already gone. Auntie Jean scrubs jam off Susie's cheek so hard she squeals and cries, 'I want my mummy' and kicks Auntie Jean's leg with her new Startrites.

Auntie Jean grabs hold of Susie's shoe. 'Don't we all, Susie? Don't we all?' She lets go of Susie's foot and slams out into the hallway.

Susie and me are left on our own in the kitchen. We look at each other. We look at the closed door.

Then Auntie Jean comes back in, tying the knot of her headscarf under her chin. 'Get your coats on, both of you, or you'll be late for school.'

After school I go to the hospital instead of straight home like I'm supposed to. The hospital bed looks very narrow because grown-ups usually sleep in double beds. Grampy has lots of white pillows piled behind his head and a tube with see-through tape squashing the veins on his hand. His eyes are closed. The hand lies limp on the bed.

Grampy's eyes half open. 'Hello, Treasure,' he mumbles. 'Help yourself to some grapes.' Grampy pats the bed with the hand with the tube attached. 'Come straight from school, have you?'

The ward is stuffy. I get my shoulders out of my blazer, letting it slip down my arms. A nurse walks down the aisle towards Grampy's bed so I wriggle it back up again.

'Want me to hang it up for you?' she asks, holding out her hand.

I take my blazer off properly and hand it over, not looking at her.

Grampy's breathing is still noisy. The skin on his neck is floppy and loose; his pyjamas aren't done up properly. There are one or two straggly white hairs on his chest.

'Come on, I won't bite.' When Grampy holds out his arms, the tube and the see-through bag move too.

I go nearer to the side of the bed, and drop my satchel on to the floor. I lean towards Grampy and his smell is dirty, wrong, like the back seat of the bus. I sniff into the neck of Grampy's pyjamas and jiggle my knee against the metal side of the bed to stop myself from crying.

'When are you coming home?'

Grampy stops patting and rubbing my back. 'Eh? What's that, duck?'

Grampy's hearing aid is on the bedside cabinet. Grampy's hand finds mine on the white sheet and holds tight. His eyes under the tufty white eyebrows are the same as always.

I look right into his brown eyes. They are purple at the edges. 'Has Mum been?'

Grampy puts a hand up to my ear, where my hand is pulling, then his head falls back on to the pillows and his Adam's apple moves. His head moves slowly from side to side. He struggles upright and leans forward to speak.

'I've missed two episodes of *Thunderbirds* while I've been in here. Might wander down to the children's ward tomorrow.' He winks. 'But can you fill me in for now?'

'I haven't seen it, Gramps. Sorry.'

Grampy's legs and feet make lumps in the white coverlet.

Grampy talks about the pretty young nurses and the hospital food that he's enjoying. 'Stay and have a taste of their Spotted Dick,' he says, his hand on the white sheet squeezing mine. I don't know what to say. No one knows I've cycled to the hospital on the way home from school. They'll get worried.

'Don't seem to have much go these days,' Grampy says with his head back and his eyes closed. 'Just have forty winks. Don't run off.' His hand goes soft and still and his head drops a little to one side and his eyes roll about under his eyelids.

There are lots of cards on Grampy's bedside table and flowers in vases. A nurse comes to change the water in one vase and she checks a see-through bottle at the side of the bed. 'Lovely Granddad you've got,' she says and smiles. She is quite pretty, Grampy's right.

Grampy goes on sleeping. I think of the high bed under the slopy ceiling in his house and Grampy's snores coming through the wall. I think about the arm of the wooden bear in the hall with Grampy's coat and hat hanging on it and the brass pot between the bear's legs with Grampy's sailor's palm and the linseed oil.

When Grampy wakes up I will ask him to tell the story of how he killed the snake in India and came home with the snake skin to hang on the wall.

Grampy should have a doctor who knows about knots. On page 75 of *The Ashley Book of Knots*, Clifford Ashley writes about surgeons. He says there are two types. Firstly, the surgeon with a nimble and intuitive mind. He is almost always endowed with light hands and sensitive fingers which enable him to tie excellent knots. Secondly, there is the methodical, reasoning mind of the heavy-handed surgeon. His clumsy fingers are only able to manage, at best, the Granny Knot.

Grampy says a Granny Knot is a False Knot and can jam very hard under strain and should not be used for any purpose whatsoever. Grampy's doctor must have a nimble and intuitive mind. I don't know how to find this out. I don't know who to ask.

Grampy goes on sleeping. His mouth drops open. The food trolley comes in and another nurse looks at the chart at the end of Grampy's bed and then puts a hand lightly on his forehead. He closes his mouth but doesn't wake up. 'He's all done in,' she says. 'He has so many visitors.'

Who else comes to visit Grampy? Mum must come, of course.

'Has my mum been?'

'Today?'

'Any time.'

'Couldn't tell you, sweetheart, sorry.'

I can't sit by the high white bed any longer, but I can't go without saying goodbye. I'll leave Grampy a message on the bedside cabinet, something that only he will understand. From the pocket of my school shorts I pull out the key to my bike padlock on its string fob. I put the key on the cabinet by the browny-pink plastic hearing-aid box. I'll have to walk home now. I pick up my satchel and slip my arms though the straps so it's on my back. I push through the swinging doors and out into the long corridor. I'll leave my blazer here too, with Grampy, so he knows I'll be back tomorrow before school.

I sleep under my bed. Susie is on a camp bed in my room because Auntie Jean is in Susie's bed.

The telephone rings in the night and Father comes out of the bedroom and knocks on Auntie Jean's door and their voices whisper. Later the front door opens and closes, a car starts up: Father going out to a patient.

In the morning there's the sound of the wireless in the kitchen. It's not Auntie Jean's Light Programme. I put my fingers up to the sack stuff on the underside of the mattress, pressing to feel the metal springs.

Auntie Jean listens to the Light Programme, but when Father is there the wireless does not go on at breakfasttime. Today there is no other noise except for the radio. There is no cigarette smoke. It is too quiet for Auntie Jean and

Father, who are always cross with each other in the mornings. Father bangs his porridge saucepan, Auntie Jean clatters her teacup and saucer together to take them out to the back porch because Father will not allow her to smoke inside. When Father's out on call Auntie Jean ignores his rules and smokes in the kitchen. She opens the window and waves a tea towel about when she's finished, pulling faces and making us laugh.

Honey's claws clatter across the kitchen lino and there's a quiet voice.

I roll out from under the bed, go down the stairs in my pyjamas and push open the kitchen door.

Mrs Hubbard looks up from where she is sitting at the kitchen table with Honey at her feet. She is not wearing her overall and she's stroking Honey behind the ears. Honey's tail begins a slow wag across the floor and a drool hangs from her mouth. Mrs Hubbard is smoothing down her skirt and asking what I would like for breakfast. She says there is porridge that Father left to soak the night before.

It's far too early for Mrs Hubbard to be here.

I pull up my pyjama bottoms. 'Where are they?'

'Well,' Mrs Hubbard's hand rises to the sausage-shaped curls at her neck and pats them. 'They've been called away to the hospital and . . .' She turns her back, goes to the stove, stirs the porridge. 'Better get ready for school now, dear. Mr Hubbard will drive you today.'

A man with his shirt untucked comes out of our sitting room holding an open newspaper in fat red fingers like the butcher's. Rain hits the windows hard.

And if they were both called away it means,

It means that

'Good morn—'

Under the newspaper, past him, to the front door as Mrs Hubbard rushes out and squeaks, 'It's pouring!' I reach for the latch, turning it, then the front path, the alleyway, the bridge, the railway line. My slippers slop so I take them off and wear them on my hands. There's pain pulling tighter and tighter in my chest like a stitch.

At the hospital there are too many doors and corridors. I get lost.

I lie down by the grey wheels of a trolley. My feet are hot and cut and bleeding and I can't find where I've hidden the stick to pick the lock to get out and something hurts very very badly in my chest and for it to hurt so badly I must have hidden the stick to pick the lock in there, in my chest, so I tear open my pyjama top and the buttons roll on the floor and I must open my chest and if don't I won't get out and I will drown in seven minutes.

I ran amok, they told me afterwards, dribbling and shrieking in the wind like a maniac. But I only remember the pain, throbbing like a wound. And a raging thirst. Mucus gathered like glue in my mouth and throat. Colours blurred, fluid in the sway of a curtain, the glitter of metal bed frames and trolleys: water. Watching a crack in the ceiling, edges of cabinets, rippling shadows on the floor. The air dripped and trickled. It would come from somewhere.

The thud of my heart: a fist. Dryness cracked my ribs, breath a sandpaper rasp. A tinkle of curtain-rings and the heave of a face as a doctor loomed over the bed.

And the thirst.

The doctor seemed to be saying something about tincture of hemp for the spasms but that couldn't be right and at the periphery of my vision, something swirled like liquid in a dark corner of the ward. Every scratch of the doctor's pencil startled me, soaked me again in a cold sweat. I had to drink.

Someone leaned towards me, lifting a metal beaker to my lips. I glimpsed the transparent menace of the water's surface, a slanting zero, and was flung from side to side. They held me down. The bed rattled with rage. Rain on the window. My back arched and twisted. My joints snapped from their sockets, bones splintered. My neck squeezed, locking. I was strangled, blood in my nails.

On page 65, Clifford Ashley describes the most suitable method for trying a delirious patient to the bedposts in order to prevent exhaustion. Strips of sheeting should be used to tie the patient spread-eagled, passing a smooth round turn about the wrist or ankle and finishing with a Bowline close up around the bedposts so that it will neither bind nor work loose, yet can be easily untied.

it's raining it's pouring the old man is snoring

A scream hurtled down the corridor and out into the black.

THERE'S A NOTE IN a plastic bag stuck to the sun-room door with a drawing pin. I lever it off with my penknife blade and unfold the paper.

FRIDAY, it says.

I look at my watch, but it doesn't tell me what day it is.

COME AND SEE ME AS SOON AS YOU CAN. IT'S IMPORTANT. SXX

I'm wet and cold from last night's walking. I probably smell. I hang the sodden sheepskin jacket on the back of a kitchen chair and run a bath.

Sometime later I wake, in cold bathwater, to loud knocking at the front door. I wrap a towel around myself, but when I limp to the front door there's no one. I'm heading back to the bathroom when the knocking starts again, this time on the sun-room door. Bloody Hell.

Her long legs. The plait with its escaping corkscrews of hair. I reach for her wiry warmth.

'God, you stink of garlic!'

'Olives. I stole some from your box of supplies – broke in. You stink yourself. Get back in that bath.' Her mouth wobbles, but it's a sort of smile.

I have never seen her cry. That's one of the things that brought me back.

281

'For God's sake!' she exclaims when there's no more hot water and when she sees my feet are blistered raw and when she picks up the sodden sheepskin jacket. She grabs the hospital blanket from the sofa, wraps me in it and holds me like a child, rubbing my back. 'Come on you, stupid man. Let's get you cleaned up.' Then she takes me by the hand to her railway carriage house.

She's not gentle. She's bossy and cross and ignores my erection.

'I suppose you've been a nurse too,' I say, as her fingers make quick circular movements over my scalp, lathering up shampoo that smells of apples. She doesn't say anything. Soap stings my eyes as she rinses the shampoo off. For a moment she holds one of my hands in hers, studying the palm, and she kisses my fingertips again, as she did weeks ago, in the sun room. Then she hands me the nail brush.

She fetches me dry clothes from The Siding. They smell of the leaf litter linoleum. 'Get dressed. Once you've eaten something, we'll talk.'

She leaves me in the bathroom and bangs about in the kitchen.

She pushes a full bowl of some sort of thick brown broth towards me. 'I've changed my mind. I'm not hungry. You eat, I'll talk. It's only left-over veggies.' She rips hunks of bread from a loaf and sits down opposite. 'I won't waste time telling you what I think about the way you've behaved.'

I look up, startled at the anger in her voice.

'No,' she holds up a hand, palm towards me. 'The deal is, you eat and I talk. You can say your bit later.' She picks up her lighter and turns it over and over. 'First things first: Susie is still in hospital.'

She shakes her head, gestures that I should keep eating.

'She had eclampsia and lost the baby but they now think she will survive. It's been touch and go.'

Susie's voice on the phone – excited as a child.

The steam from the soup dampens my face. I wipe my sleeve across my eyes.

Sarah's hand, when it reaches across the table top for her Rizlas, is shaking. She takes out a paper.

'Keep eating,' she says. 'That night—' she flashes me a glance '—Susie had driven down, alone, late, because she was worried about you. Earlier that day she'd been to the doctor's. There was concern about pre-eclampsia. Her blood pressure had shot up, she had protein in her urine, she was breathless. They wanted her in straight away. But earlier that afternoon she spoke to you on the phone and the line went dead. Richard told her she was being ridiculous. Reminded her you're a grown man, etcetera. They argued. He said he'd drive her to the hospital in the morning. He put her to bed. She crept out of the house and drove down here. The fit that she had in your kitchen was the eclampsia. Andrew, she could have died.'

I have been lifting the spoon in an automatic, measured way between the bowl and my mouth but when Sarah pauses to seal her roll-up and light it, I stop.

'She's OK?'

Sarah nods and takes a drag, her cheeks sucking in with the smoke. 'It was close. She's been moved now, nearer home.' She looks me steadily in the eye. 'Andrew, you do remember? Her convulsions?'

I try, but I can't see it.

Sarah rubs her face with both hands. 'We didn't get to hospital in time to save the baby.'

I rip some bread to mop up the last of the soup, watch the brown liquid seep into the rounded spaces left by air. I focus on these, the air pockets filling with soup, thinking that bread is a sort of froth, cooked, and how strange it is, the way the bread itself stretches and there are these spaces . . .

Sarah's voice cuts in. 'Susie said this disappearing act of yours is not the first. She blames herself, for giving you the news about your mother over the phone. Says she should have known you'd go off on one.'

Go off on one.

'You can't keep doing this to people, Andrew. I'm not saying any of this is your fault – the baby or anything – Susie already had pre-eclampsia – but . . .' an intake of breath as she takes another drag on her roll-up. I watch her hand shaking and wonder what she's been doing while I've been away.

Finally, I push the bowl aside, wiped clean, and she gets hold of my hand again. 'Now, if you've had enough to eat, we're going to bandage your feet and get straight in a taxi to the station. We're going to visit Susie in hospital.'

When she's finished with the bandages my feet will not fit back into my deck shoes. Nowhere near. We talk about using plastic bags, and I have a flash of memory, of myself as a boy and my mother tying plastic bags over my gloves so that I could play in the snow. Then I remember the wellingtons in the sun room at The Siding. I don't know whose they are, but they're huge. They'll do.

I hobble into Sarah's studio while she goes to look for the wellingtons. The studio is in darkness and smells of underground caves. The light goes on in the sun room next door. Sarah is bending to search for the boots under the table.

I can't see the concreted Jelly shoe from here, there's the cardboard box and some other junk in the way. A rope hangs from the rafters. I don't remember telling her what I planned to do with the Jelly shoe, but I must have done because the rope is hanging right over the table where I left the Jelly shoe in its concrete. And there's a noose. I can see the turns.

Part Five

THE TRAIN IS HOT and airless. Sarah's face, resting on her fist, is smudged in the dark glass as she stares out at the night.

'Any drinks? Tea? Coffee? Any snacks?' The young black guy pushing the trolley has a lisp. I catch his eye. He pauses by our table and smiles, a grin that shows teeth caged, top and bottom, in a brace. His gums are very pink. I order black coffee; Sarah chooses hot chocolate. The cardboard cups are placed with a flourish on folded paper napkins and we're given thin wooden spatulas for stirring.

'You're welcome,' the young guy says when we thank him, and he smiles broadly again before rattling down the aisle.

The disturbance is a relief. We shift position to sip our drinks, and finally look at each other across the table.

'You look rough,' she says. She takes the plastic lid from her cup and stirs her chocolate with the wooden spatula. 'Where did you disappear to?'

I try to gather my thoughts, to think of some way of telling her where I've been when I'm not completely certain myself.

'I walked. Caught a train – to Wild's Rope Walk.' This much I remember, more or less.

She raises her eyebrows in query.

'Yorkshire – where my grandfather used to work.'

'Why there?'

'Why?'

I found myself there. White splinters of frost thickened the grass blades, my left hand enclosed in the thick leather of Grandfather's sail-maker's palm. Wild's Rope Walk in Jerry Clay Lane beside Foster Ford Beck: now a straight row of terraced houses; men washing cars and women hanging washing.

I went for lots of reasons.

'Not sure, really.'

She sips her drink. I think about Sarah stirring the rich chocolate she made for me, its texture like custard. She asked the right questions then, questions I wanted to answer.

'What were you feeling?'

'Feeling?' I swallow a mouthful of coffee, weak and lukewarm. 'I was frightened.' I'm guessing that's about right. I don't remember what I felt. There was the Jack Russell cocking its leg; the black telephone receiver swinging. I don't remember much else. But words might anchor my mind. Sarah is waiting for more. 'Also, a sort of disgust.'

'Disgust?'

'Yes.'

'At?'

'Not sure.'

People fold up newspapers, collect up carrier bags and shuffle to the door. Sarah stares out of the window as the train pulls into a station. A blur of light and faces; scarves and hats and long dark coats. Nobody gets on. Our part of the train is now empty.

'Why not tell someone where you were going?'

People always want to be told.

'Didn't think it was anything to do with anyone else.'

'So it was nobody else's business?'

She sounds pissed off. I want to point out that she disappeared to London regularly but then I realise that she did usually tell me when she was going. I need to select my words with care.

'I didn't know. Didn't have a plan. Sorry. And sorry you had to deal with it all, get involved.'

'I didn't mind.' She rests her wrists on the edge of the table and leans towards me. 'That's what people do usually, Andrew, get involved.'

She flops back against the seat again and gazes out of the window for a while. Then she sighs and places both hands palms down on the plastic table top, looking at them. She opens her fingers, spread-eagled on the table; closes them again.

'There's something I need to tell you, Andrew.' Spreads her fingers wide; closes them again.

The harsh overhead light shadows her eyes. Surely she can't be pregnant.

'Because I don't know who else will find the time to tell you, at the moment.' Now she fiddles with the lid, trying to fit it back on to her cup. She gives up and sighs. 'What you told me about the accident on the beach?'

I prop my chin in my hand. On the wall opposite, an arrow points down the carriage. Next to it are symbols for a man and a woman. A third stick person sits in a half-circle.

'That's not what happened, Andrew. Maybe you were frightened by what really happened, or thought it was your fault. I'm not sure why. Perhaps gaps in your memory, things you couldn't explain, as a child. How many times have you told that story?'

Water from my bucket slopping over my shins; the stretches of wet sand; Elaine lying face down; my mother scooping her up.

'Never.'

'But to yourself? I wonder how many times you ran it through your own mind. Because Elaine didn't die that day on the beach.' She puts up a hand. 'Don't say anything. Let me keep going.'

But it's kaleidoscopic, my mind scattering into fragments that fly apart. I shove my hands in-between the rough upholstery and the press of my thighs, stare at her lips. Watch them move.

'I asked Susie. She couldn't remember anything about an accident on the beach. Seemed odd. From what I can gather you must have seen Elaine again after that day, but perhaps she was ill, or you were frightened, or something. I don't know. I can't explain it. I can only tell you what Susie has told me. And Hoggie.'

Her upper lip is fanned with fine lines. No lipstick.

'Andrew, Elaine was put in an institution, against your mother's wishes and only temporarily, but then your mother had some sort of breakdown and your father thought caring for Elaine was always going to be too much for her, too much for everybody – something along those lines, from what I can gather. Both you and Susie were taken to visit Elaine, but you had some sort of hissy fit because of the look of the place. The bars at the windows, or something. Later, Elaine went with your mother to Spain.'

Bars in wax crayon on my mother's wardrobe mirror, the wax sticky and crumbly against the smooth glass. When was that? And the photograph of Houdini, manacled and semi-naked, standing behind bars that were not real, but drawn on to the photograph – it seems relevant and I want to tell Sarah, but she leans towards me again, gripping the table with both hands.

'Wait. Just listen. Susie says Elaine was there one day and not the next. Your mother had to get your father's permission, of course, but they went to Spain to live with the man she was in love with – an artist? He'd had an accident. You know who that man is?'

I can't make sense of her words. *Spain*, she keeps saying *Spain*. I look away from her mouth. One black symbol by the arrow on the wall opposite has a square for a body, the other a triangle: a man and a woman.

Sarah is shaking her head. 'She must have had her work cut out, because later they cared for his handicapped brother too, ran some sort of care place.'

It's a little more than half a circle that the third pin man sits in, his stick arm held out as if to receive a gift. My body rocks with the train. Pinpricks of light flash past in the dark shine of the window, my face a pale smear just out of focus.

The photographs. Her belt with its silver buckle; the hat, a fan of starched white. 'She was a nurse.'

Elaine. I try to picture her – a woman, an adult – but my mind slithers.

'My mother – she was a nurse.'

'I know.'

'Elaine's living in France with my mother.'

Her throat makes a sound, choked. 'Oh shit! I'm so sorry.' She half rises, reaching across to me. Her face is collapsing.

Don't, I want to say to her. Please don't cry.

She's out of her seat, pressing my head to her belly as her hand moves over my ear. Her voice, reaching my ear, is distorted.

'No. It was Spain. Almeria. And, Andrew, no, Elaine died when she was about twenty.'

So she has been dead. There is no way I could have brought her back.

Sarah's jeans smell as if they've spent too long damp.

'Passed away in her sleep, is what your mum's friend Hoggie said. They hadn't even realised she was ill. I'm so sorry.'

I talk to the thick denim material. 'You've met her. Hoggie?' Sarah's met a ghost from my childhood.

'No – we spoke on the phone. I stayed with Richard for a while, to help with the boys.'

'At The Vicarage?' I can't imagine her, barefoot, braless, sitting down at the scrubbed pine table with Richard and the boys.

'Shove up,' she says, a hand on my shoulder as she squeezes in beside me. 'Yes.' She rolls her eyes dramatically and pouts. 'For a vicar, Richard's lousy at communication. And you're really not his flavour of the month, you know.'

'We don't get on.'

' "It is his considered opinion," ' Sarah does a passable imitation of Richard's silky voice, ' "that you are almost certainly suffering from low spectrum autism." ' She flicks her plait over her shoulder. 'His only knowledge of autism is most likely *Rain Man*.'

'The rain man?'

'The film. Dustin Hoffman.' She peers at me and snorts. 'Don't say you've never seen it! Everyone has seen it! Where have you been all your life? This is why you're so impossible!'

'Because I don't know the rain man?'

She takes my face in her hands, rests her forehead against mine. 'You OK?'

I feel the hard press of bone against bone, the slide of skin as I nod.

'It is quite appropriate though.'

'What is?' She rests her head on my shoulder.

'The rain man. I go a bit peculiar if it rains; very peculiar, in my teenage years. Richard's heard about it at great length from Susie, I expect.'

'A bit peculiar?'

'I used to run about, rip my clothing, refuse to wash, scream and yell. Generally unpleasant. My father thought I was psychotic from smoking too much dope.'

Some time I might try and tell her about it properly. Some time. Not now.

'Has Richard warned you off me?'

'A very cosy chat we had. Told him I was using your youthful body for some better than average sex.' Her breath is moist in my ear.

'Wish I *had* said that.' She exhales, her body suddenly limp. 'God, I'm worn out.' She yawns. 'Andrew, they're thinking of coming down to The Siding – talking about it anyway – when Susie finally comes out of hospital. I did remind everybody it's your home at the moment, and suggested they should ask you before they make plans to descend in hordes.'

'Richard and Susie?'

'No. Not Richard. The plan is for your mother to come over to help Susie recuperate, to look after the Boys from Hell. And they, Susie and your mother, want Hoggie there too. She's been a fantastic go-between these last few weeks, stopped things getting awkwardly emotional. But there isn't room at The Vicarage. Plus I get the distinct impression Richard is a bit pissed off that your mother has turned up like the proverbial.'

There's a suck of air as the connecting doors swish open. The trolley rattles and chinks towards us. She twists round to face me.

'What will you do?'

I stare at the trolley rattling and rolling down the narrow aisle.

'Andrew?'

'I don't think I'll stay.'

I take her hand. Her wrists are narrow and bony and she's wearing the bracelet I made for her after our first tango session on the beach, brown string threaded through a flat grey pebble.

'Undo your hair for me.'

She sits up. 'What, now?'

'Yes.'

'You do it.'

She lifts my hand from the table, turning it gently in both of hers. Then she rests the tip of her plait in my open palm and slips sideways in the seat so her back is towards me. Her plait is tight and glossy but, as soon as I begin to unwind the elastic band, the kinked strands spring apart and trickle over my fingers.

I see Susie on the veranda at The Siding, hunched against the wind, wincing and covering her ears. The boys, naked, their buckets filled with pebbles. And my mother in a headscarf, sitting on the pebbles beside a breakwater, smiling, wrists resting loosely on bent knees, a cigarette between her fingers. It will be the right place for them all.

And a lover? My mother's lover?

I cup my hands and Sarah's hair tumbles over my palms and wrists, cool and light; tickling. My limbs are weak, as if I have lain ill for a long time and need sun to warm me; blue skies. I bury my face in the spirals and curls of Sarah's hair and breathe its perfume. She's humming some tango tune we danced to, some guy singing English with a heavy accent. *It's wonderful, It's wonderful*, are the only words I can remember.

After a while, I gather the wild mass of her hair in both of my hands. 'No, I don't think I'll stay at The Siding.' I kiss the nape of her neck. 'I'll see Susie, then head back to Crete in time for Easter. They're big on Easter over there. Want to come?'

She's very still.

I begin to stroke her hair, gathering and smoothing the wiry mass of it into skeins, persuading them into three sections, preparing to weave the long plait back into existence.

'I could think about it,' she says, her eyes closed.

Postscript

HELEN WAKES IN THE half light. Curled on one side, cheek on Ian's pillow, she listens to the familiar sounds of him moving about downstairs. He must be whisking sugared milk and eggs in a bowl, she decides, making *torrijas* for breakfast: her favourite. Without opening her eyes she can see him in their tiny kitchen, bear-like and naked apart from a towel slung low around his hips, concentrating on the task. As soon as she thinks this, picturing his shoulders slightly stooped over the too-low worktop, the greying fur on his chest, she wants him. She buries her nose in his pillow.

Helen likes to surface slowly into a day's beginning. Usually, Ian will have been up for half an hour or more and she'll lie, adrift, until the dip of the bed drags her half dredged from sleep as he returns with her *cafe con leche*. If he leaves the house early, without waking her, to go walking or to begin painting before heat seals the afternoon into stupor, she'll feel wrong-footed all day; lacking in substance.

Today there is no time. Her suitcase waits by the street door. Dowsed in longing, she slips from the covers and treads, bare feet on cool tiles, through the shadowy rooms. The kitchen is warm and light, the radio murmuring. Ian is

297

dipping hunks of yesterday's bread in a bowl of the milk and egg mixture, a threadbare hand towel draped across the swell of his buttocks. Helen has always liked that he is not slim-hipped, like a boy. She loves the anchoring weight of him. The dipped pieces of bread sizzle as he lays them, one by one, in the frying pan.

He turns; smiles. And Helen wishes not to have seen it, shadowy-blue at the throb of his throat: the deep dent of his tracheotomy scar. He must have had the beard-trimmer out already this morning – his hair, too, is newly close-cropped, the snickets and gouges where it does not grow a reminder of his fragility. She's never told him, but she prefers his hair longer, the scars hidden. So, as she rests her cheek on his grizzled chest, she closes her eyes.

Too soon, she's easing the wheels of her new suitcase down the step and, calves braced for the slope of the cobblestones, she walks down towards the plaza just as the cockerels start up, triumphant and bossy. It will not, as she feared, be the rumbling of her suitcase wheels that wakens the slumbering village. The road is narrow as well as steep, built for feet and donkeys, not cars – a challenge when they first moved here, until Ian's muscles grew stronger. Recently, he has yielded to the need for a stick once more, for long distances. Slashed down the thigh's outer length by a molten rip of scar tissue, his left leg is fragmented bone held together with metal bolts. The muscle and ligaments have never regained their full strength; compared to his right leg, the left is slender. Down one side, the skin, melted and solidified, is almost hairless. She's glad that, moments before she left the house, he returned for his stick before heading on up the mountain for his morning's sketching and photography.

To keep from thinking too much, Helen makes herself notice the blue-painted wooden chair with a rush seat in the courtyard under Modesta's grapevine, Pablo's work boots side by side near his low door, Alba's blue plumbago stretching out under the archway. As she emerges from the jumble of walls and roofs and doorways, the view opens before her. Almond trees on the terraces are in blossom, the rosy-hearted white flowers fragile as confetti against the twisted, dark branches. Although the sun is early-morning low and invisible, the whitewashed walls of the *cortijo*s dotted along the winding track in the valley below are softened in its light. Alejo is baking bread already, the warm aroma wafting. She feels the scratch of the hemp bracelet on her wrist and stops to move her bag to the other shoulder. The knot inside her loosens a little.

Safely tucked into the shoulder bag is a photograph of Elaine. The one Ian took, only days before she died. He usually keeps it in an olive-wood frame, high on a shelf in his studio. Last night, over a couple of glasses of red wine, they sifted through the Amandelle tin of old photographs, choosing which pictures of her life here Helen should take to England. She thought he'd gone to fetch another bottle from the storage room tucked away in the rocks, but he came back with the dusty frame from his studio. He fiddled, bending back the pins one by one to remove the glass, and then held the photograph in his large-knuckled hands. Elaine had been their only child, the child he hadn't been able to father. He'd taken photographs of the milestones of her childhood, as any father might. As Elaine grew into womanhood the sculpted bone structure of her face emerged. Her hair, a sun-bleached blonde, grew long en-ough to pin up from her face. Ian said she had a perfectly balanced profile. His photographs, like this one, became more professional portrait shots.

In the village plaza, the blind is still down over the entrance to Lucia's store. Helen tries not to mind, waiting for the taxi, looking at her shoes, flat and comfortable for travelling and a little dusty already, and thinks instead about Lucia's black curls, lost within two weeks of the chemotherapy that has her retching into the toilet at the back of the shop. Tears threaten.

Then a toot as the taxi swings around the bend and the driver is portly, only middle-aged but probably less fit than Helen herself, grunting as he lifts her suitcase into the boot, the engine still running, pumping exhaust into the clear mountain air. She's ducking her head to climb into the passenger seat when there's a call, '*Hola!*', and Lucia hurries across the plaza, fastening her headscarf. The two women hug, rocking. Lucia clucks something about '*sus niños*' in Helen's ear and adds, with a kiss, '*Hasta luego.*'

'*Adiós,*' Helen whispers into the headscarf that smells of soap powder.

They wipe each other's eyes.

She's relieved that the driver is not communicative. He draws morosely on his cigarette and switches from one radio to another, hisses and crackles coming and going as the taxi winds down the mountains towards Almeria airport. She's free to stare through the smeary glass, to notice early-morning light raking the almond and olive groves, to stare down into dark gorges. Snow glistens on distant peaks. Gazing at the mountains, Helen glimpses the soaring, fingertipped wings of a golden eagle spread against the blue. She imagines Ian trudging up the track, the crunch of his boots on rocky ground. With his latest work he has been exploring ways to portray the texture of shadow and sunlight on rock and soil. He adds tiny, precise detail of cork oak leaves, pinsapo needles and cones. When she saw the first of these pictures, she could actually smell pine resin as she stretched out her fingertips to touch the vivid paint.

In the departure lounge, she moves through the crowds. As always, the air-conditioning chill is unpleasant and she pauses to pull on her cardigan. In the Ladies she looks at herself critically in the mirror. A tall woman in her sixties: dark eyes; skin lined through years of aridity. And the smoking, although she'd given that up after Elaine's sudden death, looking for causes and reasons for what, at the time, had seemed unreasonable. They'd treasured her so carefully. The doctors told them a cerebral aneurysm is more often than not congenital, but Helen had wanted something to blame.

She runs a comb through her shoulder-length hair, now threaded with white. Perhaps she should have had it cut. She hadn't known what to wear, had felt her choice of clothing might help her in a way to hold on to a sense of who she is. Eventually she'd settled on nothing special, a plain white shirt, the kind of over-sized, loose-fitting shirt she wears every day, untucked, over jeans: something she stands some hope of feeling relaxed in. No jewellery apart from the bracelet; Helen rarely dresses up. Perhaps she should have done, today.

'*Perdone!*' she apologises as she turns from the mirror and bumps into a little girl. The child looks up at her, thumb in mouth, bewildered, and it crosses Helen's mind that she probably now looks Spanish rather than English. And she wonders, after almost half her life lived in Spain, how much of herself really is English any more.

The escalator takes her up to the sandwich bars but, after her rich breakfast, Helen does not want food. She buys a coffee and sits at a table strewn with half-empty polystyrene cups and soiled paper napkins: the debris of strangers.

This morning, before she got downstairs, Ian had cleared away last night's empty bottle and wine glasses. He'd set their breakfast table with the colourful hand-painted crockery they chose together, years ago, from the local pottery. He put out the jars of cinnamon and honey, ready to spread over the cooked *tortijas*. The picture frame lay on the counter, now holding a photo of Helen taken on her last birthday.

This airport is like any other, a place in-between, a grey-and-white public space. The lack of colour reminds her of England, of grey sky and grey sea on days when the horizon disappears altogether. On those days at The Siding, before Susie and Elaine were born, she and Andy would lick their fingers to decide where the wind was coming from and choose which side of the breakwater to spread her old hospital blanket. If it was cold they'd be bulky in jumpers and anoraks, another blanket tented over their heads for extra warmth. They'd tell each other stories. His were often about Houdini the Handcuff King who could bend over backwards and pick up pins with his eyelashes. One time, he told her a pirate story, filled with waves and wind and stormy weather. When they got home, the front door slammed as she carried bags and suitcases upstairs and the painting on the half landing rocked on its wire. The painting was the source of Andy's pirate story, the storm and the tall square-rigged ships, she realised. Later that day she'd shown him how to make a Turk's Head bracelet, the sailor's rope bracelet said to have been worn as a talisman by the men whose job it was to climb to the very top of the rigging. After that, he always wore a sailor's bracelet, though he learned to work more complicated variations.

Andy. Now Andrew, a drifter, Susie has told her. An adult man Helen doesn't know. Over the past months there have been phone calls and letters from Susie, scrawled pages and photos of her three boys, of herself and Richard just married, standing under the green dark of a yew tree at the gateway of a churchyard. And Susie also sent one picture of Andy, a tall, gaunt man caught, half turning in a doorway, entering or leaving it's hard to say, not smiling but frowning at the camera, unshaven and with dark hair shaggy around his face: almost a stranger.

But last week, in a package with a Greek postmark, the hemp bracelet had arrived. She peered into the jiffy bag, shook out the bracelet, but there was no note. The bracelet is an alternating Crown Flat Sinnet, fastening round her wrist with a complex button knot that she thinks may be a variation of the six-strand Matthew Walker Knot. But she's unsure. These days, the knot work she learned as a small child from her father is rusty. Ian researched on the net but they'd been unable to identify either the Button Knot or the knot, formed from interconnected circles with no apparent beginning or end, that dangles from the bracelet. It reminds her of a Celtic Shield Knot. She holds the bracelet as a sign, an answer to her unvoiced question. It will be all right.

She slips Elaine's photograph out of the envelope in her shoulder bag. Elaine, hands resting in her lap, sits on the terrace where they often sat together. Her face, translucent, is turned away from the camera towards the west and the smudged edges of the line of hills on the other side of the valley. Light from a low sun picks up the sweep of her jaw line, emphasises the sculpted hollow of her cheek. Elaine's eyes are a startling blue in contrast to the tissue-paper pink of the bougainvillea flowers. When the photograph was taken, although they didn't know it, she was already dying. The slow seep of blood from a bleed in her brain was just beginning to affect her already limited co-ordination of movement. Helen knew that now. Later the same night, they'd had friends around. When Helen was feeding her at supper, Elaine leaned towards the spoon, eyes on Helen's, but something slipped, something clogged the mechanics of the familiar process and put them out of sync. Elaine closed her mouth on the spoon at an angle and meaty sauce streaked across her cheek. It was the first indication that something was wrong. Helen, distracted by the conversation around the table, thought at the time the droop in Elaine's eyelid simply meant she was exhausted, as Helen was, by the day's heat.

Below, alone on a row of chairs surrounded by milling crowds, a woman sits, rigid, tears streaming down her face. Helen recognises the solitude of grief.

It has been hard hearing Susie break down on the phone. Other things – the decision over Michael's money – have been easy. She has no right to it, no desire for it. More than that, Michael's money has no place in her life with Ian. And it is clear Susie needs her, needs some tenderness and rest during her recovery; wants mothering.

The last time she went back to the house to plead with Michael, the children were at school. She begged to be allowed to take them with her. Michael was brisk, self-righteous. He'd kept her standing on the steps. Through the open front door Helen could see Mrs Hubbard's back, the floral overall wrapped around her bony frame. She was kneeling before the grate in the sitting room, laying up the fire. Michael came out on to the top step, a hand on the knocker pulling the door almost closed behind him. Helen stepped backwards down a step as, standing above her, voice brusque, he threatened to take Elaine too, unless Helen ceased 'to persist in this vein'.

Later, she lurked in a shop doorway. She caught sight of Susie, satchel on her back, pushing her bike, surrounded by other schoolchildren leaving the grammar school. She'd waited and waited, until dark, for Andrew to come through the high wrought-iron gates. He didn't. She was almost undone by it.

Hobson's choice: to stay and lose herself, or leave and lose her children.

Helen has had to live with grieving over memories and photographs, an unacknowledged mourning. She soon learned it was easier not to tell people, easier not to feel their incredulity, their cooling towards her. Here, in Almeria, Lucia is the only person Helen has told. Lucia has listened to every detail about The Siding. She knows about Helen's kitchen all those years ago – the wallpaper, the pantry, the coal bunker. She knows about the children's wigwam, about Andy's dark head resting on Helen's pregnant belly.

'Can I listen again?' Andy had said, smoothing her dress. He put his mouth to the fabric and murmured, '*Shhhh,*' to the baby that would be Susie. '*Shhhh!* We're having a rest. Lie still. Do you like it when we all sleep together? I do.'

Helen comes to, catching the tail-end of an announcement in Spanish echoing over the tannoy. She should be paying attention. Again, the same female voice speaks, this time with hesitation, in English. The ups and downs of her Spanish accent – the weighty extravagant '*l*'s and back-of-the-throat '*h*'s – lend a flamboyance to the words. 'Passengers for flight ESY5932 to London, Gatwick should please make their way to gate number fourteen where the plane is preparing to board.'

The sound of the English language, the Spanish woman struggling to reproduce its tonal flatness, conjures up a memory of wheat fields; of moss and furled ferns in copses; high banks of silky ribboned grass.

Under a changeable sky, she will spread a rug on damp grass and make daisy chains with her grandchildren. She will see her son again and perhaps Sarah, the woman Susie has talked about with affection. Helen twists the bracelet on her wrist.

There have been more difficult things in her life than this.

Acknowledgements

I would like to thank the many who have helped, directly and indirectly, in the writing of *The Devil's Music*. For their continuing encouragement and inspiration, thank you to: tutors, colleagues and students, past and present, at the University of Chichester, particularly Vicki Feaver, Stephanie Norgate, Melanie Penycate, Ann Jolly and Maria O'Brien, who, a long time ago and over many weeks, read the beginnings of this novel; writing friends Alison Macleod, Karen Stevens and Jackie Buxton, and also Jill Dawson, Jane Rogers and Lesley Glaister, all of whom very generously gave much appreciated input at various later stages.

Thank you also to: Erica Jarnes at Bloomsbury; Penelope Beech for her knot drawings; my neighbour, Sarah Parrish, for her driftwood fence and lost-on-the-beach shoe tree; Vera Lemprez, for the tango; Mike Howarth (The Ropeman (www.ropeman.co.uk), for his knots; Lucas Cooper (www.insightstudio.co.uk), for technical input with knot pictures and the glossary; my godmother, for her name; and my parents, for the books and stories.

For all their love and support at home, thank you to my three daughters, Katie, Stephanie and Natalie Miller (thanks for the photos too, Nat) and to David Rusbridge.

Most especially, I owe many, many thanks to three people: my agent, Hannah Westland for her warmth, advice and enthusiastic belief in the novel before it was even finished; my editor, Helen Garnons-Williams, whose perceptive criticism was the best sort for a writer, pointing out what needed to be added/subtracted but leaving me with freedom to handle the details; and Kathryn Heyman, who, with her gift for language and her trademark energy and humour, has been such an inspirational and stimulating mentor and friend.

A NOTE ON THE AUTHOR

Jane Rusbridge lives on the coast in West Sussex with her husband, a farmer, and three of their five children. She taught at primary and preschool levels before returning to education herself as a mature student to read English at the University of Chichester, where she went on to gain an MA in Creative Writing. For the past ten years she has worked at the University of Chichester as an Associate Lecturer in English.

A NOTE ON THE TYPE

The text of this book is set in Linotype Sabon, named after
the type founder, Jacques Sabon. It was designed by Jan
Tschichold and jointly developed by Linotype, Monotype
and Stempel, in response to a need for a typeface to be
available in identical form for mechanical hot metal
composition and hand composition using foundry type.

Tschichold based his design for Sabon roman on a font
engraved by Garamond, and Sabon italic on a font by
Granjon. It was first used in 1966 and has proved
an enduring modern classic.